Rich Is Better

By MAX WILK

DON'T RAISE THE BRIDGE
(LOWER THE RIVER)

RICH IS BETTER

Rich Is Better

A Novel by MAX WILK

". . . I have been poor and I have been rich, and believe me, rich is better."

JOE E. LEWIS — AMERICAN PHILOSOPHER (20TH CENTURY)

New York * The Macmillan Company * 1962

W65r

First Printing

Printed in the United States of America

The Macmillan Company, New York
Brett-Macmillan Ltd., Galt, Ontario

Library of Congress catalog card number: 62-7513

1176859

To Barbara, who insisted

Rich Is Better

I

THE waiter poured the final two inches of Piper Heidsieck '52 into Marjorie's glass, upended the empty bottle in the nearby wine bucket, and sidled discreetly away.

"Drink up, darling," I said, raising my own glass. "To a beautiful woman. To an appreciative man. To the mysterious and wonderful forces that have brought them together."

She peered at me across the table. "Mr. Fleming," she commented, ". . . you . . . are behaving . . . very . . . strangely. . . ."

I smiled at her. Tonight she was wearing a dark red flowered dress, and draped across her shoulders was a metallic stole that glittered in the soft amber light. Low was her neckline, and graceful the bosom it revealed. "I have a marvelous idea," I murmured. "Right after we finish dessert, let's take a room here for the night. Better still, let's *skip* dessert. . . ." Beneath the tablecloth, I nudged her knee with mine.

She shook her head. "It would . . . cause . . . a certain . . . amount . . . of talk." Her enunciation was meticulous, and the several seconds' pause between each word was an encouraging sign that the two bottles of expensive grape we had consumed were beginning to take hold. Whisky, I have noted, merely makes Marjorie talkative. Gin gives her heartburn. Vodka can turn her into an argumentative shrew, but champagne seems to act as a benign catalyst, enhancing all her sensual qualities and bringing them to a fine, dreamy boil. I took her hand in mine. "Isn't it time we stopped worrying about other people?" I asked. "Two people in love spending a glorious night at a country inn—so we're defying convention! Who's to cast the first stone? Come upstairs with me, Beautiful."

"Do . . . you . . . know . . . how much . . . a room . . . *costs* . . . here?" she asked.

"I'm in no mood to haggle," I said, my fingers stroking her nylon-encased knee.

"Twenty-five dollars . . . and up . . ." she sighed.

"Who cares?" I insisted. "I can charge—" Suddenly, a nasty suspicion seeped into my brain. "And since when have *you* become *au courant* with the room rates here?"

Marjorie is an attractive woman, and I am far from being alone in this opinion. At most social gatherings we attend, there seems to be an endless supply of males of all ages who manage to corner her and offer hopeful suggestions that she pursue the conversation over cocktails and/or lunch the following afternoon in some dimly lit, out-of-the-way bar. Since, during these conversations, Marjorie sticks to bourbon, and not champagne, I have so far remained relatively unconcerned. *So* far . . .

"Oh . . . I've . . . heard . . ." she said vaguely, finishing her wine.

I decided not to probe further. "You're right," I said. "We'll go somewheres else. Here we're too much in the public eye." I kissed her fingers. "We'll find some place a trifle more . . . *secluded*."

She stared at me, unblushing. "Like . . . where?"

"Let's try that swanky new motel up the road . . . mmm?" I suggested.

"That's *not* . . . public?" she asked.

"We'll drive to New York and take a suite at a hotel," I suggested. She yawned slightly. "Forty- . . . three . . . miles?"

"All right, then," I said. "I refuse to be defeated by mere logistics. I'll think of something—"

"What's . . . wrong . . . with your . . . house?" she murmured.

"So ordinary," I said. "So unromantic. So full of interruption."

The waiter had reappeared and was now engaged in serving us with *marrons glacés* for dessert. The Inn may not be the logical place for a quiet romance, but the dinner had been superb. Marjorie, however, glared at her serving. "This," she said, "is . . . an evening . . . of conspicuous waste. . . ."

"The conspicuestest," I agreed.

"You cannot charge it off to business expense," she mused. "I am not a customer . . . or somebody important from . . . the Defense Department. . . ."

"Thank heaven for *that*," I said, and murmured to the waiter that we would have brandy with the demitasse.

"Then I would like to know," Marjorie insisted, "just where you come off entertaining me like this? Why, for what the crabmeat cocktail . . . and the rack of lamb . . . and the champagne . . . and all the rest of this is costing . . . one could feed the average family of five . . . for . . . at least three days!"

"Yes, but badly," I said. "Now see here. If a man chooses to take a good-looking woman out to dinner on impulse, to celebrate, as it were, the very least she should do is to have the good grace to drink up and enjoy herself and not talk price."

"*What* are we celebrating?" she demanded.

I beamed on Marjorie. What an attractive, witty, desirable female! Devoted, trusting, passionate . . . ah, how she would respond when I told her the news . . . detailed to her the remarkable happenings of this past afternoon! What would be her reaction when, as a fitting climax to this romantic tête-à-tête, I whispered into her ear that she was embracing one of the rarified-bracket taxpayers of our great democracy?

"Is it another one of those things you aren't allowed to discuss?" she was asking. "Like that device—"

"Ah, ah," I cautioned. "Shsh!"

"—or that thing you were designing for—"

"Hush!" I insisted.

She blinked sadly. "Secrets. All the time, secrets."

"You know the rules," I said. "We never discuss these things in public."

She sighed. "You'd think I was Mata Hari."

"Eat your *marrons* before they melt," I said fondly. "I'm sure you'll wheedle it out of me later. . . ."

She sipped moodily at her brandy instead. Then: "Was it a windfall?" she asked hopefully. "Did you find out you were underdrawn at the bank or something?"

"That will be the day," I observed. "No."

"None of your relatives has died and left a handsome bequest?"

"That will also be the day," I said.

She sipped more brandy. Then she triumphantly looked up and pointed her finger at me. "Walter," she said, ". . . you . . . found . . . somebody's wallet on the sidewalk!"

"*That* wouldn't do it," I told her. "It would only be full of credit cards."

Marjorie shook her head. "Then . . . I . . . am confused."

"Why?"

"Because . . . this isn't . . . like you."

"Nonsense," I said. "Just because I get an overpowering impulse to wine you and dine you and seduce you in the grand manner, don't behave like an accountant. Relax, and enjoy it."

"It's the champagne talking," sighed Marjorie. "T-Tomorrow you will rue this wanton ba-bacchanale. . . . We'll have to go on rice and beans and chili for months. . . . And you know what starches do to my figure." She put a protective hand to her waist.

"*Carpe diem,* Beautiful," I instructed. "There are no tomorrows. Your figure is superb, and let's not have any self-doubts." Backing up my statement, my hand stroked her thigh beneath the tablecloth.

"All right," she said. "I will diem . . . and stop carping . . . but"—she stifled a small yawn—"don't you think it's silly to waste good time arguing, dear?"

She made excellent sense. I signaled our waiter, who discreetly slid the check across to me. I turned it over. I blinked: $86.10.

Eighty-six ten . . . for the slop we'd had? Outrageous!

I opened my mouth to yell for the manager—and then I stifled the Pavlovian reaction. To the manner born, Walter! You're loaded, are you not? (With wealth, as well as Piper Heidsieck '52.) Here you've just spent twenty minutes lecturing Marjorie about the proper capacity for enjoyment, and now you're reacting like a peasant to this simple bit of routine gouging. . . . Now really, is *this* the attitude of a nabob?

I scribbled my signature and added a $15 tip. . . . There, that ought to show them. The *banditti!*

I took her arm and led her out toward the car, the waiter murmuring endearments in broken Hungarian as he convoyed us out of the dining room.

I gave the parking-lot attendant a dollar.

"I promised not to carp," said Marjorie, as we drove away, "but

4

all the signs point to the fact that you're tight. Really, Walter . . . a whole *dollar* . . ."

It was a soft May evening. The stars were out; the headlights reflected from masses of fresh greenery that floated on the stately elms above . . . and Marjorie nestled against me, tucking her legs up on the seat. "Okay," I murmured, "I'm tight."

"And what about me?" she asked, her fingers stroking my cheek. "I'm tipsy and defenseless . . . so let's not waste time looking for a motel. . . . Take me home. . . ."

"Check," I said.

"Sweet Walter," she crooned. "Spending money on me so extravagantly . . ."

Now was as good a time as any to tell her the news. "Shall I tell you why?" I asked.

"No," she said, and opened a button of my shirt.

"It will amuse you," I coaxed.

"I am not . . . at the moment . . . interested in verbal amusement," she murmured into my ear.

"Inform, then?" I asked. Her lips brushed against my neck. "Why don't you just shut up and pull over somewhere?" she whispered.

"We'll be home in ten minutes flat," I promised.

". . . Promises, promises," she complained faintly.

Since when had champagne caused *this* much of a reaction? I had better revise my data on Marjorie's response to wine. . . . Ah, no . . . There was the brandy. That explained it. The Hennessy was obviously detonating the Heidsieck.

I stepped on the accelerator and made it home in eight minutes, breaking our stringent speed laws most of the way, but in an excellent cause . . . and it wasn't easy, either. She was practically in my lap.

We pulled into the garage and I turned off the ignition. She pulled me down and kissed me.

"Now," she whispered, when we stopped for a breather, ". . . you go inside . . . pay off Mrs. Parker . . . and send her home."

"Sure," I agreed. "But aren't you coming in?"

"Not till she leaves," she said. "She reminds me of a house mother I had in college . . . and I'm feeling very illicit . . ."

I kissed her again and went inside.

Mrs. Parker was dozing in a chair, one of Buddy's comic books in her lap. I snapped off the television, awakened the good lady, paid her for her trusty services, explained that Marjorie had a headache and had already gone upstairs, said good night for both of us, and saw her to the door. A moment later the Parker car, a classic '47 Frazer, groaned and clattered its way down the drive.

Now. *Now* I would tell Marjorie the good news.

As I went past the telephone table, I noticed a message on the pad. Scrawled in my son's handwriting, I read: "Uncle Jerry called. He said another point. I don't get it. Your Loveing Son Buddy."

Another point? Could Jerry be serious? Must I revise my figures already? Thirty-five times *nineteen* . . . What did that make . . . ?

Beneath the message, my son had begun an interesting doodle. Two heavy black lines disappearing into a long, thin tube, the center of which was a series of round coils, and beneath the whole arrangement, in bold blocks, was printed "Internal Space Lock for Doubel . . ."

Puzzled, I studied Buddy's latest brain child. . . . What had he been pondering just before Mrs. Parker had shooed him off upstairs to his trundle bed?

Suddenly, the living-room lights were off. I was in darkness.

Damn! Another power failure!

No, there was still a faint glow spilling down from the upstairs hall . . . and a most remarkable vision on the bottom step. Bathed in the soft light, swaying slightly and humming to herself, posed a most desirable Marjorie.

"Darling," I said, clearing my throat, "I've got something to tell you. . . ."

Her stole dropped to the floor.

"Nineteen times thirty-five is . . . let's see . . ."

With one languid hand she reached behind her and did something to the waist of her dress. Eyes half shut, smiling in my direction, she gave a sudden shrug of her shoulders. Miraculously, her dress slid to the floor.

". . . three fifteen . . . plus one times thirty-five . . ." I mumbled.

She tossed a shoe at me. Missed. The second one got me in the shin.

"*Listen*, dear—" I said.

A nylon stocking, crumpled in a soft ball, flew past my eyes. ". . . six hundred and sixty-five thousand—"

"Be quiet!" Marjorie ordered, her head momentarily disappearing as she removed her slip. "There are *children* sleeping upstairs. . . ." The lacy garment was tossed aside. "Now. Come here, wasteful Walter . . ." she hummed in the darkness. "Hurry up and *carpe diem*. . . ."

Disheveled, wanton, desirable, she slalomed toward me, and I caught her in my arms, inhaling the rich fragrance of her perfume. Then my heel caught in a loose corner of the rug and we toppled to the floor.

"Beautiful," I whispered, a few long seconds later, "it's time I told you what we're celebrating. As of early this afternoon"—she was pulling at the knot of my tie—"we're rich." Her fingers plucked at my belt buckle. "R-i-c-h . . . as in money . . ."

Her arms pulled me firmly toward her. "Bully for us," she breathed languorously into my ear, and then her soft mouth covered mine.

Oh, what the hell, I thought. There's a time and a place for everything . . . and this just isn't either one for a financial discussion.

I'd tell her in the morning.

I mean, money isn't everything. . . .

2

ALL of the ensuing took place on the evening of May 18th.

To go back a few short hours . . .

May 18th, when an issue of 50,000 shares of Science Associates, Inc. was offered to the investing American public at a price of $10 per share by Lindstrom, Handvogel & Co., the underwriters, was, on Wall Street and environs, just another day.

At my home, May 18th was a nightmare.

At 11:13 P.M. of the previous night—just after a prophetic commercial on the Late News extolling the virtues of Frontol ("Banish nervous tension and soothe yourself with Frontol"!)—the downstairs bathroom facilities backed up and overflowed.

By the next morning, the stoppage had reached the upper story. Marjorie, my wife and helpmeet, her patience and her bottle of Frontol exhausted, gathered up Catherine, our youngest, and prepared to abandon ship, leaving me to go down at the helm. "Women and children first," she said, in scant defense of her cowardice as she climbed into the station wagon. "I am no pioneer wife. Call me when the men have it fixed."

I remained at my post until noontime, when the Marines came up the driveway. A brave detachment of three men from the Uhlan Sewer Co., commanded by veteran specialist Adolph Uhlan himself, arrived. They shortly excavated toward China and set to work with a hundred-foot steel snake to clear the drain. Me they stationed in the downstairs bathroom, my duty being to flush at regular intervals, in hopes that the pressure from my end would assist in opening the blocked passage. I remained at my post, perspiring and silently offering a prayer that our abused well would not choose this crucial moment in which to run dry. . . .

This grim duel with the elements continued for some little time, well into the afternoon. I heard the blast of the school-bus horn down the road, and shortly thereafter Buddy, my nine-year-old son, came trudging into the bathroom. "Hi, Pop," he said cheerfully, tossing his briefcase aside. "Miss Henderson sent me into the hall for five minutes because I talked and Harriet Lincoln talked but *she* didn't get sent out and here's a drawing of a turbo-jet racing car I made during recess and I'm hungry, what are those men doing out there on our front lawn by that big hole, where's Mom and Catherine and why are you home from your office, I'm hungry."

"Get some peanut butter from the kitchen," I told him. "Can't you see we're smack in the midst of a sanitation crisis?"

He reappeared a few moments later, clutching a jar and eating from it with a spoon. "You know, Pop," he said, "I've been thinking. The Russians are ahead of us in rockets and space technology— that's what the man said on TV last night. . . . Do you think they're ahead of us in plumbing, too?"

I have learned from previous discussions with Buddy to be damn sure of my facts, but my knowledge of Russian sanitation and its workings is derived from articles in *Holiday*, and needless to say I was in no position at the moment to do any intensive research on the subject. So for once I allowed myself the luxury of being arbitrary. "No, they're not!" I snapped. "Now, go find something to do. I'm in no mood for answering questions!"

"Strange, huh?" mumbled Buddy through a mouthful of nourishing peanut butter. "You'd think with all the scientists and engineers and thinkers, by now *somebody* would have come up with a better way to get rid of—"

"We're all too busy looking upwards to the outer galaxies!" I apologized. All around me, in the walls, the pipes were continuing to emit low, intermittent croaks. I mopped away for the nth time at the silt that was creeping out of the bathtub drain and sternly curbed my temper.

"Upward . . . instead of *down*," Buddy mused. "If the birth rate keeps going up, things're going to get worse, and if somebody doesn't give it a little thought . . . *boy!*"

9

In the living room, the telephone began to ring.

"Answer the phone, Cassandra," I said, "and don't get any peanut butter in the mouthpiece, will you please?"

He nodded and went off, still chewing.

I deserted my post and went across the lawn to the diggings. With equipment strewn in all directions, here a trench, there a series of freshly piled mounds of earth, what had this morning been an expensively kept and mown (by me) greensward now resembled a section of no man's land. Gathered about the open shaft, the three men from Uhlan Sewer, representing a total outlay of $22 an hour, bent to their task. For once I begrudged them not one cent of their wages. The price of labors such as theirs cannot be calculated in mere money, not from any aspect—philosophical, aesthetic, or merely on the simple olfactory level.

"Are we getting anywhere, Mr. Uhlan?" I asked hopefully.

"Hey, Pop!" Buddy yelled through the living-room window. "It's for you!"

"Take a message!" I yelled back.

Mr. Uhlan straightened up, wiped away perspiration, and batted vaguely at a few of the mosquitoes that buzzed about him in a joyous cloud. "Mr. Framing," he sighed, "I been in this line for thirty years and I thought I'd seen 'em all, but when it comes to mean back-ups—real *bastards*—I want you to know this baby takes the blue ribbon."

His helpers grunted agreement as they methodically continued ramming away with their steel snake. I acknowledged the dubious compliment in depressed silence.

"What you need here," opined Mr. Uhlan, "is a septic tank, a big one, with two, maybe three fields. Naw, I guess your soil is too rocky for proper drainage. Make that four fields, maybe . . ."

"Maybe I can't afford it," I said.

"Maybe you ain't in any position to argue about it," he countered with a thin smile.

"Pop!" Buddy yelled. "They want *you!* It's long distance!"

It would be a relief to be able to get away from these three harbingers of doom, even momentarily, so I went back into the house and took the receiver from Buddy's hand. "What is it?" I snapped. "I'm busy!"

"Hello, is this Mr. Walter Fleming?" asked the operator.

"Yes!" I said. "Who wants him?"

"Just one mo-ah-ment . . ."

"I *tried* to get the message," Buddy said. "I *told* her I'd take it down, but she kept calling me Sonny and asking were there any grownups home. *Boy* . . ."

"Okay," I soothed him. "Your voice will be changing in a year or so and then—"

"Hello?" It was my cousin Jerry. "Is that you, Walter, baby?"

"Yes, it's me!" I said.

"What are you doing at home instead of at the shop?" he demanded.

"I'm coping with a crisis," I told him. "Don't worry, I'll work overtime tomorrow and make it up. What the hell do you want?"

"You sound irritable," he said sagely. "Sit yourself down, pal—"

"Why should I sit down?" I demanded. "The plumbing in this crumbling colonial ruin is shot to hell. That rustic who stuck me with it misrepresented everything, and God only knows what it's going to cost me to get things back in shape—the pump's going to give out. We can't possibly live here until it's fixed, and we'll all probably have to go live in a hotel and eat our meals out and you just tell me one good reason why in hell I should sit myself down!"

"Because," said my partner and cousin, "your sewage problems are over."

"Splendid. As of when?"

"As of noon," he replied promptly.

"Yeah," I said. I've been on the receiving end of Jerry's glib pronouncements since I was a kid, and I treat them with my own form of reflex skepticism. "As of *when?*"

"Noon, buddy," he said. "Lindstrom, Handvogel & Co. put out our stock at 11:00 A.M. at ten bucks a share, remember? So guess where it is now? *Sixteen* bid, *eighteen* asked—and the specialist can't fill the orders—his books are swamped and they're coming in like the blizzard of '88! Now—tell me you're happy!"

I sat down.

"Walter, baby?" he asked. "Were we cut off? Do you read me?"

"Eighteen dollars?" I gulped. "For stock—that cost me—ten cents a share?"

"Yep, and by the end of the week, if it keeps on like this, they're figuring it should break twenty!" Jerry chortled. "So don't bother your pretty little head with plumbing problems, kid; move to a motel. Better yet, *buy* one! Call you later—they need the phone for orders."

The dial tone buzzed; he'd hung up. Slowly, I replaced the receiver in its cradle, absently flicking away at a small smear of fresh peanut butter.

"Sorry, Pop," Buddy said. "I tried to keep it off, but peanut butter is tricky stuff."

"Perfectly all right, son," I said. "It could happen to the best of us."

He stared at me. Buddy is a boy with sandy hair and sharp blue eyes that have his mother's clarity. He also inherited her directness. "Say, Pop," he asked, "you feeling okay? You're all pale and sort of white around the nose."

I lighted a cigarette with fingers that trembled only slightly. I took two puffs, inhaling deeply. It tasted very strange. By the third puff, I realized why. I gave up smoking two years ago. . . .

Eighteen dollars a share . . . wasn't that what Jerry had said? He must have been drunk. It wasn't possible. *Eighteen* dollars a *share*—for stock in a relatively new electronics firm, untried, small capitalization, no dividends, good prospects yes, but I mean—What had he said, by the end of the week over *twenty?*

Jerry *was* drunk.

But Jerry doesn't drink. Not since the ulcer. He can still chase girls, but no liquor. . . . So he *couldn't* have been drunk!

. . . Could he?

I owned ten thousand shares of Science Associates, Inc. In Marjorie's name were ten thousand shares of her own. As custodian for Buddy, I'd purchased five thousand, and as custodian for Catherine, who was right now probably making mudpies in the Barton's sandpile, another five thousand. And finally, at Jerry's insistent urging, when we formed the firm, I'd bought another five thousand in joint ownership for Marjorie and me. All for ten cents a share.

I'd fought that purchase. Sure, the price was right, but I'd been planning to use that $500 as down payment on a new station wagon, which we needed badly. But Jerry talked me out of it. He's a very persuasive talker, my cousin and partner. He can't bend Marjorie; she's tougher. But me he can usually persuade . . . damn him. Why do I always let him talk me into things?

Let him? If the dear boy wasn't drunk—why, I was sitting on top of *thirty-five* thousand shares!

Suddenly, I wasn't able to do the figures in my head. I grabbed the telephone book and scribbled on its cover. Eighteen times thirty-five . . . Eight times five is forty, eight times three, twenty-four; carry the four, twenty-eight . . . one times five is five, one times three is three, two hundred and eighty plus thirty-five; total: six hundred and thirty? . . . Just a second, add the three zeroes. . . .

On the telephone book was written $630,000.

A couple of years back, my total investment in stock, including the $500 for the station wagon, had run to $3,500.

This afternoon, with the stock on the market, while I was standing in the downstairs bathroom, grimly flushing the toilet . . . my personal worth had risen to $350,000.

And, as of this moment, according to Jerry's phone call, we Flemings were collectively worth . . . $630,000!

Possible?

"Hey, Pop," asked Buddy anxiously. "What's the matter?"

"Nothing serious," I said. "Just a new sensation I have to get used to. It's called affluence."

"Spell it."

"A-f-f-l-u-e-n-c-e."

From out on the battlefields, I heard a hoarse bellow. "Hey, Mr. Froman—get out here, fast!"

I threw open the front door, my mind spinning like a drunken IBM computer. . . . Six hundred and thirty thousand. Six hundred and thirty thousand!

I found myself standing by the crew. Two of them were wearily leaning against nearby trees while Mr. Uhlan stared happily into the gaping excavation. "Just take a look at *that*," he commanded, pointing down. "Gushing out like we struck oil or something . . ."

"Black gold," I murmured. Twice three hundred and fifteen thousand . . . six times one hundred and five thousand . . . No matter how I did it over in my mind, it always mounted up to a powerful pile of dollars. . . .

"Okay," Mr. Uhlan was saying. "We got lucky and cleared out your stoppage. *This* time. But how do we know? This ain't no permanent solution, Mr. Famman. I know these old systems—just the bare minimum. Pioneer stuff. She'll plug up again soon, and *next time*—"

"Lightning doesn't strike twice," I said.

"Now, I don't want you thinking I'm trying to sell you a bill of goods," he said, lapsing into the man-to-man gambit, "but don't you think for your own peace of mind you better let me order that septic tank? Sure, it involves a little cash . . . but think of it as an investment in your future."

Ten times sixty-three thousand dollars.

". . . I mean, is it right, a nice fella like you, healthy and all, with a family to think of, should lie awake nights, worrying about his plumbing?" pressed Mr. Uhlan.

"No, of course not," I said. "You order that tank. Order *two*."

He stared at me, suddenly wary. "Two?"

"Why not?" I replied. "It's in the American tradition! We want the best, don't we? How else can a democracy grow? From now on, we're a two-tank family!"

"Six . . . maybe seven fields . . . I could see that," said Mr. Uhlan, reeling. "But *two* tanks—I mean, I wouldn't want you to think I'm out to *overdrain* you. . . ."

"I'm going into this with my eyes open!" I told him. "In this line, there's no such thing as a bargain, right?"

"But it's going to *cost*—" he protested.

"Forget that," I said, and paraphrased one of my antecedents, another man of great wealth. "If I have to figure on what it costs to operate two septic tanks, I damn well have no business running them, do I?"

I skipped back across the lawn to the house, leaving behind me one very startled sewage specialist.

I must call Marjorie at the Bartons . . . tell her to come home.

Six hundred and thirty thousand smackers?

Oh, no. Not possible.

But Jerry didn't drink.

Celebrate. Take Marjorie out to dinner . . . the Inn. . . . Best meal in the house. . . . Champagne . . . yes, champagne! Dammit, how many days in his lifetime does a man get a phone call informing him he's only three hundred and seventy thousand paltry dollars short of being an average red-blooded American *millionaire*, eh?

I began to dial the Bartons' number.

"Hey, Pop," said Buddy, cross-legged on the floor, peanut-butter jar still in hand, the *Oxford English Dictionary* sagging heavily in his lap. "I've been looking up "affluent." Want to hear what the dictionary says?"

The peanut-butter jar dangled dangerously close to the thin pages of my prize dictionary—the one that had cost me $30.

"Sure," I said. "Go ahead and read me the definition. Read it slowly, Buddy. I want to enjoy every word."

3

A HASTILY gathered caucus of crows on my front lawn, shrilling over the pecking order of their breakfast, the corpus of some hapless mouse, no doubt, awoke me from a deep, satisfying sleep. It was not yet seven-thirty, but there was work waiting for me at the office. Compulsive to the end, I arose, shaved, and dressed. The rest of my brood were still sleeping, so I tiptoed downstairs to enjoy that rarest of meals, breakfast alone.

And a good thing, too. There, strewn across the living-room carpet, mute reminders of our wanton behavior, were Marjorie's dress, her shoes and stockings, and various other feminine articles of clothing calculated to elicit awkward questions from strangers encountering them underfoot. I policed the area and carried everything upstairs.

"Hey, Pop," whispered Buddy, as I passed his open door. "Where're you going with Mom's clothes?"

Too late. He was sitting up in bed, a paperback science-fiction novel in hand, already catching up on a little early-morning reading. "Ah—I'm putting them away," I improvised hastily. "Storage for the summer." And moved with all speed toward the bedroom.

Her head cushioned between two pillows, face downward, Marjorie groaned.

". . . horrible," she muttered.

"I'll send up coffee," I said sympathetically, and left. I knew from past experience she would not be ready for coherent conversation until some time later in the day. After dinner, perhaps.

I brewed double the usual amount of coffee, double strength as well, and while it dripped I broke a raw egg into a glass of tomato juice, added pepper and Worcestershire sauce, and stirred briskly.

"Looks like finger paint," said Buddy, who had joined me, now fully dressed. "What is it?"

"Medication for your mother," I said. "You be the Aid Man—take it up and tell her to close her eyes and drink it down all at once. Then come back and I'll feed you."

He disappeared, bearing the nostrum carefully in both hands. I was finishing my first cup of coffee when he returned.

"She says to go away and leave her die in peace," he reported. "Say, is Mom sick or something?"

I patted him reassuringly. "Just 'or something,'" I said. "What do you want for breakfast?"

He opened the grocery closet and stood reflectively staring at the eight or nine assorted cartons. He reached out a hand, then froze. A full two minutes later, I found him still there, immobile. "Don't you want cereal?" I asked. "Of course," he said. "I just can't figure out which *one*." He shook his head sadly. "I had Rice Chex yesterday . . . and the day before I had Cheerios. . . . I don't *feel* like Corn Flakes. . . ."

"Rice Krispies?" I suggested.

"Too noisy."

"Raisin Bran?" I offered. "Brimming with flavor, packed with get-up and go-go-go?"

"Sticks in my teeth," he said.

"Wheat Chex, then," I offered, handing him the carton. He eyed it, then handed it back. "Nothing to read on the box."

I cursed the ingenuity of Messrs. Kellogg and Post. "That school bus waits for no man," I prodded. "Why not blend? Make a mixture. Say, Frosted Flakes on a bed of Shredded Wheat, topped off by Rice Krinkles?"

Buddy shook his head. "For Pete's sake, why *not?*" I insisted. "Sure it's a departure from the norm, but it might work—"

"Two have sugar on them and the other doesn't," he said. "It'd be a mess."

I gave up, turned away, and dropped my two eggs into boiling water. Just because Buddy lived in a complex world was no reason why *I* should starve. "Eggs," exclaimed Buddy. "You're having eggs. Why can't *I* ever have 'em?"

"Just don't tell anybody you broke your diet," I said conspiratorially, and dropped in two more. "I wouldn't want your mother to know I was loading you up with protein behind her back."

Five minutes later, we sat across from each other, munching eggs and toast in silence. One of Buddy's unexpected virtues is his ability at times to practice Apartness in moments of Togetherness.

Then the crows came wheeling back, high up in the elm trees, screaming vituperation. I got up and shut the window.

"They have radar, y'know," said Buddy, mouth full.

"Who does?"

"Crows," he informed me. "Some kind of telepathy. I was reading about it in a natural-history book." He mopped his plate carefully. "You know what would be fun?" he challenged. "If we here down below could rig up some kind of a transmitter to tune in on their wave lengths, then we could control their minds. Can you imagine being able to send those crows up there regular messages?"

I finished my third cup of black coffee. "Not offhand," I said. "I haven't any taste for conversation with them. Merely homicidal instincts."

"I'd send 'em out on raiding parties," Buddy said. "In formation, maybe. Just think, twenty or thirty crows, all in a tight V—one crow above flying wing, just like in World War II . . . and I'm down here in the garage sending up messages, telling them where the target is located. . . ." He put the egg cup over his ear like an earphone. " 'From one hundred feet, precision bombing of Mr. Foster's corn crop! Good luck, chaps!' "

"Buddy Fleming, the Scourge of the National Grange," I said. "Incidentally, amigo, you've got egg on your chin. . . . And by the way, what was that device you were doodling last night on the telephone pad?"

He shook his head. "I don't remember."

"That 'Internal Space Lock for Double Something?' " I prodded.

"Oh, *that*," he said. "Let me see. . . ."

A quarter of a mile down the road, there came the blast of the school-bus horn. In full reflex action, Buddy jumped to his feet, retrieved his school satchel from beneath the piano in the living room, clapped his baseball cap on his head, stuffed a handful of trading cards into his pocket, and raced back to me, hand outstretched.

18

I placed his lunch money in it. "Don't you remember what it was going to be?" I urged.

"Nope," he said. "Probably had something in my head at the time, but it's gone now. Mrs. Parker said it was past my bedtime and I never got to finish. . . . See you, Pop!"

The front door slammed, and I was left to brood silently on the misplaced zeal of our over-responsible baby sitter. Would it have cost her anything to have allowed my son five more minutes in which to develop his fancy?

I poured black coffee into the Thermos jug, found a tray, added cup and saucer, and carried the second phase of Marjorie's morning medication upstairs to the bedroom.

She was lying on her back, eyes shut. I placed the coffee on the bedside table and started out.

"You were trying to poison your own wife," she muttered.

"Good morning, dear," I said softly.

"Using your own son as an accessory," she added.

"I'm off to the shop," I whispered. "See you tonight. The baby's still asleep. Turn over and get another hour. It'll do you good."

"Please stop shouting," she said, her eyes still shut. "And take that noxious mixture away with you when you go."

I retrieved the hangover remedy and prepared to leave.

"Wait," said Marjorie, supine on her bed of pain. "Would you mind filling me in on one thing? . . . It's about last night."

"A superb evening," I enthused. "I hope you enjoyed it as much as I did."

"We were celebrating?" As yet, she had not opened her eyes.

"Were we not," I said fervently. "Until all hours."

"Were we celebrating something . . . *I* should know about?" Marjorie asked.

I sat down on the edge of her bed. The sheets rustled beneath me. "Please!" she protested, ". . . the *noise!*"

"Sorry," I apologized.

"When your son delivered that ghastly brew to me this morning, he said, 'Good morning, Mother dear; how does it feel to be affluent?' " Marjorie said slowly. "He then said—and these are his exact words, 'Because we are *rich.*' "

"Your son is, as usual, right," I said, and took her limp hand in

19

mine. "Dear, we *are* rich. Since yesterday morning, when our firm's stock went on the market and rose to nineteen dollars by closing time. Now, nineteen times thirty-five thousand is . . ." I paused, and began to do the figures mentally.

Her eyes fluttered open. Though slightly bloodshot, they were still beautiful as they stared at me.

". . . six hundred and sixty-five thousand dollars," I said. "As of this morning, we Flemings are collectively worth that amount. I tried to tell you last night, but we were"—I cleared my throat—"preoccupied." I kissed her hand. "Darling, we've waited a long time for this to happen, haven't we? We worked and saved and scrimped and planned . . . but now that's all behind us. We've got it made!"

I smiled happily down at my dear hung-over wife. "Tell me, Mrs. Fleming, how does it feel to be medium rich, on your way to being stinking?"

Her eyes, without warning, filled with tears.

Poor creature. The news had been too much for her. She was swamped by emotion.

"It feels . . . awful!" she sobbed.

"Of course, of course," I soothed. "It's a traumatic jolt now, but you'll get used to it. Remember the trouble you had adjusting to having a man in the bed next to you? Then when the kids came, there were all those noises at night—and driving a car—well, that took time, too, didn't it? And now there's all this money. But don't you worry, you'll get accustomed to a big checking account."

"You're lying to me!" she moaned.

"No, I'm not," I said, and leaned forward to kiss her feverish forehead. "You're a rich woman."

She pulled away from me. "Don't touch me! I don't want to be rich!"

"Sorry," I said. "It was in the cards."

She pulled a pillow over her head. "I'm dreaming. . . . A dreadful nightmare. None of this is happening at all. In an hour or so I'll wake up and it will be time to get breakfast and clean the house. . . ."

"We'll get a bigger house," I crooned. "New furniture. You'll get the maid you've always needed . . . new clothes. . . . Maybe we'll take a long trip to Europe. . . ."

Beneath the pillow, Marjorie's shoulders heaved with silent sobs.

"Mother . . . *told* me . . . you were unreliable!" she moaned. "Go *away*."

Ah, well. We all react differently to good fortune. I pulled the blanket over her. Sleep, rich Mrs. Fleming. . . .

I tiptoed out.

4

DURING the drive to our plant, I turned on the car radio and let the news of a new day drift past my ears: A new crisis in Africa, a wildcat strike in the aluminum industry (oh, well, we had just ordered some at the plant—or *had* we?), teen-age gang war in East Harlem, Representative Somebody calling for an investigation of monopolistic practices in the frozen-food trade, tornado warnings in Oklahoma and parts of the Texas Panhandle, and last night, having trounced the Tigers 9 to 1, the Yankees had regained first place. . . .

Well, I was vaguely sorry for everyone's troubles, but on such a morning as this, that's as far as I could go. Perhaps some time next week I'd have the common decency to allow the world's ills to depress me again, but as of the moment, I was soaring too high for the flak from below to bring me down. I was a six-figure man, well on his way to seven, right? And not even the Yanks in first place again —blast them—was going to drag Walter Fleming's spirits into the ground, nosir.

But I needed gas on which to soar, so I pulled into Fizdale's Garage and stopped by the pumps.

Fingering the slight mossy growth on his upper lip that for many weeks he had been fertilizing in the vain hope that it would bring him sexual conquest this coming summer, LeRoy Quint, the attendant, peered through my window. "Fill her up with regular, Mr. Fleming?" he inquired.

"Right," I nodded.

Then . . . "No!" I amended. "Give me a tank of Hi-Test!"

"Three cents extra," he warned. "Well, it's your money."

22

He could say that again.

". . . Channel Four, tonight at eight," the announcer was burbling over the radio, "for another yock-filled toe-tapping half-hour of the Jackie Hasbrouck Party Hop, with Jackie's special guests, prize fighter Carmine Basilio doing the conga, Commander and Lady Whitehead demonstrating the Lambeth Walk, and as an added attraction the Charleston, as done by Zsa Zsa Gabor and her partner, Carl Sandburg! It's a half-hour you won't want to miss. . . ."

But with any luck, I would. The Party Hop was one of Dooley-Finch's enterprises, one that had, in various time slots, survived many seasons of the fickle electronic tube. And, in an indirect way, had been responsible for my current good fortune. The ample profits piled up year after year through the production of such entertainments by Messrs. Arch Dooley and Leonard Finch (whatever *had* become of educational television?) provided us with what is known in financial circles as "venture money."

Out of the mambo and the cha-cha-cha, the fox trot and the waltz, down from the thirty-eighth floor of 425 Park Avenue, had come Leonard Finch's certified check in six figures, and it breathed a measure of corporate life into Science Associates, Inc.

How could I have known, that hot July morning thirty years ago at Camp Ho-Ho-Ka when Screwy Lennie first walked into Tent Five, that someday he would be my silent partner, a cornerstone of my good fortune?

I drove away from Fizdale's Garage, my engine humming happily on a tankful of Hi-Test, remembering snatches of that summer at Ho-Ho-Ka.

It was an opulent camp. It had a frame dining hall, an enormous barnlike building that housed a recreation hall and a fully equipped stage; there were six tennis courts, two baseball diamonds, comfortable bunks for the Midgets, and elaborate tents for the older boys who were "roughing it." The waterfront down by the broad blue lake boasted sailing boats and canoes; there was a woodworking shop for arts and crafts, as well as a string of horses carefully chosen for their docile natures, and within easy canoeing distance across the lake there was an equally opulent girls' camp. The senior counselors were mostly Ivy Leaguers, good at sports, proficient on the ukulele, most of whom disappeared promptly after Taps in the direction of the girls' camp across the water. . . .

The fee for all of this splendor came high, but it was 1929 and my mother had been able to persuade my father to sell some of his Auburn stock and reinvest the proceeds in my summer vacation. Especially since my cousin Jerry would be a junior counselor at Ho-Ho-Ka, and he'd be able to look after little Walter and make sure the lad wouldn't drown in the lake, be carried off by timber wolves, or brush up against poison sumac. . . .

Screwy Lennie was small and plump, and his uncombed stringy hair sprayed across his forehead.

"What does your father do?" he demanded, staring at me across the confines of Tent Five and waving a large nickel-plated flashlight fully two feet long in my face.

"Who wants to know?" I replied.

"My father owns a chain of dress shops," he said. "He started with a pushcart and now we live on Central Park West, and he has a Pierce-Arrow. What kind of car do you have?"

"We have a Buick," I said defensively.

Screwy Lennie sneered and flashed the bright light in my eyes. "Cheap car," he said.

"Ah, shut up, you bragger," I said, blinking.

"*My* folks are in Europe," he continued. "They didn't want me along so they stuck me in this garbage dump for the summer. It stinks. Tent Five stinks. They moved me out of Tent Four because I had a fight, and that tent stank too."

No amount of lecturing by Cousin Jerry, who was assigned to supervise Tent Five, seemed to have any influence in changing Screwy Lennie's attitude. He made a sloppy bed; he refused to go out for sports; and worst of all, when a large box of Schrafft's candy arrived for him, he refused to share it with his tentmates.

"I don't know, Lennie," sighed Jerry. "You just don't have the proper Ho-Ho-Ka spirit."

"*You* stink too," snarled Screwy Lennie, and buried his nose in a copy of *Captain Billy's Whiz-Bang.*

After that, we all gave up. Even the silent treatment didn't seem to have any impact on Screwy Lennie. He went where he pleased, avoided organized activities, and ignored the rest of us. Which was frustrating, for when you are giving an oddball the silent treatment, he is supposed to *feel* it—not give it back to *you.* . . .

July moved along, and finally Lennie surprised us all by capitulating to group activity. Grudgingly, he joined the Ho-Ho-Ka Tribe. The Tribe met twice a week after Taps for a campfire down at the beach. There, Uncle Dan, the nature counselor, gave brief talks on the habits of wild life, explained Indian sign language, showed us how to walk soundlessly through the woods, and led the assembled Braves, squatting cross-legged in their camp blankets, in Indian songs and games. After which we roasted marshmallows.

I think it was probably the marshmallows that lured Lennie into the ranks. He gobbled them voraciously, making a complete pig of himself over them. His performance was repulsive. But they kept him in line and he continued to attend. Eventually he even deigned to begin earning a few badges. The badges were small brightly colored felt strips that we sewed to a sash (ten cents), and they represented achievement in swimming, nature study, sports, woodworking, and other manly pursuits. To win one, and to be presented with it by Uncle Dan by the orange-red light of the fire, with the cool Maine night wind fluttering the giant trees around us, was indeed a proud moment in a Brave's summer.

Earlier, I'd spent several mornings in the woodworking shop constructing my own small model of an Indian canoe, patiently gluing together the delicate frame and then stripping a piece of birch bark from a nearby tree for the skin. When it was finally done, I bore it proudly to my tent and set it on my bed.

Lennie, reading on his bunk, had sat up and examined it. Then he waved his flashlight for emphasis in my direction. "Pretty good," he said grudgingly.

Caught off guard by his unexpected approval, I mellowed. "Want me to show you how to make one?"

He shook his head. "Too much work." He yawned. "Want to sell it?"

"Why should I want to sell it?"

"To make some mazuma, you stoop," he explained. "I'll give you a buck for it."

A dollar was a lot of money to a ten-year-old, even in those lush days. It could buy twenty Hershey bars with almonds at the camp store . . . or ten rolls of Necco Wafers and ten Charleston Chews . . . or four copies of Flying Aces magazines . . . or a Scout knife with a can opener.

The canoe was the first example of my own handiwork that anyone had seen fit to purchase for hard cash. We settled for a dollar ten. I promptly spent the money and forgot about the transaction when Cousin Jerry, as assistant dramatics counselor, drafted me to help him backstage on the camp show. I spent most of my next weeks sitting up high in the musty loft above the stage, patiently sorting costumes that had been stored for endless summers in huge trunks, or chasing around camp collecting props. In a week we would be presenting a full-dress production of *The Ghost Train*, and the menial labor involved in an amateur three-act production seemed endless.

One night I was excused early from dress rehearsal for the Tribe meeting. I ran to the tent, wrapped my blanket around me, and hurried down to the lake. The bright flames and the odor of burning pine cones seeping through the darkness told me I was late—but not, I fervently hoped, too late for the marshmallows.

Uncle Dan was handing out badges. In the half-light, Braves stood up as their names were called, marched proudly over to the fire, and received their rewards. Dutifully, we applauded each achievement. Was not Good Sportsmanship the first foundation stone of a true Brave?

"Brave Finch . . ." intoned Uncle Dan. "Step forward."

A squat figure, shrouded in his blanket, scuffed across the ground to the fire. What had Lennie managed to earn?

"We do not often present badges for Craftsmanship," Uncle Dan was saying. "It is a difficult task to produce something good enough to pass the high standards of our Tribe. But Brave Finch has surprised me with *this*, which he has been working on for several weeks."

He held up a small object. I squinted at it through the uncertain light. It seemed familiar in shape. As well it should. It was my birchbark canoe.

"Hey!" I yelled, without a pause, "*he* didn't make that—*I* did!"

Amidst the blanket-shrouded Braves who sat cross-legged in a semicircle, there was a stir of confusion. Uncle Dan turned toward me. "Step forward and identify yourself."

I stepped forward and did so. "*You* made this canoe, Brave Fleming?" he inquired, his echoing voice bouncing among the trees.

"Say it's a mistake," Lennie hissed under his breath. "Shut up. I'll settle later. . . ."

In other circumstances I might have done so, but his outrageous

26

duplicity brought forth a flood of righteous accusation. I explained the details of the transaction in full.

Silence.

Then Uncle Dan turned to Lennie. "Brave Finch," he said, his deep voice trembling with emotion, "you have disgraced the fair name and honor of the Ho-Ho-Ka Tribe. As of this moment, you are no longer a Brave in good standing. Give back your sash. I expel you from our midst."

"Ah-hh—crap!" shrilled Lennie, ripping off his sash from beneath the blanket and throwing it full in Uncle Dan's face. "The Tribe stinks!"

There was a gasp of censure from the assembled Braves. Lennie ignored it. Switching on his enormous flashlight, he stalked out of the firelight, and disappeared.

He was not in his bed when we returned from the somewhat subdued marshmallow roast that followed. Jerry, tired from the rehearsal, finally appeared. Quickly he relayed the news to Uncle Jack and Uncle Harry, the camp owners. They instituted an immediate search. The camp came awake. Lights were switched on. The swimming counselor and his aides went paddling out onto the lake, and under the direction of Uncle Dan parties went out north, south, east, and west into the woods. This was no joking matter. We were surrounded by dense forest, in which a rebellious ten-year-old city boy could become very lost in a matter of minutes. Especially at night.

By 5:00 A.M., with no sign of Lennie, Uncle Jack, normally placid and jovial, was nervously discussing the advisability of calling in the nearby Forest Rangers. At six the searching parties came back, had coffee and eggs, and went out again.

Somewhat disturbed by my own inadvertent role in this dreadful crisis, I ate breakfast and then went over to the recreation hall. Since I was too small to be chosen for a searching party, and there was nothing else organized at this hour, I turned to my backstage duties.

I climbed the steps to the loft—and almost fell back down them in surprise.

There, seated on the floor, leaning against one of the trunks, was Lennie. Flashlight by his side, he was casually scanning the pages of a small paperbound book.

"Wha—" I gasped, in mingled relief and fury. "Everybody's out looking all over for you—and you're right *here!*"

"Let 'em look," he snarled. "Let 'em look all day. I hope they all choke." He beckoned to me, his mood changing abruptly. "Hey, you lousy double-crosser, want to see something?"

He held out the book, pages open.

It seemed to be some sort of cartoon book. The faces of the characters were recognizable. Jiggs and Maggie of the Sunday comic pages we all devoured—yes, them I knew. . . . But what was this they were doing, with Maggie's clothes tumbled around her, and Jiggs bending down? This, I did *not* know. But as I stared, hypnotized, my stomach began to churn, and I realized that what I was looking at—this was something forbidden . . . *defendu* . . . *verboten* . . . wrong, wrong!

"Where'd you get this?" I finally managed to gulp.

"From your cousin Jerry's trunk." Lennie sniggered. "Him and his camp Ho-Ho-Ka-spirit malarkey . . . Look what he's been reading after Taps all summer, the big faker!"

"If Jerry finds out you went into his trunk, he'll kill you!" I raged. "You're a thief! I'm going to report you!"

"No, you're not," Lennie told me. "Just you open your trap, just once, and I drop *this* on Uncle Jack's bunk and tell him how I found it on the tent floor between your bed and Jerry's—which means it belongs to one of the two of you for sure, doesn't it?"

I stared at him, caught for the first time in my young life in the clutches of an expert in blackmail. "Now," he continued, "I'll tell you what you're going to do, Brave Fleming. Because you opened your big mouth, I'm out of the Tribe. So who cares? Not me." He snorted. "But there's four more meetings before the end of camp . . . and instead of *you* eating the marshmallows, you just better save yours and bring 'em up to the tent to *me*, see?"

"I don't see why I should!" I said. "You're the one who pulled that crummy trick and—"

Lennie waved that small, disgusting, fascinating paper book at me.

So I brought him the marshmallows. It didn't much matter. . . . I was getting tired of marshmallows anyway.

And while he ate them, he let me finish reading Jerry's book, by flashlight, under the blankets. . . .

I never went back to Ho-Ho-Ka. In the fall of 1929 something had happened called The Crash, which meant that nobody was supposed to discuss money with my father, because he would instantly become irritable and yell at us.

And Screwy Lennie? Well, he, grown to man's estate, was now one of our principal silent partners. Silent, that is, in a corporate sense. In the flesh, from the first day of our meetings a year or so ago, Lennie Finch had monopolized the conversation. Sprawled on his Robsjohn-Gibbings couch in his teak-paneled conference room at 425 Park, deigning to hold court to the two supplicants before him, Jerry and myself, Lennie Finch, now fortyish, amply fleshed, well barbered, and exuding the aroma of success from each and every pore, had talked incessantly.

Inhaling a Balkan Sobranie cigarette (". . . can't trust these delicate membranes to domestic blends"), his frame elegantly swathed in a suit of navy-blue cashmere ("Spanish tailors are the only ones left who know how to cut a decent lapel and stitch it by hand"), tapping the thick pile carpet with one large foot encased in a Peel oxford, while gazing contentedly at the pleasant, tax-deductible Braque on the wall behind us, ex-Brave Finch had given quite a show.

And we listened respectfully, smiling and nodding as he told us of his presence at a select dinner party the previous evening, the guests having included two senators, the editor of *Vogue*, a tennis champion, Marilyn and Art ("damn bright girl, and he, well, maybe Art's plays are a *touch* depressing, but underneath it, he's just a sweet good-natured guy"), the Mayor and one of Texas' most powerful and shadowy financial titans (". . . mentioned a little tax situation in Florida you ought to call your broker about, boys; but don't take a flyer until you've checked with your accountant, because you may be in the wrong bracket; this is strictly a loss arrangement, see?"), and afterward Ethel came in and sang and Steve played piano for her (". . . talented, *talented* boy. Maybe he doesn't register with the great unwashed, but with the upper tenth, he has Stature").

Then he'd told us in detail of his coming two-week sojourn at the newest exclusive resort on one of the most secluded Caribbean islands. ("So it's two hundred a day, but dammit, privacy, real privacy, comes high.") We'd heard of his new car ("Rolls just yells money, but a Bentley is a touch more *muted*, y'know?") and been treated to a room-by-room description of the house his wife was redecorating in Westchester. ("Hell, I told her about the tax advantages of a co-op I know I could steal on Park—a friend of mine just took over the layout—but *she* is just not a city girl, and wants the kids to grow up *simply*.") Here, he'd turned his eyes on me.

"You know Scarsdale, don't you, Fleming?" he'd asked. "I seem to associate you with it."

"Oh, yes," I said. "I know Scarsdale."

"Unpretentious, but pleasant," Lennie remarked.

"What *do* trees cost these days in Scarsdale?" I asked. I saw my cousin Jerry throw me a warning glance, but it was too late. Lennie had already caught the needle point of my involuntary remark. "Witty, aren't you, Fleming?" he'd said, one corner of his mouth turning upward. "Tell me, where did you and I first meet?" he asked. "It was at school, wasn't it?"

"No," I corrected. "The three of us first met at Camp Ho-Ho-Ka. Don't tell me you don't remember?"

He shook his head and lighted another Sobranie with the flame of an elegant gold lighter. "Not much," he said.

"Tent Five," I insisted. "You and I—"

"Lennie," Jerry had interrupted, "the three of us have something much more important to discuss. Why don't we get to it?"

It hadn't been until an hour or so later, after we'd talked business steadily, shown Lennie blueprints of my proposed model 55B and gone over costs, prices, projected profits, tax structures, and so on, that he'd risen. "I'll have my boys and the lawyers go over your whole deal, and if they give it a clean bill of health, well, I figure we may come to some sort of basis for participation." He'd waved a plump hand in farewell "Got to run to Pavillon; luncheon meeting with Frank and Bill. It's been damn interesting; keep in close touch, and don't forget, I expect to see at least 20 per cent on my investment within two years, fellows."

"You and your sarcasm!" Jerry said, as he stuffed documents into his attaché case. "You almost blew the whole deal out the window with that snide crack about Scarsdale. And Camp Ho-Ho-Ka! Why did you have to keep harping on *that?*"

"Sorry," I said. "I couldn't help it. Maybe I just can't adjust to this Leonard Finch. I look at him and I keep getting the image of Screwy Lennie. And he *was* in our Tent—or have you decided to forget, too?"

Jerry turned around. He's several years older than I, a physical fact that at our present age—the forties—should now be decently obscured by time. Jerry has thick gray streaks about the temples and so do I, but even now vestiges of his junior-counselor attitude toward me often emerge. "Look, Walter," he said, "this is twenty-nine years later. Leonard Finch is not Screwy Lennie. He is a powerful man in quite a few areas, and it's taken me several months to get next to him. *If* we get financing from him, rather than falling into the hands of those downtown banking-house pirates, we will count ourselves to be very damn fortunate."

"I'm aware of that," I said.

"And in our future relations with Leonard," Jerry warned, "no more reminiscences. Brainwash Ho-Ho-Ka from your encyclopedic memory, will you please?"

"Okay," I said, helping myself to a souvenir—one of Leonard's Balkan Sobranies from the silver box on the table. "But he did steal your Jiggs and Maggie book. And he *was* expelled from the Tribe—"

"True!" admitted Jerry. "Now bury the past forever—and let us march forward."

We'll to the Maine woods no more I mused, and pocketed Leonard's cigarette. It was too rich for my taste buds, but I would give it to Marjorie as a token of my journey into the upper regions of high finance.

5

I DROVE into Bayport and headed for our plant.

"The Company's principal base of operation and manufacture is a modernized, fireproof two-story structure at 22 Water Street, Bayport, Connecticut," reads the spare and Spartan language of the description prepared by our lawyers for the SEC prospectus released by Lindstrom, Handvogel & Co., our underwriters. "Said premises were leased in 1958 for a period of three years, at a basic rental of $3,400 per annum, with Science Associates retaining the option to renew for three years in 1961 for three years further, at $3,600 for the fourth year, $3,800 for the fifth, and $4,000 for the sixth; and/or the right at any time during the existence of the lease to purchase said building from the owner, Biltmore Realty Corporation, for a total price of $44,500 . . ."

What our prospectus does *not* mention is the manner in which said two-story structure has figured so heavily in the past political history of Bayport, Connecticut.

Erected in 1901, it was for over five decades the proud headquarters of Hose Company No. 2 of the Bayport Fire Department. In 1952 it was officially abandoned by Mayor Raymond B. "Windy" Keller's progressive-minded administration, in favor of newer and more functional quarters for Hose Company No. 2, a spanking new colonial-style building at 38 Turner Place, erected by the Premier Construction Co. of Stamford, Connecticut.

The SEC prospectus also omits the sad details of how said structure, now a boarded-up shell, a symbol of the worst in Early

32

Twentieth Century Municipal architecture, stood empty, inhabited by a few bats, for five long years. Then, a tax-conscious electorate, inflamed by stories of waste and extravagance, fired by the shocking accusation that the Premier Construction Co. of Stamford had added two rooms and a toilet to Mayor Keller's summer cottage in Vermont without charge, threw the rascals out in favor of our present mayor, the Honorable Louis J. Bolla, who said, among other things, "My primary aim, friends, is to get our lovely town back on a sensible, financial basis, so that the Little Man will not be bled white by wanton corruption and wild extravagance!"

Our prospectus (since the SEC does not concern itself with interesting anecdotes) also omits an account of how, at a municipal auction some months later, said abandoned firehouse was sold for a price of $7,500 to the highest bidder, the Biltmore Realty Corp. (". . . thereby ridding us of this white elephant and returning it to the tax rolls, where I hope it will serve to somewhat relieve the crushing burden on the Little Man's hard-earned pay envelope!" said Mayor Louis J. Bolla, when interviewed at Town Hall).

Now since the Biltmore Realty Corp. maintains its place of business in Bridgeport, Connecticut, some forty miles away, none of the Little Men who so happily have been relieved of the crushing burden of owning 22 Water Street, have as yet seen fit to travel to the Bridgeport Hall of Records, where they might discover that the three basic partners in Biltmore Realty Corp. are one J. H. Docker, a lawyer, and Harry and Rose Loreli (the last-named née Rose Bolla, Bayport, Connecticut, in 1921).

The presence of Mrs. Rosa Bolla Loreli on the board of Biltmore Realty may be a factor in explaining why 22 Water Street, which sits smack in the middle of a primarily residential zone, received, in 1958, a variance from the Bayport Zoning Commission so that said premises qualified hereafter for light industrial use and smoke-less manufacture. Corruption? Nonsense. Progress! ("The Commission has decided, and I concur," said Mayor Bolla, following the hearing. "We must go forward! Bayport can no longer think of itself as a quiet Connecticut backwater. If we don't take such steps, we'll wake up and find that our industry has been raided by Southern carpetbaggers offering cheap labor and low tax lures, and who, I ask you, will suffer the most? My loyal friends, the Little Men!")

Can it also be attributed to progress that when parking meters were installed on the streets of Bayport's principal business area last fall, the block on Water Street on which our building stands was left free of regulation?

Or can it be that my cousin Jerry pointed out to Mayor Bolla that we have no regular parking facilities for our employees and that if we were harassed by parking meters we would undoubtedly have to move to some other plant in 1961?

I prefer to call it benevolent despotism, and since most of the residents of Water Street leave at 8:00 not to return until 5:00 P.M., I was thus able to park my car, this fine morning, directly in front of the next-door residence of one of those same anonymous Little Men whose interests Mayor Louis J. Bolla is so vigilant, twenty-four hours a day, in guarding from the inroads of extravagance and wanton corruption.

Should you ask any of our neighbors on Water Street what goes on in No. 22, you will be treated to answers that run something like this:

a. "I think it's something electric. You can hear like little motors going alla time."

b. "My kid says he climbed a tree and looked into the skylight and saw a lot of fat dames in a row playing with Erector sets."

c. "They got music playin' all the time. If you ask me, it's a bookie joint."

d. "I don't know what goes on in there, but ever since they moved in I can't ever get a place to park in front of my own house!"

There is some truth in each of the foregoing statements. But since nobody casual from the outside world is allowed past the two double-locked doors leading into the plant (part of the strict plant security that is mandatory in all our contracts), we are not one bit concerned with public opinion. The SEC prospectus will tell you that we "are engaged in the design and manufacture of various electronic devices that are components in various other electronic devices, which apparatus have been adopted by the Armed Forces as standard equipment on certain rocket-powered devices."

Clear?

Now, should you have legitimate business to transact with Science Associates, Inc., the chances are fairly good that you can get into our *outer* office. There, having identified yourself to Leo Banks, who serves as our Plant Security Officer (he is proficient in this

34

work, having come to us from thirty years at the Second National Bank of Bayport), you will be referred to Miss Rita Haverhill. As you stand in the small dusty waiting room, she will give you the once-over through the grimy glass window adjoining her busy switchboard. If, upon subjecting you to a thorough scrutiny, she is satisfied that you are not a crank, representative of a numbers ring, newspaperman, or Communist spy, but are truly here for reasons of honest commerce, she will buzz inside.   1176859

After some time, out will come either Miss Miranda S. Duffy, our General Office Secretary, or Mrs. Felicia Dinkler, Paymaster, Book-keeper, Time Clerk and custodian of petty cash, or young Miss Janice Bastedo, who is General Assistant Everything Else.

Should none of these efficient ladies be able to solve your problem and get you off the premises, you will probably, if you wait long enough, be passed along to Mrs. Hilda Bostwick, who sits guard at the desk directly outside my office and who proudly bears the title of General Executive Assistant.

Mrs. Bostwick, who served three and a half years as a Tech Sergeant in the WAC during the war, is a tall, efficient lady in her early forties. She has been able, since we first went into business, to keep S.A., Inc., operating efficiently on the management level simply because she is devoted to her job, is a magnificent organizer, and the spiritual descendant of the late Ilse Koch.

Ninety-nine times out of a hundred daily interruptions, assuming you have run the blockade of the other girls and finally got to her, Mrs. B. will be able to handle your problem and to send you pack-ing. The hundredth time, when there is nothing left but to bring you in to the boss, she will regretfully rise, throw back her shoulders, thus projecting a truly majestic *poitrine* into space, and march, with you a submissive three paces behind her, into the Executive Office.

Commercial success has reduced our executive standard of living. When we first moved into 22 Water, we had offic*es*, but now Jerry and I share this small nine-by-eleven cubicle. We also share the desk and two chairs, and we take turns sitting near the one fan that keeps the humid air circulating through our windowless cell.

In the beginning, Jerry insisted on his own office. He picked out a large area, had it partitioned off, soundproofed it, paneled it in oak plywood, and had the floor carpeted. "An executive needs a certain amount of flash," he said, justifying the expense.

Those were the early days when, with a skeleton crew out in the shop, Basil Yerkes, our engineering partner, and I were concentrating on getting our XXXXXX Model L-1 (sorry, Security) to function properly.

XXXXXX Models L-1, L-2, and L-3 all had bugs, but L-4—Eureka! She functioned according to design. Jerry had something to sell. And just in time, too. Our basic finances were severely depleted. He departed on an extended sales swing through California, Nevada, and various other Southwestern states.

Not only is Jerry a persuasive salesman, but XXXXXX L-4, bless its little electronic heart, found a ready market. When he returned, a month or so later, sunburned and triumphant, the first development he encountered was that Mrs. Bostwick had moved four new employees from Packaging and Shipping into his opulent office.

Jerry raised hell, but how could he remain angry when Mrs. Bostwick pointed out to him that the shipment of XXXXXX L-4's that the four ladies were assembling on his modern desk was the direct result of his own call on a certain customer in Dallas, Texas?

Defeated but still defiant, Jerry retreated to the conference room down the hall, a small partitioned area that Basil Yerkes and I had been using for testing. Jerry ordered an oak table and four leather chairs, equipped it with drapes and carpeting, and moved in a small portable bar. Before the bills for all this new décor came to Mrs. Bostwick's attention, Jerry was off and selling again, this time the design and working model for XXXXXX L-4A, a more efficient modification of our first success.

He stayed out on the road, selling, conferring, and exultantly firing back telegraphic accounts of his triumphs, for quite some time. Finally, surfeited with travel and expense-account living, he arrived, the conquering hero in a rented Thunderbird, to 22 Water Street. He strode through the outer office, ambled down the hall, threw open the conference-room door, and let out a high-pitched shriek of irritation and rage.

There, sitting at the beautiful oak table, drawing away and doing incessant calculations on a new piece of equipment from IBM, were four strangers, all lady employees assigned to our newly created department, Blueprint and Advanced Design. Beneath the table were the loafers each lady had kicked off for more comfort,

36

and neatly stacked on the portable bar were ample stocks of coke, 7-Up, plastic spoons, Sucaryl, powdered coffee, and Pream.

This time there was a real knock-down and drag-out, but Mrs. Bostwick remained implacable. She pointed out to my cousin that these four shoeless ladies had themselves just been dispossessed from the main factory area by the six newer ladies in Final Assembly. *What* six new ladies in Final Assembly? Why, surely Jerry hadn't forgotten the six new hands hired to help rush out our latest contract for XXXXXX L-4A's? That same profitable order that he himself had snagged for us two months ago from our newest customer in Omaha, Nebraska?

And now where would my cousin and partner, the Demon Salesman, park his attaché case? Why, Mrs. Bostwick had a temporary solution for that. He could move in with *me*.

Try to picture the resultant confusion. Take a morning, say any brisk Tuesday at eleven. Our desk is strewn with empty coffee containers and our ash tray is already stuffed with debris. I am seated across from Jerry, transacting business with one of our electrical suppliers in New Jersey, and I am shouting because the connection is poor. Jerry is dictating a letter to a client, and it is being taken down by Janice Bastedo. For lack of a place to sit, Miss Bastedo is perched on one corner of the desk, affording me an interesting view of her slightly thick ankles. Out in the hall, a carpenter is putting up a partition, cutting off what is left of the open area so that Basil Yerkes can make himself a temporary office, and the hammering is incessant. The door opens, and Mrs. Bostwick, followed by Mrs. Dinkler, marches in. She begins checking off the weekly pay roll on the office adding machine, which, for lack of space outside, has been temporarily moved into our office. She raises her voice. I raise my voice. Jerry raises his voice to Miss Bastedo. "Read back what I just dictated!" he requests. "Did you just dictate something?" asks Miss Bastedo, raising her voice.

"Please keep your voices down," barks Mrs. Bostwick. "We can't afford to make mistakes on the pay roll!"

"This guy is trying to tell me something important!" I plead. "We need an emergency shipment of cable—"

The carpenter outside switches to his electric drill. Jerry rises. "Dammit!" he yells. "This place is a madhouse! I ask you—would an executive of Minnesota Mining have to operate under such primitive conditions?"

"Please shush!" commands ex-T. Sgt. Bostwick.

Jerry glares at her. "Why should I?" he complains. "This is our *executive* office!"

"Perhaps," suggests Mrs. B., with tolerance, "it's time for you to go out and survey the market for new customers."

"Oh, *fine*. That'd settle everything, wouldn't it? I go out and sell another load of Model XXXXXX L-4A's to somebody, and when I come back I'll find you've moved both of us into the men's room!"

"Impossible," she assures him, sweetly. "I've already assigned it to Mr. Horan; he's going to use it to store chemicals."

The chaos builds to a climax. Jerry, defeated, at length leaves for a long lunch.

But on this day, with Jerry still in New York, I was a temporary Robinson Crusoe presiding over a nine-by-twelve island of solitude, coping with the business of the moment in solitary splendor.

I could study the Daily Production Report. (Two Model XXXXXX L-4A's completed as per schedule yesterday, tested and ready to ship.) Good enough. "Well," said I to Mrs. Bostwick, "even though I was called away yesterday, the shop seems to have operated smoothly without me."

Mrs. Bostwick smiled and did not bother to contradict me.

I could have a cup of coffee (courtesy of the ladies in the ex-conference room, bless their thoughtful hearts) and study my mail:

Greetings from the Bayport Chamber of Commerce, with a reminder of the upcoming monthly luncheon meeting at the Nutmeg Grill, often referred to as the Stomach-Pump Room, Honored Guest, Mayor Louis J. Bolla, who will speak on "Making Government Work." (For *whom?*)

A cheery Hi there! from my Class Secretary, requesting news and slyly suggesting a donation to the Alumni Fund (tax deductible, of course). Remembering that my son Buddy was only seven short years away from college, I shrewdly invested twenty tax-deductible dollars in his higher education.

Three bills from suppliers, for assorted amounts, which I passed on to Mrs. Dinkler with speed, a reflex dating back to our precarious beginnings.

"Dear Businessman, Would you like to know HOW I WENT FROM

38

BEING A NOBODY AT $85 A WEEK TO THE BEST-INFORMED MAN IN THE OFFICE AT $35,000 A YEAR MERELY BY CLIPPING A TINY COUPON?" (Maybe I would have last week, but today I simply couldn't care less.) Another letter on heavy parchment. "Dear Sir, It's a lovely morning. You're well, the plant is humming, orders are flowing in, and you deserve congratulations." (Cheerfully, I nod and turn to the second page.) "*But!* . . . IMAGINE WHAT WILL HAPPEN TO YOUR WIFE AND LOVED ONES IF SOMETHING HAPPENED TO YOU THIS AFTERNOON—AND YOU HAVEN'T CALLED YOUR FRIENDLY MAN FROM PRUDENTIAL AND HAD A CHAT WITH HIM *today?*" (They'd be *rich*, you sneaky bastards!)

I was opening another important communication that began "Dear Motorist, Here's the biggest news ever! PARAGON—the Clear Plastic Seat Cover for your car—PARAGON—the Seat Cover that BREATHES through MILLIONS of tiny invisible pores and VENTILATES you while you drive—" when the door opened and Basil Yerkes came in. Time for one of our sporadic Engineering Progress meetings.

He helped himself to a cigarette from my open pack and adjusted his bony structure as efficiently as possible into The Other Chair. Before we persuaded him to come into Science Associates as a full partner, Basil was one of the best engineers at one of the leading electronic outfits in Cambridge. Thank heaven Basil's wife wanted to raise their children in a rural atmosphere, for he rapidly became the glue that held together our burgeoning structure. He spends twelve or thirteen hours every day at the plant, running from department to department, wearing the same suit of Harris tweed throughout the four seasons and replenishing his energy with nothing but Hershey bars and strong tea.

"Okay, Walt," he sighed. "Where were we? Got any new ideas on that modification we discussed last week?"

"I've been kind of busy," I said. "How about you?"

He rubbed bloodshot eyes. "I was going to have a crack at it last night but Basil Junior woke up and started tossing his cookies all over the place and things kind of got out of hand."

"What'd the doctor say?"

"That croaker," he groaned. "Fifteen a house call, and leaves a sheaf of prescriptions for pills that cost a buck apiece. My kids contract only expensive viruses. Then this morning I couldn't get the damn car started."

"What was wrong?"

He shrugged. "How in hell would I know?" demanded the Electronics Wizard of Water Street. "I called a cab. Whatever it is, the damn garage will charge sixty bucks. Now, about this damn modification—"

"Basil," I interrupted, delighted to be the bearer of glad tidings, "how many shares of our stock do you own?"

"I forget," he said. "The damn certificate's in my house somewhere. Now, supposing we sit down Saturday—"

"You own exactly twenty thousand shares, and get that damn certificate into a damn safe deposit box!" I ordered.

"When I find the time," he said. "Now, Saturday, when it's quiet around here—"

"Basil!" I said. "Those twenty thousand shares of yours are selling today at eighteen dollars!"

"Good," he said. "You and I can sit down—"

"*Apiece!*" I cried. "This morning, you and Leatrice are worth three hundred and sixty thousand dollars. You're rich!"

"Rich?" he said blankly.

"Rich enough to keep your doctor on a retainer," I told him. "Rich enough to buy a new car. Rich enough to buy a summer suit and your own cigarettes. Not the office's."

"Humph," said Basil. "I hope the kids haven't ripped up that damn certificate." He rose and stretched. "Then it's settled. We meet here Saturday at ten, right?"

"Take the pack with you," I said. He did, and I watched a truly dedicated man leave my office.

Just before noon Mrs. Bostwick ushered in Mrs. Polachek, the Shop Steward. "Mrs. Polachek wants to discuss Internal Plant Conditions," she announced ominously.

What was bothering Labor now?

"Have a seat, Mrs. Polachek," I said, and waited nervously until the hefty descendant of Samuel Gompers lowered herself into it. The chair held. I relaxed.

"It's like this, Mr. Fleming," she began, her sharp eyes boring into me. "Some of the girls in Assembly got together and they were talking . . . during lunch hour, of course. Well, it came up that they would like some social activities. On their own time, of course."

"Mm-mm," I equivocated.

"So what they've decided is to form a bowling team. Now, you and I know there's nothing in the union contract about bowling." She smiled ominously. "Anyways, not *yet*. But don't you think it would be real good for plant morale if Science Associates was to provide the girls with . . . ah . . . snappy jerseys with the initials on the back, see . . . and maybe slacks—"

"Balls, Mrs. Polachek," I said.

She glared at me. "What'd you say?"

"I said the girls will need equipment. Balls, sneakers, rosin . . ." I was feeling like the Ford Foundation. "If they're going to represent us, they must be well equipped. After all, they'll be a Symbol, won't they?"

Mrs. Polachek, usually able to predict the behavior patterns of Management, was thoroughly confused by my sudden corporate philanthropy. So, for that matter, was I. "You mean . . . ah . . . you're suggesting you in here would spring for—"

"The works," I told her. "Why not? It's good advertising—all those attractive girls with a big S.A. on their backs. It'll cause talk. Pick out a vivid color scheme. Call the Sports Shop and get the wholesale prices. And remember, I'm counting on the girls. I won't settle for less than the championship!"

Mrs. Polachek rose, reached across the desk, and seized my hand. She has an excellent grip. Several of my knuckles cracked. "Mr. Fleming," she said, "this is certainly something. I mean, it's a Gesture. The girls out there are going to flip when I tell them what I just negotiated."

"What I just *gave*," I corrected. "Without any argument whatsoever. And supposing we announce it together," I added, in a little fancy footwork of my own. "At 1:00 P.M.—the two of us. Sort of a Management-Labor gesture. How's that?"

"You're the boss," she conceded.

"True." I smiled.

She relinquished my hand. Blood began to flow through it once more.

"Now it's back to the floor for me. Got to keep the merchandise rolling, right?"

She departed, leaving me temporarily triumphant. I say temporarily because five minutes later I realized why she had so readily given ground. By the time I appeared at 1:00 P.M. to make the *beau geste* to the troops, dear Mrs. P. would have had over an hour in which to spread the news everywhere, with herself as the Joan of Arc who had once again wrestled Management to the mat . . .

Ah, well, you can't win 'em all. . . .

On the other hand, my bountiful gift of bowling equipment *might* just help to forestall the much more expensive question of air-conditioning our plant in the summer months to come.

"Mr. Jerry Fleming, calling long distance from New York," announced Mrs. Bostwick.

I picked up the phone, ignoring her hauteur. "Greetings, affluent cousin!" he cried. "Would've given you a blast before this, but my head was a little fuzzy this morning. Then I had to go have a session with the tailor and other essential business. We continue to be hot; there's talk all over the Street about us—all the insiders say we're a 'mystery issue.' We're holding firm at yesterday's price in very brisk trading. Everybody's pumping me about us, but you know me: I'm the Cheshire Cat that ate the canary. How're things by the store?"

"Oh, it runs by itself, naturally," I said. "Automation has set in."

"Now, now, coz," he chided. "Omit the sarcasm. You know there just isn't room for the two of us in that plywood cell of ours, so don't resent my doing a little *outside* work. It keeps me out of your hair and you know I always have our best interests constantly at heart."

"I never need to remind myself," I said. "Your good deeds shine like a beacon in a naughty world."

"And how did dear cousin Marjorie take the happy news?" he asked. "Knocked her flat, eh?"

"That was the secondary reaction, yes," I admitted.

"And she's out getting estimates on mink?"

"Listen, are we going to see your shining face around here later?" I asked.

"We-ell," said Jerry, "let's see. I'm off to a late lunch at 21 with Leonard Finch. He's very pleased with the tone of the Big Picture Ahead of Us—"

"As he damn well should be," I said.

"—and he's got one or two people he wants me to meet. Money-type folks he assures me will do us some good. Of course, it'll drag on, and so I figured I might just as well stay in town overnight and cope with eventualities. . . . *Compris?*"

"You're going foraging," I accused.

"Now, Walter," he said, "not all of us are as fortunate as you—with a pleasant home life and a lovely, attractive wife. . . . Many's the time I've sat in a crowded room and thought: 'Jerry, you are basically lonely. What you need is a good woman, someone like Walter's Marjorie.' "

"Don't let her hear you call her that," I cautioned.

"I mean it!" he protested. "A dear, sympathetic girl. Someone to work for—"

"From whom you'd run like a thief," I said. "Face it. You're a professional prowler, an Artful Dodger. And in all my life I've never seen a better broken-field runner around marriageable-type females."

He chuckled. "Many are called but few avoid being chosen," he said. "You sound a mite jealous."

Mrs. Bostwick, bearing a sheaf of checks that awaited my signature, entered. "I'm not jealous, I'm busy," I said. "Supposing something important comes up and we need to get hold of you. Where do we locate you, or is her number unlisted?"

"It certainly is, so I'll keep in constant touch with *you*," promised the Outside Member of the Firm. "Got to run. Stay well, Affluent Cousin!"

A moment later the operator rang to verify the charges, which Jerry had reversed.

"Should anyone ask for him, is Mr. Fleming planning to be around here later?" asked Mrs. Bostwick.

"He may be tied up for quite a while," I told her. "Don't call him; he'll call us."

"An excellent arrangement," said Mrs. Bostwick. "By the way, Mr. Fleming. That gesture of yours this morning—buying the ladies bowling equipment in the name of the corporation . . . If you don't mind my pointing it out, the timing of your plan is especially helpful."

"In what way?" I asked.

"Well," said my General Executive Assistant, reaching for the checks I'd been signing, "I never pry, of course—"

"Of course," I agreed.

"—but the way it's come to me, some of the ladies out on the floor haven't been too happy about Conditions."

43

"Conditions!" I exclaimed. "We pay 15 per cent better than average rates; we give them group insurance and Christmas bonus; the plant isn't the greatest but we keep it neat and clean—coffee machines, piped-in music, fresh uniforms, a summer picnic. For Pete's sake, what's bothering the troops *now?*"

"It seems," confided Mrs. Bostwick, "that three or four of the girls in Final Assembly—you know, they're the ones who've been getting so much overtime lately—pitched in and pooled their pocket money and formed the Time and a Half Club. For a hobby."

"A club for what?" I demanded.

"For investing in common stocks," she said.

"Shades of the I.W.W.," I murmured.

"And psychologically, they feel a little hurt. The way I get it, they're quite annoyed at you for not having given them any inside information on Science Associates, Inc., stock."

"How do *you* feel about it?" I asked her, when I'd recovered from the news.

"Well, my broker was able to get me fifty shares," she replied serenely. "At twelve. But I think I can see their point. It's the principle of the thing that counts."

Hey, Karl Marx, wherever you are, I mused. *Do you dig this?*

6

I ROARED up the driveway and skittered to a stop a few feet from Marjorie. She was on her hands and knees, weeding a flower bed. "Hi, beautiful," I said. "Care to come buzz a few curves?"

"Get off the property, I'll call my husband—" she began. I took off the tweed cap, and smiled. "*Walter!*" she squeaked. "What are you home so early for in that cap and what in Heaven's name are you driving?"

"This," I told her, "is a Marci-10, designed by the great Farina himself. It is a product of fine Continental craftsmen, powered by a 110-horsepower six that combines fuel economy with the ultimate in styling." I opened the low door and extricated myself. "Care to join me in a spin, Signora?"

Trowel in hand, Marjorie stood up. She wore a bright yellow cashmere sweater and a pair of blue tapered slacks, and for a lady who had just negotiated a busy evening, followed by a dreadful morning after, she seemed extremely well restored. I offered the resilient leather bucket seat to my resilient lady. "Here, slide in."

"Walter," she said finally, her bright eyes fixed on mine, "our phone has been ringing all day. Some man called about insurance. Another man called about mutual funds. Some real-estate lady says she's got a mansion for us that's an absolute steal at sixty-nine five. I kept telling them all they had the wrong number, but they won't listen and would you mind telling me what this is all about?"

"As I mentioned before, Mrs. Fleming, you, I, Buddy, Catherine . . . the Walter Fleming family unit *en masse* is rich. We'll go for a ride and discuss what kind of mansion you'd like; what part of Europe you'd prefer to visit first; how many in help we'll need . . ."

She glanced at the opulent little Italian roadster; then she shook her head. "It doesn't make sense," she murmured. "Yesterday we're economizing on chuck instead of sirloin and today he comes home, wearing a pansy cap and grinning like a fool in this two-thousand-dollar toy. . . ."

"*Four* thousand," I corrected.

"Oh, Walter! That's wicked!"

"The hell it is!" I said. "A man is entitled to buy his wife a little *bibelot* if he's a mind to—especially a woman who's stood by his side all these years and deserted under fire only once, when the plumbing broke down."

She put a hand to her forehead. "But that's as much as we spend a year on heat and laundry and groceries and—"

"—and Buddy's allowance for the next decade!" I added. "Stop caviling. To the manner born, Mrs. Walter Fleming, and never count the cost!"

Again she stared at me. "Then . . . you weren't pulling my leg this morning? You've actually made some money?"

"Not some," I said. "Lots. Jackpot. Grand Prix. Nirvana. Capital-Gainsville, here we come!" I took her arm. "Step into your new car, dear. See how the muted maroon cunningly complements the yellow of your sweater?" I took the trowel from her hand and tossed it to the ground. "Come."

"How did we make a lot of money, Walter?" she asked suspiciously.

"We-ell," I said, "it was the skill and technological know-how of Science Associates, Inc., plus the cash of the great investing public, which seems to have developed unbounded faith in us. This spontaneous love affair has driven our stock to eighteen bucks a share, and now where may I drive *you?*"

Again I took her arm, urging her into the seat, but she pulled away and put a hand to her forehead once more. "What's wrong?" I asked. "Still hung?"

"No," she said. "My head's fine. But suddenly I have a feeling I've been through all this before."

"In another life?" I teased. "You had another husband who came driving up in a spanking new coach-and-four . . ."

46

"No. It was a Duesenberg. And it wasn't my husband." She stared at me. "It was my father. And it was 1928, when we were living in Scarsdale in that big Norman château . . . *that's* it! He came home one afternoon smelling of whisky and dragged us all out for a ride. I don't know what he was celebrating, but it was some big deal he'd just pulled off and we all went to the country club for dinner."

"Those were free-wheeling days, all right," I said. "But this is no time for reminiscence. Let's enjoy!"

"I'd like to," Marjorie said. "But I *can't*."

I helped her into the bucket seat. "Of course you can," I said. "Wait till we hit 70 in this crate—you'll get a whole new outlook on things."

I tramped on the starter, and the 110-horsepower six exploded into life. I backed up, turned, and then we were off, the trees flashing by above us, the soft May wind tousling Marjorie's hair. "Here," I said, handing her my new tweed cap, "use this. . . ."

I headed the car for the back road that winds about the reservoir, curving in and out of the tall spruce trees that protect the water supply. After the curves there was a straight stretch of three miles on which, since it was a weekday, there would be little traffic and I could put on a little more speed.

I took a quick glance at Marjorie. She sat erect in her seat, her face expressionless, my tweed cap jammed incongruously down over her hair. "Isn't it lovely?" I called.

"I guess so."

"Still reminiscing?"

She nodded.

"Ah, come on now, stop that. This isn't 1928; it's 1960. We're not sitting on top of margin and promises; we're making real dollars!"

No answer.

"Honey!" I insisted. "We're not running a bucket shop or speculating in Florida real estate! We have a product and it's needed and we make money with it. It's cash-on-the-barrel-head success!"

She muttered something. "What'd you say?"

"I said that's what my father used to say."

"Things were *different* then!" I insisted.

"I guess so," Marjorie finally admitted. "But—"

"But what?"

"I keep remembering what happened afterward," she said. "I'm sorry; I can't help it. I don't mean to spoil our ride. Let's not talk about it any more."

I patted her hand. "Okay," I said. "We won't."

So we flashed past the reservoir without any more talk about the old days, but dammit, she'd planted a cold little seed in my subconscious, and *I* began remembering too . . .

Depression.

It was a word, a thing, something almost tangible. If you were eleven years old and not yet versed in economics, it was hard to grasp its *why*, or its *what*, but even though you lived in a comfortable suburban Westchester home it made itself felt, seeping in odd ways through the insulation of your daily life.

On Saturday afternoons, for example, when your father saw to it that you went to the movies or a matinee in New York . . . That restaurant on West Forty-fourth Street . . . BERNARR MACFADDEN'S HEALTH FOOD RESTAURANT. LUNCH FOUR CENTS. DINNER SIX CENTS. *"That's awful cheap for food, isn't it?" "It isn't if you haven't got it, son."*

One morning you pass by the home of your best friend, a neat red-brick colonial. You knock on the door, expecting him to come out and go for a bike ride with you. No answer. You peer in the windows. Remarkably, the comfortable living room is shockingly bare of furniture. Where has Jackie Hill disappeared to? *"They've moved away." "Didn't they like it here, Mom?" "The Bank took the house over, dear." "Why would the Bank do that, Mom?"* (A bank is a place in which you faithfully deposit five or ten cents a week in your School Savings Account, not something that moves your best friend precipitously out of your life.) *"Mr. Hill lost his money, dear."* How? A grown man so forgetful? *"It's very complicated, dear; now, don't bother me with any more questions; maybe Jackie will write you a letter from his new address."*

Mr. Hill has lost his money, but there is still plenty in your house. Or is there? *"Pop, can I have ten cents for a copy of* Flying Aces? *There's a nifty serial in it and I want to get the next episode." "I don't have ten cents for you to throw away on that trash!" "It's not trash; it's all about the War and it's real!"* . . . Your father looks wearily up from a desk at which he is working on a set of papers. *"Well, if it's all that important to you, go earn the ten cents."*

And from your mother, no assistance. *"Your father has just had his pay cut by 10 per cent. Don't you realize what that means?"* (It means you will have to sneak a quick reading of the magazine in the cigar store, rather than buying it and bringing it home.)

And then there is another Pay Cut . . . and another . . . and another . . .

Even though this suburb is a well protected island in a sea of trouble, this thing called the Depression sometimes can appear right at the front door.

Mr. Caswell . . .

Why, I hadn't thought of him in years!

It is a bitter gray January day, and your mother is baking. (Whatever became of that comfortable colored woman who'd presided in the kitchen? Did she leave or was it again Economizing?) The doorbell rings and you answer. There stands Mr. Caswell.

He is a stooped man with steel glasses and a scraggly mustache; he has been coming to your door regularly ever since you first moved here, hefting a large worn suitcase that contains samples of canned fruits and vegetables, for which he takes orders. He wipes his feet and smiles hopefully at your mother. (No overshoes? His hands are red, and on such a cold day shouldn't an older man wear some sort of muffler around his throat?) He is opening the sample case and fumbling for his order book. *"Oh, dear, Mr. Caswell,"* your mother says, *"I'm dreadfully afraid I won't be able to order anything from you right now. My husband . . . well, you know what things are like. He says we've simply got to Economize. Perhaps next spring . . . ?"*

Mr. Caswell removes his steel glasses and with a ragged handkerchief he wipes the steam from the lenses. He sways, puts out a hand and, unseeing, sits in the nearby hall chair. "Everybody else says the same thing," he mutters. "I—I was counting on your order, Missus." His naked eyes are shiny. Tears? In your neat front hallway there is the dreadful spectacle of a worn, beaten old man . . . but *a grownup* . . . about to *cry!* And it is not polite to stare, but, aghast, you do. . . .

Your mother, no resistance to such sudden misery in her nature, fumbles in her purse. *"Mr. Caswell, I'm sorry,"* she says. *"Take this for the trouble of making the trip,"* and she presses a bill into his swollen hand. He replaces his glasses to stare at the crumpled bill. Automatically he reaches for his order pad and pencil. *"Ah, then, you'll be wanting something,"* he says. *"Some beautiful Yellow Cling Peaches in syrup . . . Say half a dozen. And how about these Kadota Figs?* Marvelous crop this year, *and so cheap!"*

"Mr. Caswell," she interrupts, *"I don't really need them right now."* He stares. *"Why don't you take the money and consider it a deposit on what I'll order in the spring?"* He shakes his head doggedly. *"You give me money for nothing, Mrs. Fleming?"* *"Why, not exactly—"* *"I couldn't just accept it that way. I don't want charity, Mrs. Fleming."* *"It's a deposit!"* cries your mother. *"Now you come into the kitchen and have some coffee and a bran muffin before you go out into that cold."*

You are sprawled on the living-room rug reading, when Mr. Caswell returns from her kitchen. You can see him pack up his shabby suitcase and close it, strapping it shut with a canvas strap that does not seem to be part of a black leather bag (peeling at the seams, it can't last much longer). Then he thanks your mother for her coffee and goes out into the raw afternoon.

But the five-dollar bill is still on the chair, where he left it.

You rush out the front door; there he is, plodding down your front walk toward the street. *"Mr. Caswell!"* you cry. *"Hey, wait a sec—you forgot something!"* Mindless of the cold, you thrust the crumpled money into the nearest pocket of his overcoat. *"No!"* he objects, *"I can't."* and then he sighs. *"Deposit,"* he mumbles. *"Tell your mother I'll be here in April for sure. . . ."* And, again, the eyes behind the glasses are wet and shiny.

He went plodding down the street, that heavy bag full of beautiful Yellow Clings and Kadotas and Oxheart Cherries and Select Asparagus (the finest, which nobody can afford), its weight pulling his body into a grotesque half-crouch as he sloshes through the street toward the house next door. (They have just moved away too.) You go back to the warmth and comparative security of your house, but where does Mr. Caswell go? Into what long dark emptiness? (*"Maybe he just forgot the money, huh, Ma? Although he kind of didn't want to take it. Why?"* *"Dear, nobody likes to get something for nothing. People like to earn what they get, and please don't tell your father about it."* *"He said to tell you he'd be here in April for sure. . . ."*)

But he was not. Nor did he ever come back again. . . .

Dammit, I wasn't going to think of things like *that* any more! Sure, I knew all about insecurity and bad times and financial reverses. But why should I let it sour my triumph now? What sort of masochism was this?

I glanced across at Marjorie. She sat in her seat, eyes half shut, letting the breeze play across her face.

"Hey!" I cried, banishing the ghost of Mr. Caswell, "how do you like the way this little beauty handles?"

She blinked, and then I felt her hand reach over to rest against the back of my neck. Her fingers tugged at my ear. "Good old Walter," she said. "Finally got your Iver-Johnson, didn't you?"

"My *what?*" I bawled, above the pulse of the engine. And then, before she could reply, I understood. "Good Heavens—you never forget *anything*, do you?"

Of course she was right. This opulent little example of Italian handiwork *was* the lineal descendant of the Iver-Johnson Speedster, that shimmering, tempting goal for which I'd rubbed my shoulders raw so long ago. . . . Oh, yes, if the boys from *Fortune* ever come to do an interview, I can always casually refer to my early Horatio Alger beginnings. How, on Tuesday afternoons, after school, young Walter Fleming shouldered his canvas bag filled with ten *Saturday Evening Post*s (five cents) and five *Ladies Home Journal*s (ten cents) and in the name of George Horace Lorimer and the Curtis Circulation Corp. went forth to earn himself a bicycle and simultaneously to do good for the reading public.

In plain truth, no Johnny Appleseed of the printed word was I; I was simply a hapless fool, trapped by lust and glib promises. As I trudged down the streets of our village, those damned *Saturday Evening Post*s growing heavier with each successive front-door turndown (who ever said this was *light* reading?) the only thing that kept my tired feet moving was the vision before me of stacks of Freenies. (Green Coupons, one for each *Post* we sold, two for each *Journal*.) One hundred Green Coupons, and the enterprising youthful salesman could convert his hoard into one Brownie. Five Brownies = one genuine A. G. Spalding Catcher's Mask. Fifty Brownies (oh, Mount Everest of accomplishment!) = (roll of drums and tattoo of bugles in the background) one blue-and-white gleaming chrome-trimmed Iver-Johnson 28-inch wheelbase Speedster bicycle!

"It's easy," promised the youthful Fagin of my early days, the Queen Bee of this nefarious web, a red-haired fifteen-year-old named Dugan who had already earned a catcher's mitt, plus a bicycle, plus a *telescope* yet! And in reward for this ferocious effort, he had been appointed Neighborhood Circulation Director. This meant that his garage was, each Tuesday afternoon, the shape-up for the half-dozen luckless drones, myself included, who'd been lured into this racket.

There was a family a block away named Frederick.

The older daughter was named Lee, and she was a beauty. Lee, who at thirteen could already fill a pale-blue taffeta party dress with an assortment of the most interesting bulges and curves, whose long brown curls bobbed rhythmically up and down as she shook her head "No" to all the local swains playing court. To an eleven-year-old, the spectacle of a beautiful fourteen-year-old girl is a throat choker. For, after all, she was Unattainable. Was it not rumored that she had Regular Dates—not just afternoon appointments to go to RKO Keith's in White Plains for a double-feature with soda afterward at the Greek's, or engagements for the monthly Dancing Class teas—but the Real Thing! Dates with tweedy arrogant Men! (There was one who was sixteen and a junior at Choate, with the use of the family's Essex Terraplane, and Heaven only knew what went on in that rumble seat.)

The Fredericks had another daughter, but nobody gave her the right time of day. A dumpy, quiet little creature whose teeth seemed permanently doomed to steel braces, she was a shadowy, silent satellite to the shimmering planet Lee, by name, Marjorie.

They lived in a large Tudor imitation, with pines along the road effectively screening the mansion from commoners passing by. (PRIVATE ROAD: NO TRUCKS OVER TWO TONS WT. By Order Scarsdale Police Dept.) I was two grades behind the Lady Lee in school, which put me on one side of a formidable social gulf, but once she had smiled at me during recess . . . and perhaps I could sell her a *Saturday Evening Post*.

I rang their doorbell. The house was so large and imposing that I couldn't even hear the sound of the peal inside.

I stood waiting, that bag with those damn unsold *Post*s and *Journal*s cutting into my shoulder like a steel wire. I rang again. No answer. So I gave up and turned away. As I did the door was suddenly pulled open. "What *is* it?" called a female voice, inside the house. "Oh, it's nobody but some *boy*, Mother."

Lee Frederick herself. And such hauteur in her tone!

"Not just some boy—it's *me!*" I protested.

In the doorway appeared an older woman, one who had once been attractive but whose eyes were now bleary and who dabbed at them with a lace handkerchief. "*Saturday Evening Post?*" I asked. "Just out, only five cents. *Ladies Home Journal?* I'm working for a bicycle, see, and every copy I sell helps me get one." "Oh my God!" cried the older woman. "On a day like this, with everything collapsing, some child nagging about *magazines*—" The door slammed shut.

What had I done? Had disaster struck the Fredericks? Was I responsible? I turned and started down the flagstone walk, the unsold magazines like an albatross around my neck. The walk wound in circuitous fashion around an elaborate flower bed in need of weeding and then through the dense covering trees by the road.

"What's in the sack?" asked a voice.

There, seated cross-legged beneath the boughs of a large spruce, her knobby knees protruding beneath an ugly pleated black skirt, sat a small girl, about nine. She stared inquiringly at me.

"Magazines," I said.

"Oh, that's interesting," she said.

"Magazines nobody wants," I added, my pent-up frustration beginning to boil over. "Nobody in this whole damn town wants to buy a *Post* or a *Journal* and they treat you like a crook or something just because you're working to earn your own Iver-Johnson bicycle!"

"I don't want a bicycle," commented the girl.

"Nobody in your house wants anything," I muttered, trying to shift my burden to the other shoulder.

"But I'll buy a magazine," she added. She rummaged in her middy blouse pocket, removing half of an uneaten Tootsie Roll, a crumpled handkerchief, and finally two pennies and a nickel. "For my mother," she said. "She's upset because something awful has happened to my father in business and he won't come home. She probably yelled at you, but don't be sore. How much?"

"The *Post*'s a nickel," I said, but it somehow seemed undignified to take the money from a customer younger than oneself. "But maybe you oughtn't to spend your money if something happened to your father."

She held out the nickel. "Maybe it'll make her feel better," she said. "Has it got funny stories in it?"

I pulled forth a copy. "There's a new serial by Clarence Budington Kelland," I said hopefully. "Maybe that'll help."

She took the magazine. I took the nickel. "Hope she enjoys it."

"Hope you get the bicycle," she called, as I started down the steps.

"So do I," I said fervently, shouldering my burden. I started down the walk, the Sinbad of preadolescent commerce.

"When you do, I wish you'd bring it around and show it to me," she called.

"Sure," I replied, without conviction.

The following week I went back, hoping that someone in the house would want to pay five cents for the next episode of Mr. Kelland's entertainment. But the Fredericks had moved away and the house was empty. . . .

"Mother never looked at the magazine," Marjorie told me, that night during the war that we ran into each other. "But I did. You know, that serial was dreadful. Did you ever get the bicycle, Walter?"

"No," I confessed, still trying to associate this trim and attractive Wave ensign in the noisy Miami Beach cocktail lounge where the glass windows were hidden by blackout curtains with that plump, middy-bloused-and-braced nine-year-old. Such a metamorphosis occurred only in fiction! "I gave up the *Post* route a month or so later. When I went around to your house, it was empty. Whatever became of all of you?"

"Oh, Lee's married and living in Chicago, has two kids and a third on the way and a pediatrician for a husband—" Vanished, then, the delicious, unattainable Lee of my furtive midnight reveries. Sad . . . But I glanced again at my new-found companion, and my now-practiced eye could recognize that beneath those severe fittings of dark blue dwelt not a stumpy little satellite but a softly rounded, well-made female. Off with the old, I thought. "But where did you people go after you left?" I asked, raising my voice to be heard above the frenetic din of other servicemen and their temporary ladies.

54

"Well, we never owned that house," said Marjorie. "Daddy finally moved us into a furnished apartment somewhere in Jackson Heights." She sipped at her rum-and-coke and made a face. "Then, somehow, he was making money again. This time it had something to do with scrap iron. He and some other man had bought an old freighter that had run aground, and figured out some special way of cutting it apart and selling it."

"To the Japanese, no doubt?"

She nodded. "That thought *has* crossed my mind. Anyhow, pretty soon he was back at the tracks, spending it as fast as it came in, and we were out of the Heights and in some big place out on Long Island, rented, of course. You know," she said, with the same candor of that long-gone nine-year-old on the front lawn in Scarsdale, "he's like Micawber. Something will always turn up. When the money comes in, he refuses to save any—in fact, he seems to *have* to get rid of it. . . ."

"Compulsive guilt complex, perhaps," said I, from the depths of my one-year psychology-course wisdom, useful in discussions of this kind and all-powerful on automobile back seats for the dispelling of female inhibition.

"I don't really know," said Marjorie. "Maybe it's a game or something. He feels that if he keeps the money in circulation that somehow it will seed *new* money. Right now he's got leases on a couple of hotels that are doing well, but there've been other times when it was a real squeeze. . . ." She stared into her empty glass. "Like my sophomore year at college."

"What happened then?"

She tapped her glass. "Can I have another one, please?" And that seemed to end the reminiscence period, and in truth, I was agreeable. Three months in a converted hotel in this dreary palm-decorated place, the steamy month of August stretching interminably on, and suddenly fortune had presented me with an attractive brunette Wave who by some miracle was sharing a two-room efficiency with only one other girl. Who could tell what delights might ensue?

But this time the pattern was reversed. Marjorie remained in Miami Beach and it was I who was yanked away, mimeographed orders in hand, to Bakersfield, California. My further pursuit of her was delayed until after the hostilities. . . . Ah, the many nights we wasted!

We were heading back toward the house now, the small Italian car buzzing happily down the road. We roared up the driveway; the tires squealed, and gravel flew in all directions.

My son leaped up from the front steps, his eyes wide. "Wow-ee!" he exulted. "A Marci-10! Where'd you get her, Dad?" He caressed the polished bonnet, his fingers leaving behind slight traces of the banana he'd been munching.

"I earned it, Buddy," I told him. "With Greenies and Brownies."

"What're they?"

"Pieces of paper, honey," said his mother.

"Tell me where you get them!"

Marjorie sighed. "I don't really know," she said. "I've always had the feeling that they're . . . printed in somebody's basement by gnomes who appear in the night."

"Jump in," I told Buddy. "I'll take you for a spin."

"You bet!" He wrestled open the door. "Say, let's whip over to Lime Rock and sign up for next month's car meet, what say?"

I grinned at Marjorie. "*He* seems to be able to take it in stride," I said. Buddy was settling himself in her lap. "Why not you?"

"I was traumatized at an early age," she said.

"Who told you that?" I demanded.

"You did," she said. "On one of those nights after the war."

"I'm a lousy psychologist," I told her. "Ignore me. And please relax. You're resisting prosperity with all the rigidity of an Amish housefrau."

She nodded. "Perhaps I ought to get myself a poke bonnet and a long black skirt."

"And a middy blouse and braces?" I asked.

She gave me a dig with her elbow. Which was an encouraging sign. It meant I had reduced philosophic argument to simple physical combat.

"Come *on!*" urged Buddy. "Don't waste time fighting. You can do that *any* day. Drive!"

We drove.

But even though the Marci-10 was, to Buddy and me, a lineal descendant of that long-gone Iver-Johnson bicycle, for Marjorie it was still the ghost of her father's Duesenberg.

7

"Do you know what this outfit needs desperately?" asked Jerry.

"New offices—" I began.

"Those *too*," he said. "But what we need right away that we can get is a base of operations in Manhattan."

We were seated, facing each other in my office, he home from his wanderings in a new suit of cashmere and wool, turning the pages of this morning's *Wall Street Journal* idly and sipping his second container of coffee, I trying to assemble a few notes on paper for my meeting with Basil Yerkes over the weekend.

"We don't need a New York office," I said. "We sell our product as fast as we make it and—"

"Who said anything about an office?" asked Jerry, examining his well-manicured fingernails. "I've already spoken to Schwartzie"— Abel Schwartz was the senior half of our local accounting firm— "and he says the whole thing could be written off as a business expense. A strictly legitimate one at that."

"*What* could?"

Jerry pulled out a pipe and began to fill it with tobacco from a leather pouch. "A hotel suite," he said. "Maybe two and a half rooms in one of those quiet little East Side joints."

"What the hell do we need with a hotel suite?"

"Here," said Jerry, proffering the pouch. "Try some. It's a special mixture they put up for '21.' Strong, but delicious when you're used to it."

"I don't smoke a pipe," I said, "and you haven't answered my question. What would we do with a hotel suite?"

"Use it for entertaining," said Jerry, placing his feet on the desk and blowing clouds of blue-gray smoke toward the ceiling. "I'm in town three, four days every two weeks; I talk to people; you and Marjorie go in to see the shows—"

"Adding up to nine, maybe ten nights out of the month," I said. "What happens the other twenty days? Do we sublet it or just let it stand idle?"

Jerry stared at his shoes, which were obviously new and very expensive. "Oh, we're ingenious fellows," he grinned. "If it bothers you to have it go to waste, I'm sure we'd find *some* use for it."

"Were you planning to hold literary soirees, perhaps?" I asked. "Or rent it out to floating poker games?"

Jerry looked at me reproachfully. "Walter," he said, "you're a good organizer and an excellent businessman, but there are times when your naïveté fractures me. Here we are, finally on top of a situation, sailing *with* the tide for a change. Our stock's holding firm at nineteen; our gross is rising, and the net, I trust, will do the same. Isn't it about time we began to *enjoy* the fruits of our triumph?"

"I'm enjoying it," I said. "I'm enjoying it very much!"

"Tsk, tsk," he said. "Such simple tastes. You bought yourself a nice little Italian sports car. Can't you think a little bigger than *that?*"

"Sure I can!" I said, on the defensive. "We're going house hunting on Sunday. Marjorie's looking for a full-time maid. I'm going to buy her a mink cape and maybe in June we'll sneak off for a week in Bermuda without the kids."

"Interesting," said Jerry. "You're living up to all your obligations, and I'm proud of you. But what about the inner Walter Fleming? The Walter you've been bottling up all these years?"

For a moment I didn't follow him. "Which inner Walter?" I asked. "There's no such person."

"Ah, ah, there *used* to be," Jerry grinned. "There used to be a Walter who didn't have to be told twice about the advantages of a cozy suite on the East Side. I remember you in full flower, old friend. Don't tell me the sap has dried up and completely atrophied!"

"Listen!" I exploded. "I happen to be—"

"—married to a wonderful girl," he said. "Loving, dutiful—"

"—and the mother of—"

"—your two attractive kids. But *don't* tell old Jerry that your eye has stopped roving, Walter. I've seen you rambling around the factory on the first day of spring, boy, taking mental measurements of every girl in the place."

"A mere reflex!" I replied.

"And a perfectly normal one, too." He blew acrid smoke from "21" in my direction. "Which proves my point. Here you are, tucked away in this backwater, coping with business five, six days a week. Is there any law that says that because you're happily married you should not be entitled to a little . . . recreation? And I do not mean golf!"

"No," I admitted, "but I've got a feeling those days are gone forever. Maybe I'm just monogamist by nature."

"*I'm* not," said Jerry, stretching his arms over his head, "and I'd be willing to bet you that if we had that quiet little two-room suite in the East fifties somewhere that sooner or later you'd find some use for it. And I don't mean just on nights when you and Marjorie are too tired to drive home after the theater."

I thought about it for a moment. Perhaps Jerry was right. Perhaps I might enjoy a free evening or so on the town . . . with license to rove. . . .

"You bastard!" I said. "You've *always* been the Lorelei in my life. Go rent your own apartment and leave me out of your fleshpots!"

He leered and leaned over to pat my shoulder, a slightly aging but still functioning Pan. "Think it over, Walter," he said. "Such a place won't cost us a cent personally, and it could return some very interesting dividends." He rose and knocked out his pipe. "I'm not going to hang around here today. Off to business."

Whistling carelessly, he departed.

What a ridiculous man, my cousin. He was pushing forty-five. Wasn't it time he stopped playing Casanova and settled down to a more sober existence . . . like mine?

An apartment in town. Nonsense. Those days were *over*. . . .

Why, I'd even forgotten what it was like.

Almost . . .

In the year 1946, when we boys had come home, and there were shortages in white shirts, new automobiles, housing, decent Scotch, building supplies, and tickets to anything on Broadway, I spent an extended hibernative period in a small one-and-a-half room apartment on East Eighteenth Street, near Stuyvesant Square.

I had returned to the office where I'd been working, just before being drafted, a large advertising agency in the Time-Life Building. All the faces there were new and they were only momentarily cordial. In that office, the little gold bird on my lapel flew only a short distance. My old job? It no longer hum, ha, existed. What had I done in the Army? Any personnel work? Say, how would I react toward taking a crack at a job in Personnel? Mrs. Strasberger down there could certainly use somebody to help her run tests and re-organize; a hell of a good spot for getting back in and learning the *feel* of the shop . . .

Outside, most of my contemporaries, released from one set of disciplines, were hurrying here and there, filling out applications and undergoing interviews, rushing to business lunches and lining up to take this course or that under the G.I. Bill, regrouping into different squads for the disciplines of peace.

But I didn't feel a bit like Personnel, and I certainly didn't want the feel of that antiseptic spot next to Mrs. Strasberger.

What did I want the feel of, then?

The catching up on my sleep, reading books without interruption, seeing good movies—even in the afternoon, eating where and when I felt like it, and mostly, doing it all with proper female companionship. After all, that was the Good Bachelor Life from which I'd been yanked, back in that grim summer of '42. And before American commerce and industry swallowed me up forever into a world of nine-thirty to five-thirty in a sober business suit, I meant to indulge myself in a tweed jacket and slacks for just a little while longer.

So, for several months, equipped with a hefty sum in Army severance pay, I was able to re-create that old cherished image of myself as Fleming, Man About Town, Gentleman of Leisure and Rakehell . . . to wallow in the exquisite pleasures of privacy and debauch . . . the privacy being the right to sleep till noon because there was nothing better to do and the debauch involving nightly attempts on the virtue of various female friends.

For the latter purpose, the apartment was ideally suited. It was a cheerful little flat, furnished in an assortment of styles by the regular tenant, with a view of a small back yard in which grew an enormous oak tree. On soft spring nights, with the windows open and the new leaves rustling in the breeze, the phonograph playing old Benny Goodman records and the sounds of the city far off, muted and still, that apartment was my island. After more than three years of continual masculine company, I wallowed in solitude. . . .

True, on certain afternoons I had to absent myself, to make room for my cousin Jerry. His right to avail himself of the premises derived from the fact that he'd found the place. It was the permanent domicile of one of his various girls, a photographer's model who'd just signed a contract with a movie studio and departed for an extended (we hoped) stay on the Coast.

In her apartment, on her furniture, to the accompaniment of her records and muted bedsprings I entertained a series of females.

I do not mean to brag. Perhaps I was striving to emulate Frank Harris, but in truth I was too lazy to operate in such a gourmandish fashion. Rather, I behaved like a cautious diner at a smörgåsbroad table, sampling and circling, trying a taste of this, having a bite of that. "I don't know *where* you dig them up," Jerry used to comment, "but the ones you chase certainly are different. Tell me, are these broads what you were fighting to get home to? It wasn't worth the battle, bud."

I rejected his scornful critique. *"De gustibus non est disputandum,"* I told him.

"I know, but you're carrying your *gustibus* a little too *far!"* he replied.

As I looked back now, they *were* a strange mixture of conquests. . . .

One was a researcher for *Time*, a graduate of Antioch who wore glasses and hid behind heavy Harris tweeds. She dragged me to small gatherings and parties where intense groups of her confréres sipped wine and discussed The Meaning of the Peace. Afterward I would take her back to the apartment and try to impress her with my knowledge of the same subject on a different level. With the help of Josh White records and a bottle of port, I could usually effect a breakthrough. Having set down her highball, put aside her current pamphlet, taken off her glasses and folded them carefully, she would lean back on the sofa and (mentally gritting her teeth, I sometimes felt) submit. She came to the field of battle with all the enthusiasm and fervor of a political spy being tortured by the police of a hostile government, muttering "Wrong . . . wrong . . . wrong!" in my ear. Later, she would rise, a triumphant phoenix, gather up her tweeds, her glasses, and her literature, and tramp off into the night, scornfully refusing taxi rides down to Jane Street (a sign of weakness).

Where are you now, O ravished Lucelady? The towering masthead of *Time* reveals that you have defected from the ranks. Perhaps to marriage and children in New Canaan? Or do you run an avantegarde paperback bookstore in the Village?

For her I served as hostile inquisitor. But with others I played different roles. Stage-Door John, for one, to an adorable aspiring actress with two lines in a current Forty-fifth Street comedy. I suppose that every man should have, somewhere along the way, one actress. We spend our early years salivating at matinees, and grow up with one universal drive: to be seen with and to bed down one of those glamorous, ephemeral ingénues. Lucky is he who can rid himself of this childishness. The endless waiting in grimy back-stage corridors, the night-after-night feeding of milady at Sardi's, until at last the moment comes. She will! And in the dim bedroom one soars above one's fellows as the delicate creature resists no longer. Oh, sweet triumph, intertwined, mouth to mouth (faint exotic flavor of Stein's Pancake Make-Up) we rise on a tumescent cloud, the actress and her adoring swain . . . and then she breaks free from that last endless kiss and, staring over one's shoulder at the ceiling, murmurs, "I wonder if George Abbott really *was* in the audience tonight . . ."

And there are men who, impervious to reality, actually *marry* these creatures! (Once, last winter, I saw mine in a television commercial. She was playing the part of a mother of a teen-age daughter, in a tense one-minute drama having to do with roll-on deodorant.)

Having rid myself of *that* fixation, I was free to explore other characterizations. For several weeks I served as Good Listener and Sympathetic Old Friend to the temporarily estranged wife of one of my college classmates. Since the rending of her once-happy marriage (he had lingered behind with a British Wren while stationed in England), this poor girl had taken up good works. In her economic bracket (upper Park Avenue) this meant charity; with her, I could feel doubly virtuous as I escorted her to various events: a tea dance at the Pierre for the benefit of some downtown settlement house, an art-gallery opening at Knoedler's where we sipped Martinis and stared at Matisse, all for the benefit of crippled children . . . opulent boat rides and buffets to raise funds for the purchase of musical instruments for an East Side mental clinic. (Some strange sort of therapy was involved here.) And as I continued to squire her in my one precious dark blue suit, gobbling and drinking, it became more and more apparent that *she* was the one who needed the therapy.

Inevitably, since even though rather a dull girl, she was a most attractive one, I made the mistake of confusing pity with desire, and after interminable pseudo-Freudian colloquies on my couch, the phonograph giving forth Debussy, and I plying her with medicinal brandy (Jerry knew a store nearby with a small stock of precious pre-war Courvoisier) I went from Good Old Reliable Listener to Lay Analyst. As I massaged her neck muscles, to relieve the tensions, of course . . . gently, gently, off came the expensive Bergdorf blouse . . . subtly I tugged away at the Bendel underclothes, and it was merely a matter of persistence before the half-bare, troubled Venus was mine, weeping softly and telling me over and over what a complete bastard her husband was.

Our unhealthy little relationship might have developed into something even more insubstantial, those tearful *mea culpa*s continuing incessantly through the long therapeutic sessions, except for the fortuitous return from England of none other than the complete bastard himself. Under the guise of "talking it all out and getting everything settled," he persuaded her to go away for a two-day stay in Southampton. They remained out of town for two weeks. Evidently he, tired of his English conquest, was most persuasive, and she, my patient, masochistic to the core, forgave.

She came only once more to my apartment for a most proper afternoon tea, glowing in her new-found uxoriousness and babbling of their plans to move to California and Start Again. For an uncomfortable hour or so we never touched, but kept our distance until, at the door, pulling on her gloves and glancing at her watch, suddenly she turned and clutched me in a fierce embrace. Swaying against me, she declared, "I'll never, *never* forget how thoughtful you've been, Walter!" We collapsed on the sofa, and when this afterpiece had ended, I had a terrible impulse to say, "And please don't forget to recommend me to any of your friends who need help." But I stifled it and watched her repair her lipstick, rearrange the décor of the proper young matron, and clatter primly downstairs in her high heels, hurrying to meet domesticity . . . and happiness? I never found out.

Her place on the couch was assumed by a procession of others, some too talkative, some too intense, all of whom vanished as abruptly as they came. Fall arrived, and with it football games and invitations to visit old college friends. Most of them were now married and busily raising peacetime babies in cramped flats or in dreadfully expensive suburban rentals, where we would spend the night boozing and reminiscing, I to bed down on the living-room studio couch and be awakened at 6:00 A.M. by a two-year-old in pajamas staring at me as if I were Gulliver. Such tastes of domesticity were reason enough to continue postponing the evil day when I must once again become a Useful Citizen.

Jerry was in public relations now, and had some vague connection with the management of a Vermont ski lodge, one that magically entitled us to special treatment and lowered rates. There we spent several weekends, foraging amid hordes of college girls, the outdoor breed, and New York office girls, up on a manhunt in the latest ski clothes from Ohrbach's. We spent the day bantering with the New York secretaries, who huddled indoors sipping hot buttered rum, and after dark we wrestled playfully with the returned amazons from the slopes.

The fall ended, dirty slush began to line the streets, and there were holiday season parties to attend. Now, as winter closed in, and I would temporarily run out of hospitable friends willing to feed and slake the thirst of me and whatever demoiselle I was squiring at the time, there was always that strange new social phenomenon, the industrial party.

Jerry's desk was littered with the proper credentials for such affairs, and he passed them over to me like some small-time Andrew Carnegie. The variety of these affairs was fascinating. Staid banquets at which ruddy-faced industrialists told jokes about Mandy and Rastus and presented each other with silver-plated desk sets; press conferences at which Hollywood starlets, coached by press agents, plugged themselves and/or their latest Technicolor epic; breakfasts at which political figures mended fences over wheatcakes and sausage; raucous gatherings at Shor's where short men in tight suits clustered protectively around a monosyllabic middleweight contender. Armed with a card from Jerry's endless supply, I might find myself gorging at an afternoon buffet where a collection of synthetic rubber galoshes was being introduced to the press, or raising a highball glass at the Rainbow Room in a toast to the newest miracle ballpoint pen. Once, in a private suite at the Waldorf, I sipped champagne as a delegation in dark-brown suits harumphed and stuttered through a plea for special tax consideration for the hard-coal industry, and three attractive girls in tight-fitting overalls and miners' caps passed out paperweights made of pieces of polished anthracite.

Oh, those were gaymad days, filled with novelty and new excitements, press releases, souvenirs, and always ample food and drink, pouring forth in the best tradition of expense-account hospitality. Who can forget the excitement of the finals of the first Pillsbury Bake-Off in the Grand Ballroom of the Waldorf, where we rooted home the winner, a wispy lady from Duluth, with her ingenious creation, Upside-Down Cheesecake topped with Jelly Beans? And what of that memorable buffet luncheon at the Astor in which an endless parade of clear-eyed American-type models, ravissante in flowing peignoires, circled the tables while the orchestra played "A Pretty Girl Is Like a Melody"? I developed a massive case of indigestion when, at given signals, each would fling open her gown to reveal the very latest in Lastex girdle fashions. Could Nero have devised a more spectacular way in which to while away the lazy noontime hours?

Equipped as I was with enough free time and a good supply of clean shirts, it began to seem that a presentable young man in a good suit might subsist indefinitely on this round of free food and entertainment. Or, as Jerry once said, "Sonny, keep it up and you will soon earn permanent membership in the Schnorr Patrol." Even when the Jewish delicatessen owner around the corner translated the word for me ("beggar, bum, good-for-nothing, boy-chick!") I wore it as a badge of prowess.

True, every so often, whispering into my ear in the early mornings as I luxuriated, unshaven, over coffee and the *Times*, a twinge of Calvinist guilt would seep through: Is this your destiny—to lounge and *schnorr* away the rest of your life, Walter? Outside, the streets were empty, everyone else gone off on the daily round, building, amassing, moving and shaking, while here sat ex-Pfc. Fleming, killing a perfectly good day until five this afternoon, when he had a date to take a model (true, not one of the $20-an-hour aristocracy, but a cheerful busty girl who specialized in young-mother fashions for next year's Sears, Roebuck catalogue) to a lavish cocktail party and entertainment commemorating Twenty-five Years of Faithful Service to You by Your Friendly Independent Neighborhood Druggist.

Come, Walter, nagged that little voice. *Capitalism calls.* Fall into formation with your fellows. Up and at 'em, over the top and across the battlefield to the upper-income brackets!

Oh, but what was the rush? There were still funds in my savings account. Get a job for what? To find myself a girl, marry her, settle down, beget children, tie myself to forty years of drudgery?

Not yet. I poured myself a third cup of coffee and rationalized a postponement of that evil day when I must answer the bugles. In the spring, perhaps, I'd start looking around. . . . Meanwhile, I had no tangible reason to pull myself out of this pleasant lassitude.

It all ended in early April, not with a whimper, but with a misfired bang.

My old college roommate, now gainfully employed in his father's wholesale meat business (and with the end of OPA, how they must have prospered!) got married to a girl whose family owned a chain of food markets in New England. It was actually more of an industrial merger than a marriage, but a truly mammoth celebration took place after the wedding, which was, of course, performed at the Plaza. In my prewar dinner jacket I attended the festivities as a stag. I had a late date with a proletarian type who was to pick me up after one of her meetings (no stickler for etiquette, she) and we would see a Russian film at the Cameo. She wasn't quite the Plaza-wedding type.

It was a crowded, happy affair, which quickly became an impromptu college reunion, with much noise and champagne and the bawling of old school songs, all of us younger people fusing happily into a wave of frenzied *recherche du temps perdu*. We laughed and reiterated anecdotes and drank and pounded each other on the shoulder; we danced and clustered about a piano and sang all the songs from the last Drama Club show of '41. I was finishing the last

66

intricately rhymed chorus of "Gentlemen and Scholars (to the end)" when I felt an urgent tug at my sleeve and I turned around.

There, no longer in Navy blue but glamorous in a smart ball gown, smiling broadly and crying out "Private First Class Fleming, is it not?" . . . Marjorie.

"Ensign Frederick, as I live and breathe!" I shouted, and we clutched each other in a convulsive bear hug. I snatched a passing bottle of champagne from a tray and led her to a quiet corner. Where had she been? Wave no longer, she had stayed a few months in San Francisco, but now she was back in New York, sharing a flat with two other girls and working in the advertising department of one of the larger stores; in fact she had come straight from her job, and wasn't this a lovely party and what was *I* doing with my new-found civilian status? Not much, just looking around, I told her, and admired her excellent figure and wondered what sort of guy she'd come with and how soon I could get her phone number.

Eventually, apologizing for breaking off our flow of reminiscence, she glided off to find her escort. I shrugged and went back to the piano for more community sing. It was getting late. The bride and groom had departed, and people were discussing whose apartment to go to for further festivities, and suddenly Marjorie was back, an apologetic smile on her face. Her date, it seemed, had disappeared. (Foolish man! Off in search of greener pastures on the other side of the ballroom?) Well, I still had time to kill, and we fell again to chattering and more champagne.

I don't know what time it was when we left, because we were by now both quite tipsy. I found one unopened bottle of champagne in an open bucket near the bar and quickly tucked my dripping prize beneath my coat. Giggling conspiratorially, we departed.

I should have taken her home, but I had no taste for small talk with roommates. Why not an hour or two at my place? "Yes, but I can't stay long," she said. "Have to be up early for a nine o'clock meeting." So, still talking fondly of the old days, we made our way downtown, where I decanted the champagne into highball glasses and turned on the phonograph. Affectionately misty with sentiment and more grape, we fell to dancing somnambulistically back and forth across the tiny floor between the sofa and the ugly, overstuffed armchair, and then, quite remarkably, for was this not the friend of my childhood, the small girl in middy blouse with braces on her teeth cross-legged under that Scarsdale tree? . . . Marjorie and I were kissing.

Gone the dumpy nine-year-old and gone the chummy Wave, and in their stead, a luscious creature redolent of Chanel and Piper Heidsieck with warm lips and (perhaps it *was* the wine or a Pavlovian reaction to the situation that caused my first tentative caresses) a surprising depth of response. . . .

The phonograph, untended, revolved accusingly in the corner, but we paid it no mind. We were stretched quite naturally out on the sofa, our hands learning each other's topography "This is so *wanton*," she murmured. "Two hours ago we hadn't even met and here we are . . . like two high-school kids. . . ." My fingers had encountered the involved fastenings at the waist of her evening gown. "Sorry," I said, ruefully, "I'm ruining your party dress."

"True," she whispered, and pushed my hands gently away. She sat up and brushed her tousled hair from her eyes . . . and I was full of guilt for my evil intent. How callous had I become, that I should automatically have begun to try and seduce the younger sister of one of my childhood dreams? But before I could make my apology, Marjorie's hands went behind her, I heard the sound of a zipper, and before my astounded stare she stepped out of her long skirt . . . and like a demure, well-trained house guest, folded it and set it neatly down on the nearby chair.

Question this? I rapidly readjusted my attitudes; all those years in the Waves—an attractive girl who filled her uniform as well as she would surely not have remained a maiden indefinitely, would she? . . . She was coming back to the sofa now, humming softly, kicking off first one slipper and then the other, spilling deliciously out of her slip, which gleamed in the faint light, a smile on her face as her arms reached out for me. . . .

She fitted herself against me. "We wasted *so* much time, didn't we?" she murmured. "Kiss me, darling."

Seconds later, a key turned in the lock and Jerry pushed open the apartment door. We were drenched in light. "Well, here we are, Dollface," he cried, and led a lady into the room.

"For God's sake!" I gritted, but he had already snapped on the switch and we were revealed, sprawling in our dishevelment. There stood Jerry, beaming foolishly at us, holding in his hands a large greasy bag of delicatessen sandwiches and a quart bottle of beer. "Don't you ever *knock!*" I fumed, while behind Marjorie scrambled for her dress. "Sorry," said Jerry. "Really damn sorry, old buddy. Miss Trimingham and I were fixing to have a snack, and you *did* say you had a date and weren't using the facilities—"

"We weren't 'using the facilities'!" I snapped.

Jerry chuckled.

"Shut up!"

Miss Trimingham, a tall, angular blonde in lavender tweed, around her shoulders a savagely crimson stole, had the good grace to pluck at Jerry's arm. "Let's blow," she said. "This is a private party, so stop staring."

"No, please stay," said Marjorie through the folds of the dress she was pulling on. "I'm just leaving. . . ."

"Ah, come on; stick around, baby," said Jerry cheerfully, oblivious to my angry glare. "We'll make it a foursome." But Marjorie had disappeared into the tiny bathroom.

Jerry sat down and sighed. "The nervous type," he commented.

"Have a little respect," said Miss Trimingham sternly.

Jerry sat down and patted the sofa. "I am a true believer in romance," he said. "But I also believe in a healthy attitude toward sex."

There ensued a dreadful four or five minutes of sporadic small talk, as Marjorie repaired herself behind the door. Miss Trimingham seemed to have something to do with fashion, whether high or low I couldn't make out, and when Marjorie finally emerged (what a difficult entrance *that* must have been for her) her hair in place, her lipstick fresh, Miss T. cried out in admiration. "*Adorable*, honey!" she gushed. "You have a *mar*velous color sense!"

"Thank you very much," said Marjorie, hunting for her purse.

"Have a corned-beef sandwich, doll," said Jerry from the kitchen.

"No, thanks, not hungry," she replied.

"Ahh, don't go away mad," he said, coming forward with a paper plate of food.

She found her purse, retrieved her wrap. "No, I've really got to get home."

"Shank of the evening!" Jerry cried. "After all that exercise, you're probably starved."

"Jerry, why don't you just shut up!" I snarled, but he burbled right on: "—and besides, baby, you can sleep late. Do like Walter here; he never opens an *eye* until ten-thirty."

"Oh, and what sort of work are you in?" inquired Miss Trimingham, turning to me.

"He sleeps and eats and drinks," said Jerry, his mouth full of corned beef. "It's a process called readjustment. Only, with Walter it's taking a little longer than with most. But more power to you, cousin. As long as you can get away with being a bum." He stared at Marjorie, who had put on her wrap. "You could model, honey," he commented.

"Thank you," she replied. "But I'm just a white-collar girl who has a steady date with a typewriter from nine to five." She glanced at me. "Don't bother about me, Walter," she said. "I'll pick up a cab at the corner. Good night all."

I hurried after her down the stairs. "Marjorie!" I pleaded, hoping to patch up the ruined skein of the evening. "Please. Don't be sore. It was just a stupid mix-up, a coincidence—"

"You and he ought really to work out a more efficient schedule," she replied. "All this traffic coming and going—you're doing a bigger business than Grand Central.

We were down on the street now, and I was trying to stay abreast of her as she click-clacked on high heels, a small upright Cinderella marching with precision toward Second Avenue.

"Oh, *don't* be sore," I repeated. "It could happen to anybody."

"It wasn't *any*body, though, it was *me*," she said, and hailed an oncoming cab.

"It won't happen again," I swore.

"*That's* true," she said, as the aged, prewar De Soto Skyview clanked to an anguished halt at the curb.

"Okay!" I said, suddenly losing my temper. "The evening was spoiled and I'm sorry, but you don't have to stay mad forever—"

She turned to stare at me. "That's *not* why I'm angry," she said, and then she yanked at the bent doorhandle. She hauled herself inside.

"Well, enlighten me," I persisted, holding open the sagging door. "What the hell *is* bothering you?"

"Finding out you've turned into such a *bum*," Marjorie said from the depths of the back seat. "One ten East Seventy-sixth," she told the driver.

"As soon as the bum here lets go the door, lady," said the driver.

"I'm not a bum, buddy!" I told him.

"Get a lawyer and sue the lady for slander," commented the Bronx Mark Twain. "Shut the door. Don't slam—*shut.*"

"With pleasure!" I said, and heaved it shut. It immediately bounced open again.

"Take it easy!" yelled the driver, as, furious, I pulled back to let it fly again. "Maybe *you* don't care if my kids eat, but I can't make a buck without no door on this heap!"

Chastened, I shut the door with care. But before I could lean in to say anything further to Marjorie, the engine wheezed and off went the De Soto uptown.

I didn't go back upstairs for a while. I walked around the block three or four times, oblivious to the cold night air, and then I went for coffee at Riker's and sat, staring at myself in the mirror, wondering why the word "bum" in the mouth of my cousin Jerry had no effect on me, whereas when Marjorie Frederick . . . that pompous little middle-class twist, really nothing more than a casual acquaintance . . . why should I be so upset?

Then I went back upstairs, having allowed Jerry and Miss Trimingham a decent interval, and joined them for a nightcap. . . .

Might there have been any relation between Marjorie's use of that word and my decision, a week or so later, to go chat with one of my college acquaintances at National Radio Supply in Queens about the possibility of a job as Junior Executive Trainee? Perhaps.

But more plausible was the simple truth that I was bored with the partying and the free-loading and the aimless laissez faire.

No, I cannot point an accusing finger at Marjorie.

For there was another extended period of over two years during which we saw nothing of each other, months in which I was busy in the Trenton plant learning the radio business from the subbasement up and she was serving a tour of duty in her department store's new Los Angeles branch. And although we never discuss it, I am sure that an attractive girl like Marjorie did not sit at home and wait for her phone to ring while in California. Nor did I in Trenton. The hours I put in at the factory were not for the love of a good woman. My motive was salary.

In fact, if we had not met at that Easter fashion show, where the company had sent me with a crew to keep an eye on our first primitive television equipment and her store had assigned her to provide the announcer with copy, we might well have continued to go our separate ways. But there she was, pounding a typewriter in one corner of the improvised studio in Grand Central Palace, and as I stared at the delicate architecture of her . . . (demurely folding the ball gown neatly on one end of the couch and coming toward me with arms outstretched) . . . I gave myself a swift mental kick. And so must she. I no longer had a convenient bachelor flat on Eighteenth Street, so for a day or two we were affectionate, friendly, and platonic. But I managed to get two tickets to *South Pacific* from a gyp broker (perhaps Jerry could have used his influence, but I was trying to do without his help this time), and we went the following evening after work.

Completely under the spell of Mr. Hammerstein's lovely couplets and Mr. Rodgers' lovely strains, we wandered out of the theater and were silent all the way uptown to her place (she had returned to New York and been fortunate enough to nab a sublease on two pleasant rooms in an old brownstone). At her door I bent to kiss her a simple good night. Simple and chaste. For the first few seconds . . .

We woke up very late the following morning, all the old unfinished business completed at last.

"We are very late for our gainful employment," I observed. She yawned and stretched luxuriously.

"Call up and say you're in bed with a cold," she murmured.

I pulled her over to me. "A most remarkable lie," I whispered into her ear.

And so, as it must to all bored rakehells, domesticity caught me by the ankle, and my nose has been applied to the grindstone ever since.

Oh . . . probably it *was* Marjorie all the time. That forthright disapproval of hers, on the sidewalk on Eighteenth Street, had probably been rankling deep inside me, nudging me on to prove myself as a sober, reliable citizen, a non-bum.

Behind every gainfully employed taxpayer, hands outstretched, stands an aggressive consumer, his wife. Why, if it hadn't been for her use of the word "bum" I might still be *schnorring* my way through industrial cocktail parties, massaging misunderstood wives, and in general wasting my life. Without a little woman and kids to house and clothe and feed and educate and discipline and cope with and . . .

(And be having a hell of a time *on my own?*)

Shut up with that subversive talk, Walter. Stop picking on Marjorie and your offspring. It's not their fault you're a successful industrialist, who meets a pay roll each week and has given up the Indolent Life.

True, I agreed, mournfully. I simply wasn't cut out to be a full-time bum.

And I *love* my wife. And as for having the key to a permanent two-room house of joy somewhere on the East Side, why, the idea was repellent. Disgusting! Jerry, naturally, would put it to use. Heaven only knows what shameful goings-on he'd initiate. But me? No, thank you. I am fulfilled, fairly clean-lived, and I was certainly getting too old for That Sort of thing.

Jerry was born to be a Philanderer. I wasn't. So why must I be his accomplice?

Two rooms on the East Side. A childish indulgence. To hell with him.

I picked up the Daily Progress Report and began to study the problems of the day.

On the other hand . . .

If we *did* have such a place . . .

(Tax deductible and not paid for out of pocket) . . .

It might be . . . stimulating . . . to know that if I ever *did* get the impulse . . . or if the opportunity simply presented itself . . . I mean, not that it was likely that such a thing would ever *happen* to a fulfilled, clean-living successful, happily married executive like me . . .

But that the apartment was *there*, ready and waiting . . .

I mean, how could it possibly *hurt* to have such a place?

(All those nights when Marjorie and I dragged ourselves home from a night at the theater, red-eyed and tired. I was getting too old to drive late at night . . . fall asleep at the wheel . . . run off the

73

Parkway. . . . Think of the poor kids . . . Buddy and Catherine, orphans at such a tender age!)

Maybe, for once, old Jerry was right. . . .

Damn him.

8

Now that we were successful small electronics manufacturers, we had of course joined the National Association of Small Electronics Manufacturers. That meant we got trade bulletins, a monthly newsletter, and an imposing invitation to the Annual Conference of NASEM, which was scheduled for Monday through Thursday, the first week in May, at Riviera-in-the-Mountains, an opulent place in the Catskills.

"Speeches, Swimming, Golf and Tennis, Round-Table Discussion, Dancing, Broadway Entertainment, and Informative Panels. Bring Your Lady and Go Home Stimulated and Refreshed," read the brochure.

"*You* go," Jerry said, flipping it back across the desk.

"No, thanks," I said. "It sounds more like your sort of do."

"Couldn't possibly," he said. "All that rich food—it's Hypertension Hall." He winced. "But a crazy place. Haven't you ever been to the Riviera?" I shook my head. "Well, you owe it to yourself and Marjorie at least to go take a look. It's like Cleopatra's barge—with air conditioning. Crazy."

"I'll go if you go," I said. "Make it a threesome."

He shook his head. "I've *been* once, and besides, at a convention, things are very dull. Unless you go for married women, which I do not."

"And besides, you now have a New York base of operations," I sniped.

He ignored my reference to our newly leased "business suite" (oh,

75

yes, I'd finally agreed to it) and he fell to consulting a tiny new black leather date book. "Oh, and another reason: that Thursday I've promised Lennie Finch to drop by his apartment. He's giving a small soiree."

"To which I wasn't asked?"

"Actually, it isn't your dish of tea, Walter. Lennie and Beatrice have just bought an abstractionist sculpture from Saline Bernardi and they're having an unveiling. With a buffet and dancing."

"How chic," I said. "What's it like, cha-cha-ing with an abstraction?"

"Don't be middle-class," he chided.

"You're pushing me up to a convention in the Catskills," I answered, "and what could be more middle-class than that? Besides, how can I walk out of here for three or four days without somebody to keep an eye on things? You'll be out playing footsy somewhere; Basil Yerkes and I still haven't licked that modification problem—"

"You know what's happening to you, Walter?" Jerry said, stuffing his expensive new briar with tobacco from a small Dunhill can labeled "My Mixture." "You're developing the typical Businessman's Syndrome. You've invaded a small terrain, mastered it—"

"For the moment, at least," I hedged, not without a soupçon of pride.

"—and proceeded to create a subconscious image of yourself as the Father of it all. Next, you'll begin to believe you're indispensable, and *that's* when the tentacles begin to clutch. Your fear of failure will start to inhibit you; you'll tense up, get wound tighter and tighter into a ball of compulsions, lie awake nights, lose all your capacity for enjoyment—"

"Scratch a partner, uncover Dr. Rose Franzblau!" I said.

"No," he said, suddenly grinning. "Just a dynamite salesman making an oblique pitch. Go take Marjorie and have yourself a rest. Study humanity at play. Who knows? You might even pick up some information from one of our competitors who's had too many Martinis. And remember, the entire four days is—"

"—deductible," I finished.

He patted my arm. "Cousin, you're learning."

Mrs. Bostwick had knocked and entered, a folder of papers in her hand. As she laid them before me, her nostrils twitched disapprovingly at the expensive, acrid smoke from Jerry's pipe. "Besides," he went on, "if you're looking for a supervisor, how about Mrs. B. here? She'll run a taut ship for you, won't you, ma'am?"

"I beg your pardon?" she asked.

"Mr. Fleming is going to the NASEM meeting for four days," said Jerry. "Assure him you can keep the plant from coming apart at the seams until he gets back."

"Will *you* be here?" she asked him.

"Oh, no," said Jerry. "I've got meetings and such in New York. . . ."

Mrs. Bostwick's shoulders moved slightly back. Chin up, stomach pulled in, "In that case," she said, "we can manage." For a moment, I fancied we had just given her orders to take command of the Lost Battalion. She about-faced and marched out.

"There," said Jerry. "Now you've *got* to go. You certainly wouldn't want to deprive the old Sarge of her chance to lead the troops, would you?"

Partly because of his persuasion, partly out of curiosity, and mostly because I *was* tired and wanted a change of scene, I sent in the reservation card (with a company check).

Persuading Marjorie to go along wasn't quite so easy. She fought a hell of a delaying action, throwing up barriers all the way. I now discovered she'd been reading travel folders and dreaming of the Champs Elysées this summer. Psychologically, she was not prepared to settle for four days at Riviera-in-the-Mountains. It took a large amount of persuasion to convince her that this was not going to be our annual vacation for this year. I assured her that our new financial status would certainly enable us to make more than just the usual trip to the Cape. But the ghosts of years of annual budget chats had to be banished. Finally, we crossed that barrier. Then up rose another. Responsibilities. "I've got an Up-Zoning Committee Meeting, and I promised to work on that fund-raising project for the PTA, and heaven knows what else."

"Can't it wait four days?"

"The PTA is teetering on the brink of bankruptcy," she said, "and I promised Mrs. Delancey Hook to work on an emergency project to save it from going under. Poor soul, she's desperate."

"She needs a *business* head," I said. Marjorie beamed at me gratefully. "All right!" I said, trapped. "Get her to table the crisis and *I'll* sit in when we come back." So down went Barrier Two.

77

Up came Parental Guilt. "We really ought to take the kids along, too," she suggested. "Buddy's got such good marks this semester and he's earned a treat.

"*Believe* me, dearest," I said, plunging back into the fray, "he'll be happier at home. Kiddies also need to get away from their parents; remember that article in last month's *Reader's Digest* you made me read?"

"Yes, but—"

"And as for a reward, I'll buy him that kit he's been pestering about and he'll be much happier building his own Junior IBM computer than he would be learning to mambo." So that took care of P. G. but Marjorie didn't give up quite so readily.

A few moments later she aimed and fired at me with Fear.

"But will they be *safe?*" she demanded.

"The Geisha Girl is very reliable; she'll take excellent care of them and she sure knows how to use long distance—look at last month's phone bill." (I was referring to our newest status symbol, a genuine sleep-in housekeeper and cook, a stout oriental we had ransomed at fearful expense from a local employment agency. Mrs. Kee, a westernized Butterfly, wore slacks and a home permanent, smoked filter tips, never missed "Gunsmoke," and baked an excellent mince pie.) "Besides, darling," I insisted, "we're only going to be gone for four days, not *forever*."

"And that's *another* thing," she rebutted, bringing up her heavy artillery. "I just don't have a damned thing to *wear!*"

Aha! at last we were down to bedrock. This I could cope with.

"Simplicity itself!" I soothed. "Just take a blank check and spend the afternoon at Loehmann's!"

Loehmann's is a legendary store, once based in the Bronx and far out in Brooklyn. It now maintains a branch in Norwalk, to which, with glad cries, station wagons full of knowing local ladies make eager, sporadic foraging expeditions. There, from plain racks, are suspended row upon row of high-fashioned clothes, mostly designers' samples and one-of-a-kinds, sold for cash on a strict no-return basis. For a fraction of their cost at the more expensive department stores, these dangling treasures can be sought out, tried on in the fitting room, and then borne home like some prize from the gods by the sharp-eyed madame who can still wriggle herself into a 14. An intelligent husband will never argue with his lady about the cost of these Norwalk expeditions. He knows that not only is Loehmann's the Las Vegas of fashion, but that also, for Marjorie and her fellow hunters, the store is a stimulant for frayed female nerves, a feast for the depressed ego, a salon of Miltown in which rising tempers can be miraculously soothed by the discovery of a brand-new, genuine high-style Norman Norell, a Trigère, a Larry Aldrich . . . an honest-to-God Sophie or a Hattie or a Nettie, just arrived, marked down to $28.90 from the original $79.50 tag it wears this very week at Bonwit's . . . and look!—in the right *size!*

"Loehmann's?" murmured my Marjorie, her eyes brightening at the broad vista of a long afternoon to be spent pawing through rack after rack of cut-price *haute couture*.

"With a blank check," I said, closing in for the kill.

She ran up a white flag. "That's *different*," she surrendered. "Then I can go."

Riviera-in-the-Mountains lies some fifty miles above New York City, deep in the pleasant, rolling Catskill countryside. It is easily reached from Connecticut by driving across the Tappan Zee Bridge and then going on to a broad new express road known as the Thru-way. According to its chatty ads in the New York *Times* travel section, the Riviera had "Everything, but EVERYTHING, you could ask for to make your hard-earned vacation a memorable experience. If you don't find it somewhere on our lavish 110 acres, friends, then believe us, it's not worth looking for! Ask singer Ethel Merman, Industrialist Harry Cogan (Long Island Building Supply) Novelist Al Morgan, Ambassador Ralph Bunche, Skating Champ Sammy Locke, TV Producer Marshall Jamison, Lyricist Alan Sherman, Broadway Newshawk Sam Zolotow, and the hosts of others who had fun and frolicked here at the Riviera last weekend!"

We crossed mile upon mile of soft farmland, covered with dairy herds and billboards. Modesty is a misprized virtue among Catskill innkeepers.

THREE MORE MILES TO

SINGER'S-IN-THE-PINES

RELAX AND ENJOY

STEAKS—CHOPS—LOBSTER

NEW ELECTRONIC ELEVATOR
COMPLETELY FIREPROOF
COMING NEXT WEEK
IN THE FABULOUS LIDO ROOM

XAVIER CUGAT & ORCH.

PLUS

FREE 2-HOUR SEMINAR

"MAKING MARRIAGE WORK"

"What was that about relaxation?" asked Marjorie.
Then we read:

HEY POP! HOW ABOUT THIS?
MOM AND THE KIDS CAN PLAY ALL WEEK LONG
  AT BENSON'S SHOREHAVEN LODGE & COTTAGES
AND FOR JUST PENNIES MORE
YOU CAN JOIN THEM FOR A WEEKEND OF TOGETHERNESS!

"Only a masochist would accept that offer," I murmured.
"It's nice to know where we stand," Marjorie replied.

AFTER YOU'VE TRIED THEM ALL
  YOU'LL COME HOME TO THE PEACE AND QUIET
  OF   GERSHGORN' RETREAT

Swimming, Dancing, B'way Stars, Golf,
Tennis, Boating, Steam Bath, Health Club,
Bingo, Arts and Crafts & Free Cha-Cha Lessons

"I would like to discuss the definition of the word 'retreat' with
Mr. Gershgorn," said Marjorie.
"He's probably resting in New York," I replied.
And now a somewhat cosmopolitan flavor began to creep into the
culinary scene:

RUDY'S RUSTIC BLINTZATERIA

SLOW DOWN! JUST AHEAD!
FARBSTEIN'S VILLA D'ESTE

ENJOY! ENJOY!
AT AUNT LENA'S HUNGARIAN FARMHOUSE

WONG'S CHINA DRAGON TEAHOUSE
MANDARIN CUISINE
(Dietary Laws Strictly Observed)

Somewhat defiantly:

O'CONNOR'S SHAMROCK BAR & GRILL

And then back to:

SAMMY'S (FORMERLY OF LINDY'S) DELICATESSEN
BEST PASTRAMI EAST OF THE HUDSON!

THIRSTY?
ONLY TWO MILES TO
THE BORSCHT BUCKET

"Whatever became of Howard Johnson?" Marjorie asked.
"Abdicated the area, I guess."
"He's here, but under an assumed name," she mused.
Then, at last, we saw a small sign:

Riviera-in-the-Mountains
One mile
Need we say more?

"Just in time," said Marjorie. "Another mile and I'd have indigestion."
But the hotel itself, so modest in self-advertisement, was in reality enough to stagger the mind.
We drove up its entrance road and then rounded a sharp bend. There stood a nine-story building, easily a full city block long, jutting upward from the tender green hills. Picture the Flatiron Building set in a meadow, or the Hotel Astor picked up from Times Square and dropped, by some whimsical tornado, into a forest glade, and it may convey some sense of the incongruity of this massive concrete and steel zeppelin hangar in the pines.

81

"Wow," breathed Marjorie. I could only nod.

We were ushered through the massive portico by a crew of bell-boys. Once inside, the countryside receded completely. Banks of elevators, a balcony with brightly lighted shops, high marble columns, an acre or so of open carpeted lobby dotted with rows of armchairs and sofas, and towering over it all, a staircase of marble which jutted at least three stories skyward.

"Good Lord," murmured Marjorie as we plodded toward the reservations desk, made of mahogany and easily sixty feet in length, "it's as if we'd just come aboard the old *Normandie*."

It was very quiet.

The room clerk, a small dapper man, signed us in and handed us both plastic badges marked NASEM-1960.

"Very quiet," I commented.

"Quiet?" he replied. "Mister F., checkout time last night we had paying up at the cashier eleven hundred and ninety-two people."

"Where did they all go?" I asked.

"Where should they go?" he replied. "Home."

"To recuperate?" asked Marjorie.

He ignored the witticism. "You're hot from the trip, have a swim in the pool. Take a little nap. Your people meet in the Skylite Lounge for an opening cocktail party with dancing, then dinner in the Main Hall at eight, followed by dancing in the Place Pigalle Room until midnight, and for tomorrow's schedule, consult the billboard, enjoy yourself, we're a simple friendly place, Mr. F., so far so good?"

"Yes indeedy," I muttered.

Our room was opulent, with soft double beds and a gleaming bathroom. But all around us was silence. We could hear no one stirring in the hall outside or in the rooms next door. I looked out the window onto a deserted countryside. Even the huge parking lot below was dotted with a mere handful of cars.

"It's *eerie*," said Marjorie, stretched out on the bed, rosy and glowing from her shower.

I stretched out alongside. "What is?"

"This feeling," she said. "It's like that movie we saw: Buster Keaton and a girl all alone on an ocean liner . . ."

I stroked her through the soft folds of a new negligee. "Hotel rooms always bring out the real you, don't they?" she sighed.

"Loehmann's?" I asked, tugging at the sash. She nodded happily. "Lovely," I said, pulling it open.

"Thank you." She yawned. I began to forage further. "I thought this was a business convention," she murmured, her eyes closed.

"The man downstairs said to *enjoy*," I reminded, and leaned over to kiss her.

But she was already asleep.

Some women just don't know the true meaning of the word *relax*, I thought, and went out to explore.

Except for the hundred-odd delegates to the NASEM get-together, the enormous Riviera was almost empty. Badge on lapel, I wandered through its extensive facilities. I nodded and smiled at other Small Electronics Manufacturers and their ladies who were also idly rambling through the card rooms, the lounges, the indoor pool, peering into the Place Pigalle Room and the Skylite Lounge and on and on. . . .

After a bit, since most of the NASEM-ites had arrived and completed registration, some of the usual convention spirit began to take over. Even though we seemed a relatively small group, somewhat dwarfed by the size and scope of our surroundings (*some* place the Ways and Means Committee picked this year!), we small businessmen weren't going to let the Riviera awe us, no, sir. All sorts of complete strangers began to grin at me and seize me by the hand. I met a sunburned group in careless sports clothes (Doc Kitchell, Harry Dillard, over here's Lew Harms, we're partners in Arizona Technics, fastest-growing little outfit this side of the Rio Grande and sure it's hot where we are but brother, that climate is certainly what the doctor ordered for sinus!) . . . A couple, more sober types, indoor-complected, in dark-gray suits, one with a goatee, the other wearing thick glasses (Dud Hasbrook and Art Gordon, Audiosonics, Inc., Route 128, just outside Boston, of course . . . Ah, yes, we *have* done rather well with our microwave rigs this year, but chalk it up to damn good luck and the breaks, old man) . . . And Leo and Dante Fuselli, of Long Island Electronic Supply (We hadda get out of radio and teevee repair, the bastards was cutting the little man's throat, so we figured what the hell, we get into bed with the military, right?) . . . And then I found my hand pumped and around my shoulders went the arm of Ben Chatsfield, Space

Components, Inglewood, Calif. (Say, we just jetted in, the missus and me, and by our time it's still only 2:00 P.M., right? So how about we go find ourselves a wee lunchtime drink, mmmhmm?) By now my throat was just as dry as his, so we proceeded a quarter of a mile through endless halls to the Skylite Lounge, where we all found seats at the imposing Great Wall of China of a bar. I say "found" because the Riviera management had not yet seen fit to turn on the Skylite itself, and the room was as dark as Yankee Stadium at 2:00 A.M.

By the eerie orange light that reflected through banks of bottles, I found a house phone and called Marjorie to brief her on my new location. She said to start without her while she dressed, and we did. Over Dewar's and water Chatsie and DeeDee, his wife, an ample, deeply tanned California matron, and I cemented our new-born friendship. What exactly did my outfit produce? Ah, ah, top secret, fenced I, and what about his Space Components? Ah, ah, likewise, he chuckled, and now we were fellow conspirators in the grand design of National Defense. I suggested we banish shoptalk. DeeDee agreed enthusiastically, and we began a minute appraisal of the L.A. Dodgers and their chances this season. Then we discussed the L.A. system of freeways, skipped lightly over the L.A. smog index, and debated the difference between living Connecticut style as versus the good life in L.A. Then we peered at pictures of each other's offspring and compared their progress in school. The Dewar's continued to flow, and so did this conversation until a female voice on my other side broke in. "Excuse me," it said, "but you sound just like a man I used to know named Walter Fleming."

"That's strange, because I am he," I said. DeeDee and Chatsie were amused. "But how can you recognize anyone in this Black Hole of Calcutta?"

"Voices don't change," she said. "How's Cousin Jerry; still fooling all the people?"

"Who are *you?*" I inquired.

"The two of you run Science Associates in Connecticut," she said, out of the dark—very oracular. "Hot little firm, too. Earnings projection up 32 per cent over last year. Honestly, I never thought you boys had it in you, Walter. Congratulations." Her voice wasn't familiar. This encounter in the gloom was becoming Kafka-esque.

"And who might *you* be?" I asked.

"Don't say anything, boy," injected Chatsie. "Lady might be from the Eff Bee Eye, y'know . . ."

While he and DeeDee chortled over that one, I lighted a match and peered at my questioner. She was a small blonde in a tailored suit.

She smiled. "You'll burn your fingers, Walter," she said. "I'm Betty. Betty Lawrence." The match went out and I was back in the dark. "Betty *Lawrence?*" she insisted. "Don't tell me eleven years have aged me *that* much?"

"Of course not!" I said, and desperately riffled through the mental card index of my past. Actress? Schoolmate? Ski companion? Dammit, nothing. Either because of Dewar's or because of disuse, my file of old conquests was no help.

"Stop torturing yourself," she said. "I was Jerry's secretary at Mackintosh & Bates, the PR shop."

"Of course!" I said. "Theater tickets, cocktail parties . . ."

"Just call Betty," she said. "How do you think I remembered your voice?"

"Nice to see you in person!" I said. "What are you up to these days?"

"*There*'s a blow to my ego," she wailed. "Here I am, syndicated in fifty-four papers all over hell and gone, and to you I'm still tickets to *Finian's Rainbow.*"

"Say, are you *that* Betty Lawrence?" interjected Chatsie. "Never miss reading you, honey. Memorized your series on Thirty Ways to Save on Taxes. Framed it and hung it on the Accounting Department wall next to my picture of Dick Nixon!" He introduced himself and DeeDee.

"Oh . . . Space Components, Inglewood?" Betty inquired.

"Boy, what a file-cabinet mind!" said Chatsie.

"Nope, three researchers," said Betty.

"We better watch ourselves, Walt," said Chatsie. "This little lady is dynamite."

"Absolutely," I murmured. In truth I was feeling foolish. Too foolish to ask Betty how this transformation—efficient secretary into high-powered daily columnist—had ever come about.

"Say," Chatsie was asking, "I thought you only hobnobbed with the wheels from IBM and GE and Standard Oil. . . . What're you doing mingling with the peasants?"

85

"Doing a series on Small Business: the Cornerstone of Growth," she explained, "so I'm up here prowling through the grass roots."

"*Here* you are," said an accusing voice at my shoulder. "Why didn't you warn me to bring a guide dog into this coalbin? I've been accosting complete strangers in here for the past five minutes."

"Gotten any offers?" said Chatsie.

"Enough," said Marjorie. "Who are you?"

I introduced her to Chatsie, DeeDee, and Betty Lawrence. "Guess what, dear. Betty here was Jerry's *secretary*," I explained.

"*That's* interesting," said Marjorie. A brief silence.

Then: "Don't worry, Mrs. Fleming," said Betty. "I've since gone straight." Another hesitant moment, and then they both laughed. "I see we understand each other," said Betty.

"Perfectly," said Marjorie.

"Darling, that's a marvelous dress," said DeeDee. "I mean, even in this rotten light."

"Oh, do you really like it?" purred Marjorie.

"It's heaven. Where did you find it? Saks?" asked DeeDee, thus firmly cementing *their* friendship.

Chatsie insisted that Marjorie catch up to the rest of us, and we continued to down Dewar's (although, as Betty slyly pointed out, the bartender could just as well, in this gloom, be serving us Breath of the Heather and how would we know the difference?)

Some time later, the shadowy bartender emerged to inform us that it was dinnertime. He gave us detailed directions, but Chatsie wouldn't leave until the man had drawn us a map on a bar napkin. Armed with that, we signed the tab, trooped out into the bright hallway, and our brave little band set forth on its first expedition to that nerve center of Riviera living: the dining hall.

At last we came to its entrance. A headwaiter consulted his map at the doorway, nodded when we insisted that we all wanted to eat together, and sent us off across a veritable sea of white table-cloths to join the rest of the NASEM folks.

I once attended a meal in the old Twenty-first Street Armory, a political banquet at which eight hundred-odd diners sat down together . . . and a college friend of mine once invited me to lunch at the mammoth old Yale Freshman Commons, where a thousand or so undergraduates broke bread simultaneously, but neither of these mass feedings prepared me for the sight of the Riviera dining room, which consisted of easily two full acres of tables-for-eight, stretching away into the horizon like a section of the Nebraska prairie.

And tonight, most of them standing empty.

We were led far down the aisles to a section over which had been hung a small banner: WELCOME NASEM! There, a noisy clot of us, a Custer's Last Stand of our cohorts, were already eating. We were ushered to a table, and as we seated ourselves a gangling white-jacketed bus boy immediately set down dishes overflowing with loaves and fishes. "Hello, folks," he said, "I'm Larry. If you don't see it on the menu, don't hesitate to ask, okay? Okay!" He reappeared shortly with a serving of butter. "This is strictly, but *strictly* against the law," he whispered conspiratorially. "But the management figures nobody's around, you people don't keep kosher, so we'll just pretend like it isn't here, okay?" He passed out menus.

Chatsie stared at me. "What's *that* mean?" he asked.

"I think he's referring to the dietary laws," I explained.

"Now what the hell kind of a local ordinance is that?" he complained.

"Honey," broke in DeeDee, "this is the longest menu I've ever seen and I do not understand one word of it!"

"Why, is it in French or something?" he asked.

"I don't know *what* it is," she said, "but I'm going to need an interpreter!"

"Hello everybody and welcome to the Riviera," said a stout, bespectacled waitress, "we certainly hope you enjoy your rest here and what'll it be tonight if you don't see it don't be shy just ask Bessie."

DeeDee looked gratefully up at Bessie. "Excuse me," she said, "but just what is this . . . Stuffed Derma?"

"Derma," replied Bessie, "it's a tasty piece Derma that the chef God watch over him spent the whole afternoon stuffing. You'll take an order?"

DeeDee wasn't persuaded.

"Say," said Chatsie. "What's this stuff Chopped Lungen?"

"Nectar from above," said Bessie, "the chef picks from the calf a nice piece of lung—"

"We'll have honeydew melon," DeeDee said quickly.

Bessie turned to the rest of us. "You folks could use a little Stuffed Calves' Head in Jelly maybe?"

87

We thought not, and said we'd try the Chopped Liver instead.

"You'll never regret it," said Bessie.

"What's a Canapé of Nova Scotia?" DeeDee inquired.

"Honey, you can't be serious," said Bessie.

"It's smoked salmon," said Marjorie helpfully. "It's also called lox."

"Oh, no it's not!" said Bessie.

"What's the difference?" Betty asked.

"Roughly forty cents a quarter-pound, darling," shrugged Bessie.

We continued to pick our way through the ensuing maze of courses. Soups? There were Mushroom and Barley with Mandlen ("Like little hard nuts, very tasty") . . . Chicken Soup with Kasha ("Kasha is . . . well, Kasha is *Kasha!*") . . . Chicken Soup with Kreplach ("Kreplach? The Chinese stole it from our people and call it Won-Ton. You'll try a nice bowl?" "But I don't like Chinese food," said DeeDee. "I'll bring you matzo balls so you shouldn't be confused.") Then: "Larry will bring you all Greek salads while you're waiting and I'll bring a few portions of chopped herring you'll taste you'll enjoy and now let's get to the main course what'll be?"

"Excuse me for being stupid," said Marjorie, "but what exactly is Boiled Flanken in the Pot?"

Bessie winked. "Not tonight," she said. "Listen to Bessie. Where are you both from?" We told her Connecticut. She nodded sagely. "You two I'll bring a beautiful cut of roast beef and in case that shouldn't fill you we'll sneak out a side order stuffed cabbage and some baby potato knishes. *You*, darling," she said, smiling at Betty. "Watching the waistline, right? You'll enjoy a broiled lobster stuffed with crabmeat." She turned her attention back to the confused Chatsfields. "Where are *you* people from? California? So tell me, how would you like the chef to do your sirloins?"

Then she was gone, whirling off to the kitchen.

We stared at one another.

"I'd like to hire that dame as a salesman," commented Chatsie.

"But I don't have the faintest idea what we ordered!" DeeDee complained.

"That's why she could make me rich," said Chatsie, buttering another roll.

Some six or seven courses later, we all pushed ourselves away from the table and, in a semicomatose condition, tried to rise. "Feeling better, folks?" encouraged Bessie, our Lady Bountiful. "Go have fun see you all in the morning and you better start already thinking of what you'd like for breakfast."

Marjorie reeled. "Metrecal," she muttered.

"Ah, ah, darling, up here that's a dirty word," said Bessie.

Our little band trudged wearily down the aisle, back across the vast dining room, headed for the exit. Suddenly, a disembodied public-address voice surrounded us stereophonically. "Good evening, guests of the Riviera. With your pleasure in mind, we have a marvelous program of events planned. Tonight, there will be a program of Broadway entertainment in the Riviera Showtime Theater followed by dancing in the Place Pigalle Room, cards in the Card Room, bingo in the Lounge, and for all you couples, remember, the special Midnight Plunge in our famous heated pool, with poolside mambo and cha-cha tournament, lavish prizes to the lucky winners . . . And finally, don't forget, at 1:00 A.M., be the guests of the Riviera at a special gala Chuckwagon buffet. Enjoy yourselves!"

"This may be only our first day at the Riviera," commented Betty, "but it feels like the last day of Pompeii."

There is nothing like a private hotel room to bring out the latent beast in the most normal married man. He and his wife enter a luxurious, dimly lit chamber, aglow with several after-dinner brandies; he is secure in the knowledge that there will be no interruptive phone calls from the neighbors, no sudden kitchen crises, no small children quarreling downstairs and running up to hammer on the locked door with loud requests for an adjudication. . . .

For the first time in months, Marjorie and I went to bed very early and got to sleep very late.

Around nine-thirty the following morning I awoke, stretched luxuriously, snapped on the bedside light, and glanced at the printed NASEM program for the day:

10 A.M.

Opening Address
"Small Businessman, What Lies Ahead?"
Harry L. Conover, FedPlastOnics, Des Moines, Iowa

"Wha'?" murmured Marjorie, blinking in the glare of the bed-side lamp.

The bedroom door was still locked and I was drunk with power. "Good morning, darling," I said, and reached for her.

"Not *now*—" she protested. "Must get childrens' breakfast. . . ."

"They are not here, angel," I assured her. "They are safe and well at home."

"Oh, lovely," she said, and came into my arms.

"Beautiful nightgown, darling," I said.

"Loehmann's," she sighed into my shoulder . . . "And please don't tear it," she added, ever practical.

By the time I arrived downstairs, the noontime panel on Auto-mation was just breaking up in a welter of indecision. I felt a faint pang of hunger, so I made my way across the plains of the dining room. At our table, Bessie was waiting for me. "You missed break-fast!" she scolded. "The body can't function without nourishment, shame on you!" She began to shower an assortment of rolls, cream cheese, smoked fish, fruits, and breakfast pastry upon the table. "Here, Bessie looked out for you, so where's the little woman?"

"She'll be down later," I assured her.

"A living doll," said Bessie fervently. "Do you know what a lucky man you are? You take good care of that little girl, hear me, and what'll you have for a main course?"

It was a bright clear day, and after my meal I didn't want any panel discussions; I wanted exercise and fresh air. I made my way through the lobby and started out the front door. "Walter?" called a voice. "Wait for me!"

Betty Lawrence, wearing slacks and a heavy sweater, most un-executive and completely outdoorsy in the approved Abercrombie & Fitch manner, caught up to me. "I've had a morning full up to here with technical discussion," she said. "Take me out for a walk, will you?"

We tramped across the parking lot and headed for a birch-framed archway over which hung a sign reading "This Way to the Glorious Riviera Mountain Trails."

They even had the woods organized.

"Where's Marjorie?" asked Betty.

"Back at the hotel," I said. "Decided to go for a swim and then treat herself to the works at the Health Club. Steam bath, rubdown, you know."

"Nervous tension?"

"Not at all," I said. "Just general muscle fatigue."

Betty smiled.

"And what is that smirk for?" I demanded.

"Your choice of words," she said. "I noticed you weren't at any of this morning's meetings . . . nor was she."

"We overslept," I said.

"More power to you," said Betty. "The two of you are helping to revive my faith in romance. . . ."

"What does that mean?" I asked.

"Simply that it pleases me to see you both behaving with such gusto," she said. "And married for this length of time, too."

"I thought you were a financial columnist, not Dear Abby," I said.

"Don't be so defensive, Walter," she said. "I meant it strictly as a compliment." We were passing through a grove of pine trees, and she stared off at them. "*I* should be as lucky as Marjorie."

"You will be," I assured her. "A girl with a mind like yours—"

"Oh, Walter," she said, "you still haven't learned the ground rules, have you? Men rarely loll until noon with brainy-type girls."

"You're thinking negatively," I told her.

"And thank you, but you're simply being gallant," she replied.

"Nonsense," I said, and glanced at her neatly kept figure encased in stretch-nylon ski pants. "Given the proper set of circumstances, I'd enjoy lolling till noon with you enormously, Betty."

She turned to me, her eyes widening with surprise. "Why Walter," she said. "You satyr. How pleasant. How extremely nice of you."

"And I am not trying to give your ego a rubdown," I insisted. "I mean it."

91

She nodded. "I know," she said, her voice softening. "You're not out to sell me on writing your biography or promoting a new product, or to get me to publicize your flourishing business. You don't have any angle, so you must be—oh, Dammit, there I go analyzing it!" She shook her head ruefully. "You're simply being spontaneous, and I'm so calloused I can't accept spontaneity any more!"

We tramped on through deep woods, inhaling the fresh air and relishing the absence of a public-address system. "I can't believe you operate in such an unappetizing jungle," I commented. "What the hell, people aren't so dreadful, are they?"

Again she turned to stare at me. "Walter," she said, "keep talking this way and you'll send me right back to the Campfire Girls."

"I don't get you, dear," I said.

She shook her head with disbelief. "Here you are, successful, affluence oozing out of every pore, your stock selling at a stiff price, and well on your way to a paragraph in *Who's Who*. In the normal course of events, you should be pompous, arrogant, and a Republican. Instead, you're still the good soldier Schweik . . . a lovable schnook. Thank Heavens!" she added, patting my arm. "And thank *you*, Walter . . ."

"Who's a soldier schnook?" I demanded.

"You are," she said, "and I use the word in its most constructive sense. Oh, be glad you're a schnook—and not a schlemiel like . . . oh, like your cousin Jerry—"

"How did *he* get into this discussion?" I asked, now thoroughly bewildered.

"Because he's your opposite number!" she said.

"Now you have lost me," I said.

"Look," she said. "This is a business convention. You're here—ostensibly for business, right? Where's your cousin and co-worker?"

"In New York," I said.

"Working . . . like you?"

"He's making contacts—and pulling strings—and—"

"Of course!" she said. "Ducking his responsibilities and having an expense-account ball while you keep your nose to the grindstone."

"I'm on an expense account, too!" I protested.

"But you don't pad yours," she said. "And you're here because you really believe you can learn something at a convention like this. You're still honest and upright. You are one of the dear patient schnooks who stand quietly in line, waiting for the door to open, but Jerry is one of those who know how to get inside without waiting."

"Thank you for the personality profile," I said, and had trouble repressing my resentment.

"Don't be annoyed, dear!" she said, taking my arm firmly. "The world is *built* on the backs of you and the rest of the standees! You work hard, you think of things, you stay up nights and get them rolling. . . . If it weren't for all of you standing there, there wouldn't be a line for the bastards like Jerry to make an end run around—don't you see?"

"Why are you so down on Jerry?" I asked.

The trail had circled through the woods and now it had begun to wind its way back down again.

"I guess," she said, softly, "because I've never realized how fond I could be of a good soldier Schweik."

"Keep Walking, Folks," read a small sign on a tree. "Only Five More Minutes to the Fabulous Riviera."

"You'll have to excuse me," I said. "I thought the fresh air would clear my head, but after half an hour in the woods with you, I'm hopelessly confused."

Betty stopped and turned toward me. And then she reached up and kissed me firmly on the lips.

At any other time, this onslaught would have stimulated me to further explorations, but today I was in something of a euphoric state to begin with. The embrace remained chaste, and she finally released me.

"Sorry," she murmured. "All that talk about lolling until noon . . ."

"Don't apologize," I told her. "Even though I may be confused, I enjoyed it!"

She held out her hand. "Handkerchief?"

I reached for one. "Now, don't cry, Betty, please—" She began to mop away at my mouth.

"Emotional I've never been," she commented wryly. "But practical? *God*, can I be practical!"

"What happened to you this afternoon?" asked Marjorie, as the two of us relaxed in our room that evening, whipping up strength to hurl ourselves into the gustatory breach once more.

"Oh," I said, casually, "I went for a walk in the woods, then sat in on a few dull meetings, making contacts, as they say. What about you?"

"I came up here and collapsed," she said. "After that two hours in the Health Club, I'm a complete wreck. Walter, it was unnerving. Do you know what *happens* in the ladies' section of a steam bath?"

"No, my folks never let me see that play," I said.

"First I had a sunbath, and then a swim, and then they gave me a towel, took away my suit, and pushed me into the Steam—not the Dry—but the real torture chamber—the Wet. Well, I walked in, with my towel clutched around me, and sat down . . . and it was like Dante's Inferno. There were these four old ladies sitting there and staring—all naked, with towels, sort of like the gargoyles from the top of Notre Dame Cathedral, remember? Only *uglier* . . ."

I winced at the mental picture.

"So there we sat, all perspiring away, and then they started cross-examining me! Who was I? Where did I come from? How many kids, and what business were you in, and how much did you make, and were we happy together . . ."

"Sweating it out of you, so to speak."

"I never felt so . . . *naked!*" Marjorie exclaimed. "They got more and more personal. Finally, one old harridan—she must have been at least seventy, and obviously the Dowager Duchess of the Wet Steam Room—said: 'Honey, your towel's drooping open and I'm getting a good look at what you got, and I wanna tell you, darling, for a dame with two kids, you got a nice built on you—I'll bet you know how to take care of the old man, huh?' "

"Give me her name; I'll be glad to drop her a testimonial," I said.

"Oh, shut up," said Marjorie happily. "Then she said, 'Take it from me, tootsie, if you want to hang on to your husband, lay off starches and keep that shape, believe me!' Then she waved her arm at all her friends sitting there, who were all nodding and snickering, and said: 'You don't believe it, take a look at the girls here. Darling, don't ever let this happen to you!' "

"A superfluous warning," I observed.

"*Thank* you, dear," said Marjorie, stretching luxuriously.

94

"Because, according to insurance statistics, women in any shape whatsoever are outliving their husbands by almost five years. And already own 53.6 per cent of the nation's wealth . . . by inheritance."

"You have an answer for everything, don't you?" sulked Marjorie.

"Ah, ah, there," I breathed into her ear, "my beautiful, relaxed, open-pored, fragrant wife, mother of my children, well-preserved lady with such a nice built onto her . . ." Between us there was an elaborately lacy peignoir. "Mmm . . . this is new, isn't it?" I asked.

She nodded.

"Loehmann's," I said, plucking at its fastenings.

"The same," she said. Before long we were well on our way to being late for another meal.

Then the bedside telephone rang.

"Long distance?" I repeated, irritated.

Instantly, Marjorie reverted from Cleopatra to Cornelia. "Something's happened to the children!"

"Relax," I told her, "it's Mrs. Bostwick calling from the factory. . . . How are things in the shop, Mrs. B?"

"Tiptop," she said. "I hate to butt in when you're involved in such an important business conference, but a Major Willoughby from Army Procurement has been calling all day yesterday and today to talk to somebody in Management. I held him off, but I've taken the liberty of giving him your whereabouts; he should be in touch with you either tonight or tomorrow. I wanted to warn you."

"Okay," I said. "I'm braced. Does it sound like something important or is this Willoughby just on a routine bird-dog expedition?"

"He's a major," said Mrs. B, her WAC reflexes rising to attention. "I hardly think he'd be calling you merely to pass the time of day, Mr. Fleming."

Marjorie looked inquiringly at me. "Some joker from Washington," I said, after I'd hung up. "It could be important."

Marjorie shook her head sadly. "Just as I was beginning to relax, too . . ."

"We're not going home *yet*," I said.

"No," she agreed. "That's true, isn't it?"

We were late for dinner after all.

But after another Gargantuan repast, when we were all holed up again in one of the smaller bars, sipping therapeutic crème de menthe, the major got through to me. "Tried to reach you for forty-eight hours," he said. His was a brisk, no-nonsense manner. "Can't discuss this with you over the phone, but it's quite important. If I hopped a plane up tomorrow, do you think you could be in your shop Thursday at nine for a meeting?"

I belched slightly. "Sure," I said. "In the interests of my country, I'll be glad to make the sacrifice."

"Thank you, Fleming."

"Not at all," I said. "I was headed for hypertension anyway."

I rejoined DeeDee, Chatsie, and Betty. "Farewell drinks," I said. "We've got to evacuate the premises tomorrow morning. Duty calls."

"But tomorrow's the best part," said Chatsie. "We're having a demonstration of a bill-posting machine by IBM! I hear it's great!"

I shrugged. "You know these Government contracts," I said nobly.

Betty Lawrence sipped at her drink. "Can't Cousin Jerry handle it?" she asked.

"No, he can't," I said.

"Oh. Too busy with—other activities? Well, it figures."

"What does *that* mean?" I asked.

"Nothing, Mr. Schweik," she replied. "Marjorie, why don't you stay an extra day and come home with me? No reason why you should have to go tearing home, just because Walter has to cope."

"Thanks," said Marjorie, "but I'll have another vacation sometime soon. Won't I, dear?"

"Of course," I said. But I could tell from the look in her eye that she did not believe me.

Just then a small, sun-tanned gentleman in a dark-blue suit, a large panatela held lightly in his hand, approached our table. "Excuse me for butting in," he said, staring at Marjorie. "I don't mean to interrupt, but I have to ask this lady a personal question."

Marjorie looked up, surprised. "I beg your pardon?"

"Madame, what made you buy that particular number you're wearing?" he asked.

Marjorie, completely bewildered, mumbled something about having liked the design.

96

"It caught your eye?" he inquired eagerly. "It stood out from the others? Was it the scoop neck? Or the drape of the skirt? Or maybe the discreet trimming?"

"I just liked it," she said helplessly. "Did I do something wrong?"

"God forbid!" he exclaimed happily. "Madame—it's extrasensory! I mean, it's as if we had you in mind when we ran it up! The perfect mating of customer and design. Oh, I tell you, when I see one of our creations end up on a lady like you with such a result—" He patted his dark-blue breast pocket. "It gives me a warm feeling here, y'know?"

Marjorie beamed.

"Your dress?" asked Betty.

The small gentleman bowed. "L. M. Harris of Champs-Elysées," he announced.

All three girls were enormously impressed.

"I *love* your clothes!" said Marjorie.

"So stylish!" bubbled DeeDee.

"And well made," said Betty.

"My pleasure," said Mr. Harris. "May I buy you all a nightcap?"

Going up in the elevator, Marjorie suddenly dissolved in a fit of silent hysterics.

"What is it?" I asked, concerned.

"I was just thinking about Mr. Harris"—she giggled—"and what he would . . . have looked like . . . if I'd told him . . . I bought his beautiful dress . . . in *Loehmann's!*"

9

BEHIND every great scientist there stands a woman, unseen, unsung, and usually unpopular.

Behind our partner and inventor, Basil Yerkes, existed such a female, his wife. Mrs. Yerkes, however, did not stand behind Basil; most days she could be found lying down with a dreadful migraine.

When Leatrice Yerkes (née Cunningham) was some three hours old, her mother, a devout romantic and avid moviegoer, offered the ultimate sacrifice to her gods and goddesses by naming her new-born in honor of the most glamorous motion-picture star of that year.

The counterpart of vivacious, seductive Leatrice Joy the future Mrs. Yerkes was not to become. As her early years passed, she did not blossom forth; she merely grew into an earnest girl with a firm mouth, slightly myopic eyes, and straight, unyielding brown hair.

Whereas some of her contemporaries who were no more beautiful than she managed to become known as "good sports," or "buddies," or "lots of fun on a date," the sad truth about Leatrice Cunningham was that she was never popular with either sex. Mrs. Cunningham, still a romantic, kept on trying, all through Leatrice's formative years, to induce a butterfly from her cocoon of a daughter. Obediently, the child would allow her stocky figure to be swathed in various shades of tulle for endless, fruitless high-school dances. Patiently, she would stand at one end of the gym, waiting for the arrival of some male assigned by a thoughtful chaperon to lead her through a duty dance. Doggedly, she would allow herself to be whirled three times around the floor by the silent partner, inevitably to be returned to the nervous knot of unassigned females. Leatrice went through this pointless ritual merely to avoid arguments with her mother; in her heart she knew the whole process was a complete waste of time. In the parlance of the sports world, Leatrice was a loser.

Since it is a statistical fact of population that there is a larger percentage of unmarried females (spinster) in the Commonwealth of Massachusetts than there is of unmarried males (bachelor), it would ordinarily have been more than likely that Leatrice Cunningham of Duxbury, Mass., would spend the middle years of her life as a book-keeper or a dental technician or a schoolteacher, sharing an apartment with two other unmarried females, arranging small parties at Schrafft's for the luckier girl who had just bagged herself a mate, and for kicks going to Boston for a matinee.

But statistics represent human beings, and every so often, Fate can make a monkey out of the census taker.

Upon her graduation from Katherine Gibbs Business School, Leatrice went to work in a Cambridge bank as a stenographer. In a matter of four years, she worked her way up to be personal secretary to the manager, which is as high a post for the young career girl in banking as the ordinary young career girl is likely to attain.

One day in 1950, the monotonous treadmill on which Leatrice was plodding stopped for a moment. Into the bank came Basil Yerkes, a postgraduate student at M.I.T. In his hand was a sheaf of canceled checks and on his face an expression of complete bafflement. A genius in applied physics, the pride of his teachers, a brilliant creative technologist with a long record of scholarships and awards for his imaginative work in the theoretical structure of the memory core (as yet unperfected), an intellectual in the upper .01 percentile, Basil Yerkes could not balance his own checkbook.

At the sight of the tall Harris-tweeded Ichabod, this awkward and embarrassed egghead full of theorems and equations, Newtonian Law and Lobachevskian dreams, this visionary who had been so rudely brought back from outer space to Cambridge by an over-draft of $7.93 . . . something in Leatrice Cunningham responded. This bony male had Problems. He could not cope with them. She could. Instinctively, she rose from her IBM Electric typewriter and hurried forward to answer the cry of a fellow human in pain.

Under the guise of taking her coffee break, Leatrice led Basil out

99

of the bank, away from the tentacles of finance that were waiting to bring him down. Over coffee and cake at Bickford's she audited his checkbook and brought order to his accounts, quickly finding the mistake in a check that Basil had drawn to his laundry and forgotten to enter.

Basil thanked Leatrice profusely, made restitution to the bank in cash, and hurried away down the street toward M.I.T., back to his monastic workbench.

The following month he was back, overdrawn again to the tune of $6.82. Since he had discovered someone to help him out of these mundane annoyances, he came, like a well-trained retriever, and laid his problem in Leatrice's capacious lap. And since she enjoyed the sensation of being needed, like the retriever's mistress, Leatrice responded. Again they went next door to Bickford's, had coffee and cake while she again audited his checkbook, and again he thanked her and left.

One financial crisis led to another, and by the fourth one Basil discovered that he too was enjoying these meetings. Leatrice was saving him valuable time with the audits, she was pleasant company, and Bickford's coffeecake was tasty. (Basil's normal diet consisted of Hershey bars, instant coffee, and an occasional helping of sardines, eaten from a can at the lab.)

It is difficult to document exactly when the physical entered this fiduciary relationship. Up to this time, it had occurred to no male to try to take from Leatrice a girl's most precious possession. As for Basil, his interest in sex had thus far been confined to lab studies of the mating habits of herring, conducted in large tanks. (One of his colleagues had hit upon the notion of herding fish, which are essentially one large ear, with ultrasonic waves, the theory being that if the herring could be forced into one another's company on a regular basis, their rate of reproduction could perhaps be increased.)

Leatrice Cunningham knew little about the mating habits of herring, but she had read enough Erskine Caldwell and John O'Hara in paperback editions to know that, in order to increase human mating activity, there are times when a spinster cannot rely upon sonic stimuli, but must take the initiative upon herself . . . even in Massachusetts.

She decided to take a bold step. She wanted Basil. He was hardly the knight on a white charger she had once imagined for her very own, but at her back Leatrice could hear time's wingèd chariot hurrying near . . . so she devised an intricate plan.

When Basil next showed up, on a cold, drizzly January afternoon, for his monthly auditing, Leatrice feigned a heavy head cold. Instead of adjourning to their customary meeting place at Bickford's, she suggested that Basil accompany her, after banking hours, to her apartment. By extremely fortuitous circumstance, her roommate, a schoolteacher in suburban Brookline, had taken charge of the Seventh Grade play, and was staying late for rehearsals, thus assuring Leatrice an uncluttered theater of operations.

At first, Basil resisted. He did not wish to take advantage of Leatrice's good offices, especially if she had a bad head cold. She should, he believed, go home and get under the covers. Since this was exactly the goal Leatrice was building to, she insisted that he accompany her. How could he allow his financial difficulties to lag? They must do his audit forthwith.

By the time they arrived at the two-room flat on Gray Street, Basil, sans raincoat, was a mass of soggy, steamy Harris tweed. Leatrice suggested that he slip out of his wet things lest he, too, become prey to the deadly virus. Thus Basil shortly found himself seated on the sofa, draped in one of Leatrice's old flannel robes, the window blinds drawn (to keep the chill out) and in his hand a hot toddy.

Leatrice excused herself. A few moments later she made her reappearance, her bankers'-gray suit discarded, wearing her roommate's most prized possession, a Chinese robe of robin's-egg blue silk. She rustled across the room to the sofa and sat down next to Basil. As she picked up his checkbook and began figuring, the soft fragrance of her rain-drenched hair wafted into Basil's nostrils. . . .

He gulped the remainder of his hot toddy.

Leatrice interrupted her calculations just long enough to refill his glass. Then she was back at the sofa, this time even closer. As she bent her head over his checkbook, Basil shot her a nervous glance. By some accident, the sash of the silken robe had come undone, and the garment gaped open revealing several inches of pink nylon tricot and an inch or two of pink Leatrice. . . .

Basil reached over to put his glass down on the coffee table, and his hand accidentally brushed against Leatrice's knee. He felt a shock. His hand recoiled.

Static electricity?

The phenomenon interested him as a scientist.

Gradually, Basil reached his hand out to touch Leatrice's knee again.

Another shock.

Basil blinked. What an interesting manifestation. Fact One: A man, slightly damp, without rubber soles on his shoes. Fact Two: A slightly disheveled young woman three inches away. Fact Three: Man's hand touches protective coating of robin's-egg blue silk, encounters electricity. Hmm. What can have caused this static charge? Had it merely been an accident, or was there some deeper scientific explanation?

For a true researcher, the situation called for further investigation. Basil was a dedicated scientist. His hand moved toward Leatrice's knee for a third time.

Ah ha . . . Once again, shock!

This must mean that—

Basil's ratiocination was interrupted by a most remarkable corollary phenomenon. This electrically overcharged female in the billowing silk robe had dropped the checkbook on the floor, had turned, and seemed to be embracing him!

Most unscientifically, but with the directness of a Nike missile on target, her lips were moving toward his . . . and what sort of a reflex was this? She was *kissing* him!

Yes, indeed. Not only was she kissing him, but the once-demure banker's secretary had him pinned in an embrace tighter than a safe-deposit time lock. Well, mused Basil, in the interests of science one must pursue this strange behavior pattern and see where it led. . . .

Reeling beneath the determined thrust of Leatrice Cunningham's piledriver onslaught, Basil Yerkes, the dedicated researcher, found himself jammed tightly into a corner of the sofa, her lips searching for his. Great merciful heavens—this experiment had gotten out of control! From a simple charge of static electricity, this lady seemed to be generating massive bolts of lightning! Overcome, he attempted to fend her off . . . and then, whether it was the touch of the young female accountant's caresses, or merely two glasses of toddy at work, a strange reaction took place within Basil. The filing cabinet of his conscious mind slammed shut; the Thinking Man retired, and the Animal appeared, to embark on a series of remarkable and unfamiliar actions. Gone was intellectual curiosity, to hell with scientific research! Basil went to work on a simple physical inventory.

And did not stop to take notes as he went along, either. . . .

Shortly after this fierce Cambridge afternoon, Leatrice and Basil were joined in holy wedlock. All in one well-planned passage-at-arms, Leatrice had achieved her many goals: she had gained a brilliant budding genius for a husband, found a provider, a father for her unborn children, and had also knocked a slight dent into the Massachusetts statistics on Females, Unmarried.

Upon their return from a brief four-day honeymoon (which they spent in Atlantic City, attending a meeting of the American Research Fellowship), Basil deposited Leatrice in their apartment, waved goodbye, and went back to his lab at M.I.T.

As the years passed and Basil went from a twelve-hour day in a lab at M.I.T. to a twelve-hour day as engineer with Techni-Devices, Inc., in New Jersey, and thence to a twelve-hour day with Electro-Lab, in Cambridge, Leatrice began to have doubts about her marriage license. True, it maintained she had a husband . . . but it did not seem to guarantee his physical presence.

He arose at 6:00 A.M. and disappeared. By 7:00 or 8:00 P.M. he would return, exhausted. After washing his face, he would lower himself wearily to the supper table and, with a technical manual in hand, gulp down his food. The conversation usually ran like this:

"How did it go at the factory today, dear?"

"Fine."

"What are you working on over there now?"

". . . A reverse diode capacitator."

"Oh." Long pause. "What *are* reverse diode capacitators, dear?"

"Here." Basil would hand the 286-page manual to Leatrice. "Read all about them." He would rise, disappear into the spare bedroom, where all his own lab equipment was set up, close the door, and remain there until midnight.

The dishes done, Leatrice, in a freshly ironed nightgown, her hair brushed, and with just a soupçon of perfume behind the ears, would take to her bed, one eye on the capacitator manual, the other watching the door to the spare bedroom.

At the onset of the witching hour, Basil would stagger out of his lab, stumble into the bedroom, shuck off his Harris tweed, kick off his shoes, absently pat Leatrice on the forehead, and drop like a discarded fuel tank into his own bed.

". . . Darling?" whispered Leatrice.

". . . 'a' minus 'x' to the twelfth power . . ." mumbled Basil.

She reached out a questing hand . . . and encountered a tightly shut eyelid. The scientist had worked himself into a dreamless coma.

Fortunately, there *were* variations to this routine. On Christmas and New Year's, the plant would close, and Basil was forced to spend the day at home. Several days ahead of the holiday, Leatrice prepared a powerful batch of Tom-and-Jerry. . . . Which may explain why both Yerkes' offspring celebrate their birthdays in September.

But the fact that for the remaining 363 days of the year Basil was firmly married to his work may serve to explain the origin of Leatrice's backaches and her increasing migraines. Even after he progressed to a partnership in the new firm of Science Associates, Inc., and they moved to a pleasant little home in Connecticut, he remained a dedicated man, showing no signs whatsoever of slowing down at his bench.

The months passed, the children grew, Basil left the house at six and worked until midnight . . . and Leatrice lay alone in her bed, a technical manual instead of a husband by her side.

She had married an inventor who treated sex as an interesting experience . . . and then had gone on to more complicated problems, leaving her to cope with the by-products.

Who can blame Leatrice Yerkes, stretched out on her lonely bed at 11:00 P.M. of a warm spring evening, with Basil still locked away in his basement workshop . . . the migraine beginning to flicker in her frontal lobes . . . for musing that perhaps that bank job in Cambridge, with its group insurance and hospitalization and retirement on half-pay pension at sixty wasn't such a bad deal at all?

For she had come to realize one dreadful fact: The role of wife and helpmeet to an inventor is not designed for a woman. It is not a job for a human; let IBM invent a device that will operate a seven-room split-level, raise the children, see to their education, cook, clean, market, mend, and taxi . . . and manage the household finances as well. Why, there was not even a technological advantage in being married to a scientist like Basil. If something went wrong with the electrical appliances, she had long since learned not to rely on her husband but to call an electrician. Should something go awry with the plumbing, Leatrice promptly called for a plumber. Perhaps, mused this depressed Connecticut Molly Bloom . . . with Basil locked in his workshop and me lying here feeling like this . . . *again* I should call the plumber.

"Absolutely not!" I told Marjorie, as we sat at the dinner table. "Basil and I are meeting tomorrow at nine sharp and we'll be up to our hips all day in calculations."

"Tomorrow's Saturday," she said. "And you promised Buddy days ago the two of you would have an outing."

"I also promised Major Willoughby that he and the Army would get a pilot model of a modification," I said. "And we're in a hell of a bind delivering it."

"A pilot model of a modification of *what*, dear?" she asked.

"Sorry," I said. "Classified."

"Have you worked it out in theory yet?" she asked.

"No," I sighed. "And we've been at it for almost three weeks."

"But how can something you haven't worked out yet be classified?" Marjorie asked.

Our latest maid, a muscular Swedish girl named Katrin, stamped into the dining room. She dropped a pot of coffee and cups onto the table, and stamped out.

"Is she working out?" I asked.

Marjorie made a face. "Let's talk about your modification."

"Can't," I said.

"Other men bring their problems home and thrash them out with their wives," said Marjorie. "Whenever I ask you about what's happening down at the factory, you make me feel like a cell member."

Katrin reappeared, bearing a covered tureen. She placed it in front of Marjorie and started out. "Spoons," said Marjorie sharply.

Katrin turned and gave us a blank stare.

"For the pudding," said Marjorie.

No reaction.

"To *eat* with," said Marjorie.

A vague smile broke over Katrin's face. "Oh. *Ja. Sure,*" she said, and padded out in house slippers to repair the deficiency. When we had spoons and Katrin had retired to her coffee in the kitchen,

Marjorie heaved a sigh. "I don't know," she said. "For the first week or two she was such a jewel; it was like a dream come true. But in the last few days, she's begun to come apart at the seams."

"So's our modification," I murmured. I was thinking, with some dread, of Major Willoughby, the tall, bespectacled ramrod from West Point. Upon my return to the plant from the Riviera, we'd held a top-level conference with him. He'd quite clearly indicated that the Defense Department was not pleased with our lack of progress. While the Major, in the course of that five-hour session, hadn't exactly come right out and said it, his manner inferred that the entire space program was stalled on the launching pad, waiting for Science Associates to deliver that miserable modification of XXXXXX L-4. With all possible speed, we were to fall in, tote that XXXXXX, lift that XXXXXX, and carry the ball over the goal line for a technological touchdown.

"Why don't you take the afternoon off and go to the movies with Buddy?" suggested Marjorie.

"Dearest," I said, sipping my black coffee, "I'm spending the next forty-eight hours with Basil Yerkes."

"Why can't Cousin Jerry fill in for you?" she inquired.

"Cousin Jerry is off somewhere negotiating," I said. "Besides, he'd be no good to Basil and me. He's not a technological type; he's Sales."

"If the Army is panting so to get its hands on this, I simply can't see what you need a salesman for," Marjorie said.

"Let's not go into a discussion of what Jerry does or does not do at Science Associates," I said. "In the interests of national defense, our son Buddy can go to the movies by *himself!*"

She did not answer, but shot at me that disapproving look employed by most cunning American wives and mothers—that withering beam of scorn that is calculated to instill a deep sense of guilt in one's mate, to prove to him that no matter how successful he is in the outside world, as a father he is Inadequate.

"Cut!" I told her. "Turn off the ray! You know better. Under most circumstances, Buddy and I are Good Pals—we have plenty of Mutual Projects; we find it easy to Make Contact with Each Other; and we never have had difficulty in finding Joint Interests. So lay off!"

Marjorie finished her coffee. "Agreed," she said. "And since your relationship is so ideal, *you* go have a nice Father-and-Son Chat . . .

and *you* explain to that poor boy why *you*'re breaking the date."

If one were to believe in the transmigration of souls, there are times it would be quite possible to deduce that my wife is the reincarnation of Clarence Darrow.

I went up and knocked on Buddy's door.

"Come in, whoever you are," he said.

It took me a minute to locate the boy. He was lying on his bed, the only comparatively open space in a sea of clutter. The walls were tacked solid with an array of photographs: airplanes ranging in age from the World War I Sopwith Camel and Fokker D-7 to the B-56 Hustler; Casey Stengel, the Los Angeles Rams, Ted Williams, Lassie, Chuck Connors, Dr. Albert Schweitzer and the Harlem Globetrotters next to Scott Crossfield; a pennant from M.I.T. cheek by jowl with a banner reading "Sunset Hill Day Camp," encrusted with campaign buttons from the last two local elections and the traditional Pullman card reading QUIET IS REQUESTED FOR THE BENEFIT OF THOSE . . . The chairs, the desk, the shelves, the bureau tops were a jumble of models, a sea of plastic miniature antique cars, gaily decorated hot rods . . . battleships, atomic powered subs, a clipper ship, half-tracks and tanks and armored vehicles, an intercom set, a ship-to-shore telephone, a model microscope with slides, a chemistry set, several pieces of HO railroad rolling stock, and a two-transistor radio, once alive, now dead, resting in peace atop a shoe box full of baseball cards, and a three-year store of well-thumbed "Atomic Boy" and "Masked Phantom" comic books.

In the midst of this graveyard of satisfied whims, my son lay flat on his back on the bed, his hands locked behind his neck, staring up at the ceiling. I walked over to him, ducking my head to avoid colliding with a suspended model of the Graf Zeppelin. "What're you doing?" I asked.

"What's to do?" he replied.

"You're bored?" I asked.

"I like to lie here and think," he said.

I sat down on the bed next to him.

"Listen," I said, "things've been a little hectic around here the past few days. Lots of activity at the plant . . ."

He nodded. "You and Mom have a good time up at that convention?" he asked.

"I suppose so," I said. "Why?"

"It was kind of a relief, mm?" he asked. "Did you good to get away from home and the kids for a few days."

"What gave you that idea?" I asked.

"Oh, I don't know," said Buddy. "You see it all the time on television—those family shows. About once every couple of months, the mother and the father decide they ought to get away from the kids for a vacation *alone*." He grinned.

"Those shows aren't much like life, though," I warned.

"No," he agreed. "Because the kids always end up going along. On television, that is." He sat up. "What'd you come up to discuss, Pop?"

I felt dreadful.

"Well . . . it's about Saturday," I began, wondering how to equate the needs of the Defense Department, the pressures of the electronics business, profit and loss and other such adult intangibles with the unpleasant task of disappointing a nine-year-old child.

"How about Yankee Stadium?" Buddy suggested. "A doubleheader with the Indians—we could drive down in your new Marci-10 and go somewhere first for kosher frankfurters, huh?"

I looked in his expectant face and thought, Damn you, Major Willoughby . . . damn *you*, Mr. Khrushchev . . . why don't *you* explain why I can't go to Yankee Stadium with my own son? The phone rang.

"Honey!" Marjorie called. "Will you get it? It's probably for you, anyway."

"Hold it a second," I told Buddy, and went to pick it up in our bedroom.

First I heard the muted symphony of a wailing two-year-old, and then I heard Basil Yerkes. "Walter?" he asked. "We still meeting tomorrow?"

"Sure we are," I said. "What made you ask?"

"Uh, Walter, I'm in a squeeze over here at the house," he said. "Leatrice is down with some kind of a bug. Doc was here—just gave her a tranquilizer—damn things cost a fortune—says she should stay in bed tomorrow. I'm stuck over the weekend with the kids. Got the woman next door to come in and take care of the little one, but what do I do about Basil Junior? I mean, there's no school tomorrow."

"Wait a minute," I said, and yelled downstairs to Marjorie.

"Honey, can you handle some kids here tomorrow? It's Basil and he has a problem—"

"And *I* have a problem too," she yelled back. "Katrin just quit and please get off the phone; I have to put an ad in the Classified. I've got eight women here for tea for the Community Chest steering committee meeting and you've simply *got* to take Buddy off my hands—"

"Basil," I said, "can't you for heaven's sake get hold of a Mother's Helper somewhere? If it's money you need, I'll see that the firm defrays the cost—"

"I had one lined up to come in next week but she just ran off and eloped," he whined.

"Why in hell did she elope?" I demanded.

"I, uh, think it was an emergency," he said.

And I should try to explain this all to Major Willoughby? Christ, the problems of the Small Businessman!

"How would it be if I, uh, brought Basil Junior over to the factory while we work?" he suggested.

"We keep one eye on him and the other on the drafting board?" I snapped. "Impossible."

"What are you going to do about Buddy?" Marjorie called.

"Well . . . I guess we're hung, then," said Basil mournfully.

My back was to the wall. "We are like hell," I said. "Bring your kid along."

"For the whole day?" he asked, hopefully.

"From 8:00 A.M. on!" I said, and hung up.

I walked purposefully back to Buddy's room. "Old boy," I asked, "what's your allowance running these days?"

"Thirty-five cents a week," he said, "and I haven't had a raise in months."

"We're renegotiating your contract," I said. "As of tomorrow, I'm raising you to fifty cents. How's that?"

He sat up. "Cool!" he said—and then eyed me. "Ah . . . what do I have to do for the extra loot?"

"Oh, it's merely a little extra assignment," I told him. "You know how you've always wanted to see what happens in Dad's factory?" He nodded eagerly. "Well, tomorrow I think I can arrange it for you to hang around there for a few hours."

"As a technician?" he asked.

I patted his arm, diplomacy oozing from my hand. "Eventually, yes," I said. "Naturally, you can't go into the restricted areas, so tomorrow I'm starting you in on the ground floor of the electronics business. I want you to keep an eye on Basil Yerkes, Junior. He's eight."

Buddy's lip curled. "He's younger than I am."

"It's very important that we keep him occupied all day," I said.

He nodded. "Baby-sitting," he said, cutting to the heart of the matter.

"If you want to call it that," I said.

"*Sixty* cents a week," he said.

Oh, well, in a way I was glad to see he was acquiring a certain business acumen. Lord knows, it wasn't hereditary. . . .

Basil and I set to work early, the deadline staring us implacably in the face. We had the modification fairly well thought out, but there were certain miserable little bugs in the XXXXXX which so far had defied solution.

Drs. Gesell and Ilg might not have approved of that Saturday's child-care pattern I improvised, but I was too busy to worry about it. During the morning I assigned Buddy to the outer office, where he was to keep an eye on Basil Junior, a stubby, frenetic little monster. I assumed there were enough avenues of amusement in Mrs. Bostwick's domain; Buddy had carte blanche to bang on typewriters, run up columns of figures on the electric adding machine, talk into the dictation equipment, and write up imaginary orders. Plus an unlimited supply of cokes and crackers from the vending machine in the hallway. Heaven knows whom they called on the office phones. . . .

Leo the watchman allowed them to make the rounds with him, and when I came out of the conference room at noon, he was teaching them the rudiments of poker. I sent the two down the block to a nearby Polish delicatessen where, with folding money at their disposal, they gorged on some ghastly unbalanced meal and brought us back sandwiches.

That carried us till 1:00 P.M. And by that time the movie was open. I shipped Buddy and his charge off to the Bijou for a double feature.

Under ordinary circumstances, Brigitte Bardot in *The Girl in the*

Chemise, double-featured with *The Attack of the Giant Plastic Men*, might not have been the most suitable entertainment for those two impressionable young minds, but what was I to do? Let those two intellects, with their two sets of active hands, roam at will through the factory? Leo wouldn't be back on duty until five-thirty.

Apart from basic considerations of plant security, never was there such an opportunity for kids to wreak havoc . . . an open field of 101 Things a Bright Boy Can Do. So many pieces of expensive, intricate one-of-a-kind equipment: testing rigs, the deep-freeze box for cold and the insulated ovens for heat, tiny power tools, that electronic numbers board we call the Tote Machine with its glass face of numbers across which lights are constantly flickering, testing, retesting . . . One touch of an uneducated hand, and the rig would be out of whack for weeks. All those tables covered with bins of tiny diodes, wires, capacitators, modulized electric motors and intricate plastic-molded blocks that contain an entire chassis the size of a sugar cube—and heaven knows what else we keep in inventory—all neatly arranged in order, requiring only one nine-year-old with itchy fingers to stall Monday's production line for five or six hours.

So off went the Bright Boys to the Bijou, and back we went to the drawing board and workbench, pacing up and down and staring at the equations Basil had scrawled, then fitting a piece of XXXXXX to XXXXXX L-4A and then spending an hour or so checking out that tiny step.

"If we could only lick *this* phase of it," said Basil, several hours later, "then I could see daylight." He stared at the pieces strewn on the blackboard. "Say," he said. "Supposing . . ."

"Go, Basil, go," I murmured. I recognized his trancelike state. It was a sort of pregnancy in Basil, out of which usually emerged an important breakthrough. But unlike the female cycle, Basil's period of gestation could never be predicted.

The phone rang. Irritated, I was about to rip it out of the wall when I suddenly remembered I'd told Buddy to call us from a pay phone if he got into any trouble with Basil Junior.

"What's up, son?" I said.

"Why, Dad, I didn't know you cared," chuckled my Cousin Jerry. "Hibernating in the shop on a Saturday afternoon, eh? Were you really worried about me?"

"Hardly," I said. "I've been too damn busy coping with your problems."

"I detect a slight pouty edge in your voice," said Jerry. "Go home and have a cocktail; you'll feel better."

"I can't afford that luxury," I said. "Basil and I are working our asses off on the Willoughby project—"

"And I'm here in New York, working my ass off on the Fleming project," Jerry said.

"Listen, I'm *busy*," I said, impatient to get back to work.

"Oh ho, you think *I've* just been tomcatting around town—expense-account living it up? No, sir! I've been deep in cheery meetings with Leonard."

"That's a form of work," I conceded.

"And we are working on a little arrangement that will warm the cockles of your petulant heart, Walter," he chortled.

The phone buzzed again. "Hold it," I said, and punched the button. Immediately a querulous voice asked, "Is Basil Yerkes there, please?"

"Hello, Mrs. Yerkes," I said. "Basil's kind of busy—"

Basil was mumbling to himself: "Assuming that xxxxx is the co-efficient of xxxxx . . ." His eyes were glazed. There were all the signs of an impending accouchement in his manner.

"I *have* to talk to him!" Mrs. Yerkes insisted.

"I'll have him call you back," I promised.

"No, I'll hang on!" she said. "It's important!"

"Okay," I said. "Hang on. . . ."

I punched Jerry's button. "Listen, Jerry, whatever it is, let it keep until I see you."

"Oh, no," he said quickly. "This is hot. Leonard and I want you down here Monday for a conference."

"Out of the question," I said. "Don't you understand, we're in a bind! We have to deliver a modification!"

"Will three hours kill you?" he asked reasonably.

"Look, if you two are so anxious to see me, why don't you come up here and pitch in?" I snapped.

"I'll call you back when you're in a better frame of mind," Jerry said.

"A dandy idea," I told him, and punched Mrs. Yerkes' button. "Mrs. Yerkes," I said, "can Basil please call you back?"

Basil had risen and was slowly walking to the blackboard, one finger pointing hesitantly. Something was about to gush forth. . . .

"I want to speak to my husband!" Her voice ripped from the phone.

Basil stopped. He turned in my direction. He blinked vaguely.

"Go on," I urged.

"Sounds like Leatrice," he commented.

"I'll tell her you'll call back," I said. "Keep going with what you're doing—"

He shook his head. Still mesmerized, he came and took the telephone from me. "Yes, dear," he said. "Mm-hmm . . . Basil Junior? He's all right, I guess . . . Lunch? . . . He had something . . . Hot? I don't know . . . Home? . . . I don't know exactly when . . ."

"I'll take over!" I said, but he shook his head.

"Dinner? . . . I don't know . . . We could eat home, I *guess* . . . No, I don't care . . . Make anything you like . . ." There came a series of irate remarks. "Okay, we'll go out then," he said. "But I don't *know* what time we'll be home . . ."

Good God! Was Galileo plagued with this sort of thing? Were Wilbur and Orville Wright forced to cope with a nagging telephone and a house full of domestic problems?

And instinctively, without consulting the encyclopedia, I knew the answer. Of course they were.

So how come, I asked myself, were they able to function so much more successfully than we twentieth century eggheads?

Basil hung up. Eagerly, I pointed him in the direction of the blackboard. "Now," I said. "You were standing right here—something was cooking in your frontal lobes—your finger was pointing right there—"

A pause. Then he turned to stare at me. "Yeah," he said. "What the hell was it?"

"Basil," I grated. "I am now going to shut off that damn telephone, right?"

"What the hell, Walter," he said. "Don't pick on my wife. . . . I wasn't the only one who got a call."

"You could have postponed it!" I told him.

"You could have postponed *yours*," he replied.

We glared at each other. We were tired and depressed, and our nerves were beginning to wear thin from equal parts of overwork and frustration. "Let's not squabble about it," I said. "We're grown-ups, and we've got a problem, and it's getting late." I had a sudden thought. I glanced at my watch. Five forty-*five?*

Where the blazes were the kids?

I went out to the waiting room. Empty. I peered down the street. No sign of them. They should have returned by now.

Worried, I went back inside.

Leo, the watchman, came limping up, puffing on his rancid Italian twist. "Leo, have you seen the kids around?" I asked.

He shook his head.

A street fight? The kids in this neighborhood were tough. Buddy had money in his pocket. Might he and Basil Junior have been way-laid on their return trip?

I started back toward the conference-room. Call the police, perhaps. Or the movie house.

There was a faint light burning inside the factory proper. "Hey, Leo—did you leave the lights on inside?" I called.

He came up beside me. "Nope," he said. "I'll go investigate."

I hurried inside ahead of him.

A few feet away from the main doors is a small area of tables that is used as a staging area for Shipping. The walls are decorated with the usual array of photos of nearly nude demoiselles, cultural poses clipped from *Playboy* and tacked up by our work force to serve as constant inspiration in their daily labors.

Beneath an outsize thirty-inch-long blonde, teetering happily back and forth on a stool, sat Buddy, a pile of fresh comic books in his lap. "Hi, Pop," he said, looking up. His eyes were bleary. "We stayed through the French picture twice; then we came back. The doors were open, and I figured you were busy, so we just came in here to wait for you, okay?"

"The . . . doors were open?" I asked Leo. "How did that—"

"Oh, I went to the john a second, a little while back," he equivo-cated. "Mighta left them open then."

Buddy yawned. "Pop, you all finished?"

"Where's Basil Junior?" I asked.

"Gee . . . that's funny. He was here a minute ago," said Buddy.

"Where is he *now?*" I demanded.

"I don't exactly know," replied my son.

"You're supposed to be baby-sitting!"

"Ah, Dad, I got *tired* of baby-sitting," he complained. "He's a drag. Got scared during the attack of the plastic men . . . then he got bored during the French picture and he ate too much candy and got sort of sick and annoyed everybody around us—"

"Sh-sh!" I said. In the distance, I thought I heard a faint buzzing sound. "Basil Junior!" I yelled. "Is that you out there?"

Silence. Then the pad of footsteps running and a stifled giggle.

"Basil," I crooned, forcing cordiality into my voice, "come on out of the factory. Be a good boy and get yourself out of there."

A pregnant silence. Then . . . "No."

"Hey, Basil, don't be a drag; come on out!" offered Buddy.

"You shut up!" piped Basil Junior.

"You see?" said Buddy. "A real drag."

"Basil!" I called. "Come on out of there, you little monster—" I caught myself. Psychology, Walter. Use your head. Menace will get you nowhere. . . . But if it won't—what *will?*

"What's up?" asked Basil père, coming up to me.

"Your son is roaming around loose out there! We've got to flush the little monster out before he does any damage!"

"Walter, don't call my little boy a monster," said Basil.

I might have paid some heed to the edge in his voice, but I was too irritated to be subtle. "We'll argue semantics later!" I told him. "Before the brat gets his clumsy little paws on something—"

"He's also not a brat!" said Basil.

"—exercise your parental authority and get him the hell out of there!" I said.

Leo had gone to the master switch. On flickered the fluorescents, and in their white glare was revealed the open factory floor, our valuable equipment stretching quietly, ominously still, off into the distance. Silence.

And no sign of a small, potentially destructive Yerkes.

"Basil Junior," called Basil. "This is Daddy. Where are you?"

No answer.

"Time to go home, Basil."

Silence.

"You coming with Daddy?"

Some distance off, a voice piped "Nope."

"Why not?" asked his brilliant, logical father.

"More fun here."

"Oh," said Basil Senior helplessly.

Here was child psychology at work!

Well, it was too late for rational behavior. Basil Junior must be evacuated before he did some serious damage. I tiptoed down one side of the factory and signaled to Leo to go down the other. Basil hesitantly started down the middle aisle.

Stealthily, middle-aged commandos all, we crept through the maze of testing equipment, stacks of components and power tools, past workbenches laden with XXXXXX L-4's in various stages of completion.

I turned a corner. I might have gone right past him, except for the sudden short burst of wind that was passed in my ear. I wheeled.

There, standing mesmerized by the flashing lights on the face of our most intricate device, the Tote Machine, was Basil Junior.

And he was reaching out a grubby hand to flick at one of the control knobs.

"Stop that!" I yelled, dashing toward him.

Startled, he turned to stare at me. "Look at this funny television set—" he began.

I body-checked him at least three feet into the air.

As he landed, he let out a loud wail.

Basil rounded the corner, just as his son burst into convulsive sobs. "He hit me!"

"What'd you do to my kid?" Basil demanded.

"What do you think?" I answered, furious. "Fooling with testing equipment—did you think I was going to stand here and allow *that?*"

"He didn't mean any harm!" Basil said, steely-eyed.

"He had no business in here in the first place!" I bawled, my frayed temper now shredding hopelessly.

"He wouldn't have *been* here in the first place if *your* damn kid had kept an eye on him, the way he was supposed to!" Basil yelled.

"*My* kid?" I countered. "How did it get to be *his* fault? He wouldn't have had to keep an eye on *your* kid if *your* wife hadn't had another one of *her* damn migraines!"

"My wife wouldn't have migraines if I didn't have to spend all *my* spare time bailing *you* and your stinking cousin out of this mess with the Army and *why did you hit my kid?*"

"Bail *us* out!" I yelled. "You're the hot-shot engineer we made a partner who's supposed to have kept us advanced enough so that we didn't have to redesign a modification of XXXXXX L-4 in the *first* place!"

We snarled like two aging tigers. Half an hour ago we had been working side by side; now, remarkably, we were spitting fire at each other. "And I hit your kid because he was playing with this goddam delicate piece of machinery!" I roared, taking a fighting stance.

Basil's fists clenched. He raised a threatening hand . . . and then his eye flickered over my shoulder across the face of the Tote Machine.

"Go ahead!" I snapped. "You started something—now finish it!"

"Oh, Christ," he moaned, staring at the flickering numbers. The scientist in Basil had displaced the latent Rocky Marciano. "Look at those figures," he said. "All bollixed up. The damn thing *is* out of whack . . ."

And no longer Ingemar Johansson, but once again the harassed businessman, I too stared at the machine. "Thirty-six hours at least to get it back into adjustment," I moaned.

We relaxed. Now that the damage was done, what could be gained by arguing?

Basil put an arm around his sniveling offspring. "Come on," he sighed. "I'll take you back to Buddy."

We slowly trudged out of the factory proper.

"Basil," I said, swallowing my bile, "I'm sorry I pushed the kid. It was an accident."

True, I was demeaning myself, but I wasn't being completely altruistic. Science Associates, Inc., could hardly do without a head engineer. . . . Not *this* week, anyway.

He nodded. "Forget it, Walter," he mumbled. "We were both tired."

"True, but we're both sensible, reasonable thinking men," I said. "Let's shake."

He gave me his hand. "I was just thinking about that modification," he said casually. "Supposing we took XXXXXX L-4 instead of XXXXXX L-4A and tried it with a <u>capacitator</u> . . ."

I stared at him.

"Do you think that makes sense?" he asked.

"Let's try it," I urged.

We deposited Basil Junior and Buddy with Leo, and dashed back to the conference. With a burst of furious energy, Basil began to scrawl new sets of equations on the blackboard.

Some minutes later, he dropped exhausted into a chair. "There," he said. "How does that look?"

"You're the engineering brains," I said. "How does it look to *you*?"

"I think we better start building the sonofabitch!" he said triumphantly.

"Tomorrow," I said. "It's been a long day."

We stared happily at the blackboard. "Basil, darling," I said, "if this is what comes of fist fights, we ought to go fifteen rounds more often."

"Physical violence is the weapon of intellectual children," he said.

"You're absolutely right," I told him.

And thank heaven *that* breach is healed, I thought.

But I forgot that Basil Junior had a mother to whom he could tell his troubles. . . .

10

IN HALF a lifetime, from that moment when he first learns to use his vocal chords, the normal man can and will make many masculine friends.

And they can be of remarkably different backgrounds and character.

The kindergarten snot-noses with whom he learned to play London Bridge or Tag, or Doctor (with that forward little minx in a basement down the block) . . . Pimply fifth and sixth graders with whom he went hiking and traded pulp magazines, passed a football, and grabbed a furtive Lucky Strike while speculating on what one's older sister looked like while taking her bath . . . The college classmates with whom he competed for positions in the social and academic sun, or argued all night with in strident bull sessions . . . That bewildering cross section of contemporaries from forty-eight remote states, with which he was paraded about and yelled at and incarcerated with in the various phases of his military service, at home and overseas . . . The eager beavers and the toadys and the good joes and the company men and the deadheads with whom he has worked, bench by bench in the shop, or desk by desk in the home office, or bar stool by bar stool out in the field . . . Casual bachelor playmates with whom he has got tight and/or gone prowling for available prey . . . Briefly encountered companions in the club car or the locker room or on the deck of a fishing boat . . . The neighbor from down the street with whom he serves on a Boy Scout fund-raising drive, or the intellectuals from across town who are interested in Art and Truth and Better Schools . . .

All these are called friends.

From the vantage point of one's late thirties, one can even project into the future and foresee what new companions/friends/buddies will emerge as one grows older. There will be fellow members of boards of directors, middle-aged cruise-ship cronies, that chap you will sit with at a testimonial dinner, fellow pallbearers at the funeral of a mutual friend. . . .

As long as one has a hand with which to shake that of the new arrival, a bottle of whisky with which to oil the machinery, a date-book in which to file the new name and address, the well of masculine friendship will not run dry.

As new faces and telephone numbers appear in the pocket secretary, the Christmas-card list loses a few names each year by erosion. The childhood friends have long since married and moved away; the classmates and bachelor friends and Army cronies have gone their separate directions. Poker partners find new games in which to play; social friends move into other spheres, either upward or down, and in one's world of business affairs the rapid turnover is too dizzying to contemplate.

One becomes increasingly aware of this ebb and flow of the social tides as he grows older. A man is left with the realization that he is fortunate to have one, two, perhaps three lasting friends—men he has known longer than since the last cocktail party his neighbors threw.

So, in the face of this constant human flux how is it possible that the relationship between me and my cousin Jerry has lasted and remained firm for such a long time?

Regard the two of us.

Jerry is glib and witty and quick.

I am slow, thoughtful, and careful with a dollar.

Jerry was and still is good at games and sports.

I am able to break 85 only after years of intensive practice . . . and on a very good afternoon.

Jerry has never had much use for stated routines, discipline, and order.

I can go quietly mad if a box of paper clips is missing.

Jerry has never stayed in love with the same female for more than three consecutive months.

I am (so far, at least) a married monogamist.

Jerry will always buy whatever he needs at lower than list price.

I am the one who trembles when my mail brings a notice of a routine examination by the Internal Revenue Department.

Examined rationally, we offer each other nothing.

Oh, I know that our friendship can be glibly explained by the old theory that opposites attract each other. . . .

But perhaps there is another bond that welds us together—one a little less pedantic:

Might it be that Jerry subconsciously represents all the things that I yearn to be? Wastrel, Artful Dodger, nimble broken-field runner across the sensuous byways of nonsuburban life?

Perhaps . . .

Then what about me? If I am such a stodgy bastard, so much of a white-collar bore, then what is there about gray Cousin Walter that attracts twinkle-toed Jerry?

Well, I might just be a symbol for him, too. A constant reminder of the middle-class world he is always avoiding. I could be Walter the Good Provider, the Shackled Male, the Trapped One whom he likes to have in constant proximity, so that he can glance at me and reassure himself: "There, but for the grace of my own fancy foot-work, go I."

Whatever strange alchemy it is that has kept my name in his address book all these years, I can grant Jerry one tribute. He has never bored me.

Even if I've bored *him*.

The Tote Machine was miraculously back in working order by Tuesday morning. After twenty-eight hours of forced-draft work, the blueprints for the new modification were complete, and Basil was already started on the building of our new XXXXXX L-4 (modified).

For the first time in days, I sat back at my desk, put up my feet, sipped some instant coffee, and relaxed. Now there was nothing to do but wait—sweat it out until Basil built his modification and proved it, God willing, to Major Willoughby's satisfaction. Then we could embark on manufacturing it for a decent profit.

And none too soon, either.

For the original contract for XXXXXX L-4 had practically run its course. If the new modification *didn't* prove out successfully, we would be in a very vulnerable spot. Science Associates, Inc., was far from being the only small firm engaged in this particular field of research and manufacture. In the past few years competition has cropped up like milkweed all over the landscape. The New England woods are full of bright young technicians and ex-college instructors huddled together in small one-story buildings, putting in twelve hours a day on the solution of technological problems that will automatically render their competitors' products obsolete. In this constant game of technological leapfrog, bankruptcy awaits the firm in second place.

Ah, well, thanks to Basil we were still holding onto our lead. . . .

The intercom on my desk buzzed. "Mr. Fleming," said Mrs. Bostwick, and her ordinarily firm tone of voice was a trifle shaky, "There's a man outside with a Rolls-Royce who says he's come to take you on a trip."

I sat up slowly. "Mrs. Bostwick," I said, "the last few days we've all been under tension, and I'm as aware of the need for an escape valve as the next person, but let's not lapse into silly practical joking."

"Go outside and see for yourself," she snapped.

Parked at the curb on Water Street, surrounded by an assortment of awestruck urchins, there was indeed a sleek, black, and indubitably genuine Rolls, and at its wheel a short chap in discreet matching black livery. "Mr. Fleming, sir?"

What was this handsome couple doing in our dingy environs?

"I am he," I said, affected in spite of myself.

"Any time you're ready, sir," he said, touching a finger to his cap, "we can be off."

There was a tinge of E. Phillips Oppenheim in all this.

"Would it be indiscreet of me to ask where you and this car came from, and where we're supposed to be going?" I asked humbly.

"Not at all, sir. You're to be at 335 East Sixty-third, New York, by three sharp. I believe you will find your cousin Mr. Teel awaiting you there."

"And whom—I mean, who is footing the bill for this expedition?"

"Oh, Mr. Teel is, sir," he said. "Shall we be off?"

"But what *happens* at three sharp? A meeting at the summit?"

He handed me a small envelope. I ripped it open. On a card, in Jerry's handwriting, I read, "Dear Walter. I couldn't think of any other way to lure you out of the woods for an important meeting with Leonard F. Sit back and enjoy the ride. Jerry.

"P.S. The Rolls is rented. Yes, Virginia, there is a bill and it is coming to Science Associates. But it's deductible. Okay?"

What normal, red-blooded overgrown American boy could resist a ride to New York in a spanking new Rolls, driven by a liveried chauffeur?

A fiendish man, my cousin.

Ten minutes later the Rolls purred its way into our driveway and up to the front door. Chambers, the driver, opened the door and I got out. "Won't be a second," I said. "Just to change my shirt."

"Of course, sir," he said.

I must stop this obsequious deferring to him! Just because he drove a Rolls . . .

I strode up the front steps and inside. Marjorie was crouched over the living-room telephone, a pile of notes near her hand, a harassed expression on her face. As I walked in, she turned. "What are *you* doing home?"

"Madame," I said, pulling her to her feet, "come for a ride to New York at sixty miles per hour, with the only audible sound the ticking of the dashboard clock."

"I'm busy," she said, pulling free. "I've got no time for your games; I've been calling employment agencies, canvassing for the damn Community Chest, and why aren't you at the factory?"

I pulled her to the window. I pointed at the imposing English import in our driveway. "Just *regardez cela*," I said.

"What'd you do? Trade in that silly Marci-10 *already?*" she demanded.

"I am on my way to New York for a meeting," I tried to explain.

"You couldn't just take the New Haven Railroad like anybody else?" she asked. "I know! You had a few drinks at lunch and you were feeling restless so you went out and bought that. Oh, God, I married a lunatic!"

"Come on, sweet," I urged. "To the manner born. Climb into something chic and dash up to town with Pater—"

"You *are* drunk!" she said. "Who's to stay with the kids? And clean the house and cook the dinner and raise money for the damn Community Chest?"

"We're rich!" I said defensively "*Hire* somebody!"

I ran upstairs to find a clean shirt. She followed me. "It's very easy for *you*," she said. "You feel like tossing your work aside and

123

having a good time; you go buy a Rolls-Royce and start dashing around the countryside. But it's different for me. I'm the one who's got the responsibilities and the marketing and has to cope with the help—"

"The Rolls is *rented!*" I said, recoiling from the force of her attack.

"—and if you really want me to come to town with you," she continued, "we'll have to wait until Buddy comes home from school."

"Out of the question," I said, donning a clean shirt. "I'm due for a meeting at three with Jerry. . . ." I started downstairs, knotting my tie. It was the wrong time and the wrong face and though her face was charming it was the wrong face.

Marjorie followed. "What kind of meeting?" she asked, suspicion thickly coating her voice.

"Well, if you promise not to spread it around," I said, tucking in my shirttails, "I'll tell you. He's taken a suite in a cheap hotel in the fifties under an assumed name, and there are these two sisters, friends of Jerry's, models . . . very sweet girls, really, but when they've had enough champagne, they're absolutely uncontrollable—"

"Very funny," said Marjorie, but she was smiling. "Will you be home for dinner, dear?"

"I'll call you by four and let you know," I said, and kissed her fondly. "Leonard Finch has a bad habit of droning on and on, but with any luck I may be able to duck him."

"Oh," she said, making a face. "Leonard *Finch*."

"Exactly," I said.

"I don't envy you the afternoon one bit," said Marjorie.

"I'm glad you understand," I said, and started out toward the waiting Rolls.

As I climbed into the front seat, Marjorie followed me out.

"Is that beautiful thing really rented?" she called.

Chambers turned and bowed. "We prefer the term 'hired,' madame," he said.

An elegant hour and a half later, I was gently deposited on the sidewalks of Sixty-third Street. Chambers closed the door behind me and tipped his cap. "I'll wait for you here, sir."

I glanced up and down the street, solidly lined with cars. "You're simply going to stand here?" I inquired. "Won't you get a ticket?"

"Oh, no, I shouldn't think so," he said, with a faint, tolerant smile. "Not in *this* car."

Well, Walter, take a lesson I told myself. The Rolls owner double-parks with *droite de seigneur*. At last you are tasting some of the flavor of the rich full life. . . .

I rang the doorbell of our corporate snuggery.

I heard laughter; then the door opened and an extremely beautiful young brunette peered out. "You from the liquor store?" she asked. "Bring it in here, lover!"

"I—I must have the wrong place," I said. "Looking for a Mr. Teel—sorry—"

"You're *Walter!*" she trilled. "Come *in* sweetie! We've been waiting and waiting for you!" she clutched my arm and tugged me into the room. "Jerry, he's here!" she called. "He's got a touch of gray at the temples and he's tweedy and it's terribly becoming, isn't it, Bettina?"

Seated on a low couch was an equally stunning girl with a glass in her hand, her long and beautiful legs extended and resting on a coffee table. On the same table a large bottle of champagne was chilling in a silver bucket. She looked at me and blew me a kiss. "Yes he is," she said. "Pour him a little grape and make him comfy, Marilyn."

The brunette handed me a glass of wine. "Here, cutie," she said. "Drink up, you're bottles behind us. Isn't he, Bettina?"

". . . Bottles and bottles of bubbly," said Bettina, and patted the couch next to her. "Sit down and rest, Walter; you businessmen keep up such a rapid pace. You must be exhausted." She hiccuped happily. "Scuse me. Wouldn't you like Bettina to rub those tense old neck muscles for you, doll?"

"Now, Bettina, just back off," said Marilyn, moving in on the other side of me. She patted my arm. "Jerry specifically said that *I* was to be nice to Walter, so you concentrate on your champagne and leave his therapy to me."

"Oh, there you go, using those dreary old words again," sighed Bettina. "I *wish* you wouldn't keep calling it therapy. It makes sex sound like Blue Cross or something, and I don't think it's medicinal at all, is it, Walter?"

I hadn't found my voice yet.

"My analyst said—" began Marilyn.

"Your *an*alyst," said Bettina, with a wealth of scorn. "From what you tell me, he should be paying *you* the twenty dollars an hour." She smiled over at me. "Isn't that collar a little too snug, honey?" she inquired, touching my neck with her cool fingers. "Why not slip off that jacket and be more comfy, mm?"

"Dr. Gebhard is *not* a dirty old man," pouted Marilyn. "He's very understanding. He's helping me understand why I've always had this urge for self-expression."

Bettina hiccuped again. "Self-expression?" she remarked. "Everybody knows those quiz shows were all rigged."

I stared at Marilyn and finally found the use of my vocal chords. "You were a quiz contestant?" I asked. At this point in my journey through never-never land, I would have accepted her as anything.

"Oh, no," she smiled. "I was *part* of the show. See, first I started as a simple Leader—On—you know, the one in long black chiffon who brought the people on from backstage. And then when the show got real intense, the producer liked my work so much he promoted me to being a Paying Teller. Don't you remember me now?"

"Afraid not," I said.

"Why, I was the one who handed them their check from the Chase Manhattan Bank!" she said, her eyes bright with memories of past glory. "And then, if they lost, I was Key Bringer. I gave them the keys to the Consolation Cadillac, and helped them into the front seat. At the end, I was Door Slammer, too!"

"How could I have forgotten?" I apologized.

"Those investigations really torpedoed my career," Marilyn said, gazing glumly at the carpet.

"Walter!" came Jerry's voice from somewhere inside. "I'll be out in a minute. The girls taking care of you all right?"

". . . Show business is for the birds," Bettina was saying as she leaned back, one arm clasped behind her blond head. From where I sat, the view was superb.

"Fine, fine!" I gasped, remembering my manners sufficiently to answer Jerry's question.

"A girl who wants a future should get into *heavy* industry. Isn't that right, Walter-baby?" Bettina asked.

"That's what they tell me," I said, mesmerized by the scenic route. "What, er, line of endeavor are you in?"

"You didn't see me at the Coliseum?" she pouted. "At the Construction Equipment Sell-o-Rama? I was a smash. I started as Miss Power Shovel, and when Miss Pay Loader got the virus, I took over for her. I did so well I was given the Miss Bulldozer spot, too. I'm already signed for next year. How's *that* for security?"

"As a taxpayer and a businessman," I said, "I'd say our highway-construction program couldn't be in better . . . hands."

"You're sweet," giggled Bettina. "Now, how about a little message?"

"Bettina," said Marilyn, warningly, "you're *poaching* again."

"Well, you're neglecting this nice man, and I'm just filling in for you," said Bettina. "Until you get over your depressed period."

"Please, ladies," I insisted. "Don't fight over me, I'm not worth it." But Marilyn had begun to unbutton my coat. "If it's attention he wants," she said peevishly, "I'm perfectly capable of easing his basic tensions."

"Thanks heaps," I said, pulling away, "but—"

"Now, you mustn't let your inhibitions take over," Marilyn scolded, her fingers dismantling the knot of my tie. "They just narrow your horizon and keep you from expressing yourself. . . ."

Before she could extend my horizon further, Jerry, immaculate in a new dark silk suit, bounded into the room.

"Well, Walter, how do you like the way I've decorated the place?" he inquired.

"It's a little busy," I said, fending off Marilyn.

"I see you two girls have made friends with my country cousin," he said. "That's very good thinking."

"We'd like to, but he's full of latent hostility," said Marilyn.

"Oh, Walter," sighed Jerry. "Relax and enjoy. Who's to know?"

"I'd relax," I said, "but I thought we had a business appointment!"

"It can wait a little." Jerry smiled. "We've got at least an hour before we meet with Leonard."

"Oh, good," cooed Marilyn. "A whole lovely insane therapeutic hour!"

I took both of her delicate hands in mine and held them firmly, thus suspending her tactile peregrinations. "Thanks," I said, "but Jerry, you and I had better do some serious talking. I need briefing."

Marilyn stared at me. "Lover," she sighed, "you *are* inhibited."

Damn her and her analyst. They were both right; my horizon *had* narrowed and I *had* forgotten how to express myself. Could it be that I was getting too old and settled in my ways to blast off into a new orbit? How depressing to encounter this sudden insight!

I turned back to Marilyn, prepared to release her hands, and myself as well, but it was too late. Reason had set in and the initiative was no longer mine. "Walter's right," Jerry was saying. "Sorry, chickens, but he and I have to do a little business."

"If it's heavy industry," asked Bettina, "may I stay and listen? A girl can always learn. . . ."

"No, dear," said Jerry, helping her up and kissing her forehead. "This is strictly high finance and it would make your head spin." She pouted. "Walter, is the Rolls still downstairs?" he asked. I nodded. "Good," said my cousin, the last of the great spenders. "*Mes enfants*, tell the driver to take you down to 113 West Thirty-seventh, eighteenth floor, Town and Country Furs, and ask for Manny. Pick yourselves out a little knick-knack each—"

"A mink coat?" asked Marilyn happily.

"*One* skin," said Jerry. "Then if you're good, you get another skin next week, and another the week after . . ."

"What kind of coat is that?" she asked.

"It's a special do-it-yourself job," he said. "An Add-a-Mink . . ."

Marilyn gave me a chaste goodbye buss, and then the girls were gone, wafted away on a champagne cloud to a wholesale-house heaven.

When the door had shut behind them, I looked at my cousin. "One question. Are those two . . . ladies . . . by any chance *sisters?*"

"I seriously doubt it," said Jerry. "If they are, it's only by profession."

"Thank heaven," I said. "I was beginning to think I had developed extrasensory perception."

Jerry shook his head and smiled tolerantly. "From where I sat, Walter, it seemed like merely a very bad case of scruples."

Although the houris had vanished, all around us in the small, expensive expense-account living room their soft, insinuating fragrance lingered on, inducing in my mind, like forbidden scenes from an uncut French art film, lustful visions of what this afternoon might have been.

"I'll thank you not to rub it in," I told him. "Now, see here. You've been very cute in kidnaping me in a Rolls and bringing me down to show me how badly Science Associates needed a New York base of operations. But the party's over and let's get down to cases, Diamond Jim. First, the modification—"

Jerry had been pouring the last of the champagne into my glass. "Walter," he asked, "how would you like to be rich?"

"I *am* rich," I said. "At least, that's what you told me when we talked last. Which, I may point out, was some time ago. For an officer of this firm, Jerry, you certainly have made yourself conspicuous by your absence when the chips were down."

"Stop being peevish," he said. "Of course you're rich, but only *small* rich. Ordinary rich. Only six figures. Middle-class rich."

"It's a very satisfying feeling," I said. "I enjoy it. That is, when I get time away from business. Which isn't often. Jerry, I'm warning you, if Basil's modification should develop bugs, we're in a hell of a bind with Major Willoughby and the rest of his boys."

"How would you like to be *really rich?*" he cooed.

"Don't split your infinitives," I said. "Don't you see, if the XXXXXX L-4—"

"Oh, brother!" sighed Jerry. "At a time like this, he's a grammarian! Walter, get your nose out of McGuffey's Reader and join me up in the stratosphere with the big boys!"

I began to lose my temper. "I don't know why I put up with you, Jerry," I told him. "You're unreliable, you're arrogant, you're crude, you're lazy, and simply because of an accident of genetics, whereby your mother was born my father's sister, we've been shackled to each other for all these years—"

"When I say 'rich,'" Jerry said, "I mean seven-figure, capital-gains, vested-interest, backbone-of-the-Republican-Party rich. Now, does *that* sort of wealth interest you, Genetic-Accident cousin of mine?"

"Legally?" I inquired.

"Sufficient to satisfy even young Robert Kennedy," he replied.

He was a worse siren than either Marilyn or Bettina would ever be. How could one fight Jerry? At the moment, I *was* worth six figures, exactly as he had predicted I would be, that day not so long ago when we had embarked in business for ourselves. And although I had sufficient moral fiber to withstand the temptations of an attractive young siren . . . Seven-Figure Rich was a dazzling lure.

"I am interested," I told him.

"Good," he said. "Finish your champagne, and then we're off to see the wizard."

"The who?"

"The Wonderful Wizard of Moo . . . Leonard Finch."

I winced. "Oh, no. Listen, it's been a long day, and my stomach can't handle—"

"Swallow your pride, Walter," said Jerry, taking me by the arm. "Keep your eye on the Big Capital Gain Up Yonder. Leonard is merely a means to an end. Bear that in mind and it will sustain you."

I allowed myself to be led to the tumbril.

II

———

". . . When the definitive history of the Plasticist School of twentieth century American painting is written, the name of Sim Torgen will loom as large as, if not larger than, that of any of his contemporary Plasticists. This young twenty-nine-year-old rebel, bursting free of the shackles that have fettered so many of his fellow painters, is almost single-handedly responsible for the massive artistic revolt that took place in the late fifties, in the now famous colony of lower East Side New York painters. Torgen it was who proclaimed, in his original manifesto, 'Break down the walls and free the painter from his age-old enemy, namely, paint. Let us explore the uses of completely new materials—everyday objects, the things we live in, of and by . . . fragmenting them into their components and thus forcing them into new shapes!'

"With this stirring, if somewhat belligerent, call to action as his keynote, Torgen began, in 1957, after his expulsion from the Art Students' League under circumstances that are unimportant here, his first attempts to contribute to the mainstream of art. His historic first works, 'Composition A,' 'Composition B,' and 'Composition B Plus,' were all done on beaverboard, with colors secured by the grinding up of powdered eggs, stale blue cheese, and shoe polish of black, brown, and ox-blood shades. In a letter to his discoverer and later mentor, Axel Dougherty of the *avant-garde* Dougherty Galleries, on East Ninety-third Street, Torgen wrote, '. . . A painter must not only eat—he must also be able to use what he eats!'

"Moving rapidly forward after these first experiments, Torgen proceeded to his next stage, or Plasto-Cuneiform Phase, in which he completed the series known now as 'Cold Frames.' These arrangements were of chicken wire, stretched between tomato stakes, onto which the artist affixed cunning festoons of wet toilet tissue, molded and left to harden in a variety of interesting shapes.

"Thereafter, Torgen moved rapidly to an attack on the problem of dimensional space, in his Chiaroscuro, or Tinkertoy-Fantasy series ('Hammerlock,' 'Scissors-Grip,' and 'Kidney Punch,' all presently in the collection of A. G. Spalding & Sons) in which the artist made bold new use of powdered Jell-O, in all seven colors, brushed across such hitherto mundane materials as a glass shower door, the back of a 1936 De Soto sedan, and an official National League catcher's chest protector.

"The latest work of Torgen, which is on display in the show opening this afternoon at the Dooley-Finch offices, is an exciting demonstration of this artist's never ending, restless search for new forms, new materials, new techniques. Hung on the walls are a series of his latest efforts, on which he has been furiously at work in sporadic bursts of energy for the past twelve months. They are titled by Torgen 'The Fargo Experiments'; accomplished, in his own words, in the following manner: '. . . In the back yard of my winter studio in North Dakota, I have been using the sides of old packing cases. On cold winter mornings, just before the sun has risen, to take full advantage of that ugly gray light, I go outside at five in the morning. There, in a bucket, is pancake syrup in which I have already begun to mix my colors, made up of powdered instant-gravy mix, cigarette ashes, mercurochrome, and chili. It has been hardening all night long; now I take handfuls of this material, aim, and fire it against the rough pine board, some thirty feet away. The results have helped me to express the confusion of my inner eye, the sense of agony that surrounds us, and finally the completion, or perhaps Satori, that comes after a hard morning's painting. I call it my "World Series." '

"Even though none of the Torgens on display here today is for sale, having already been purchased by such eminent collectors as the Guggenheim Museum, Mr. and Mrs. Leonard Finch, and the Purchase Fund of the General Foods Corporation, art lovers are indeed fortunate to be able to have this bleacher seat, as it were, at the flowering of a major American Plasticist talent. Following this current exhibit, Mr. Torgen plans to travel to France where, as he himself has said, 'I shall begin experimenting with gourmet materials. . . .'

"All proceeds from the sale of tickets and of catalogues at this week's show here in the offices of Dooley-Finch, Inc., will accrue to the benefit of the Summer Tenement Fund of New York, Inc., which has for many years supplied cold drinks and tennis shoes to slum children here in the hot city."

—ANNA RANKIN PERLOWITS, critic, *Art Herald*

"Sorry we have to confer in here," said Leonard, ushering Jerry and me into a small back room of the sprawling Dooley-Finch offices, "but this Torgen opening is such a success out there that things have got a little out of hand." In his immaculate industrial-olive suit, silk shirt, and discreet Charvet tie, my one-time Camp Ho-Ho-Ka bunkmate resembled a smug, well-dressed Buddha.

We found ourselves in a windowless cubicle, an architectural afterthought with a desk, three Eames chairs, and a bookcase crammed with what were obviously discarded manuscripts. On the wall next to me was a small hand-lettered inscription: "HOROWITZ IS AN EXISTENTIALIST"

"One of the writers works in here," Leonard apologized, as an attractive secretary swiveled in, bearing a tray on which was a decanter of Scotch and three Steuben tumblers. The decanter bore a silver collar: "*Mr. F. Private.*" She deposited it on the desk, and left. "And how did you like the Torgens outside?" Leonard asked, pouring.

"Damned interesting," said Jerry. "Mm . . . Delicious Scotch."

"What about you, Walter?" Leonard inquired. "Did *you* get Torgen's message?"

The condescension in his voice chafed me. "Message?"

"Walter loves them," Jerry said hastily, pushing a glass of Scotch into my hand. "He hasn't been able to stop raving about them since we got here."

Leonard tilted back his chair and rested his bespoke Peel oxfords on his writer's desk. "To tell you the truth," he said, "I myself didn't see too much in them when I first got to look at his work. But it's just as the critics said, Torgen *grows* on you."

"Like poison ivy," I murmured, thinking of those angry swirls of dirty ox-blood and brown, the sunbursts of soggy Delsey, the crusty pancake syrup oozing onto raw pine boards. "It looks like the inside of a supermarket after a tornado."

"Drink up, Walter," Jerry said, forcing the glass toward my mouth. "Now, Leonard, since Walter has been occupied with various other matters these past few weeks"—*such as earning a living for you two*, I thought savagely—"perhaps we ought to bring him up to date, eh?"

Leonard nodded indulgently and cleared his throat. "Walter, old boy," he said, "let me start by saying that I as well as others have watched your accomplishments with a very solid sense of satisfaction." *From where?* I wondered. *A banquette at 21?* "And pride." *And profit, you pompous ass.*

"Thanks a lot," I said, with a sycophancy that hurt.

"Not at all," said Leonard, sipping his whisky. "I always believe in giving credit where credit is due, and all that jazz." He lit a Balkan Sobranie with his gold Dunhill lighter and exhaled a thick plume of expensive smoke. "Now, Walter," he said, "it's time we discussed the architecture of the future."

"Whose future, Leonard?" I inquired, coughing.

"Why, ours," he said. "We're all in Science Associates together, aren't we?" *Of course we are. Me working in my shirtsleeves around the clock and you sitting back on your fat corporation with your bloody English brogues on the desk. . . .*

"Now here's what I've been kicking around in my mind," continued Leonard. "Of course, I haven't hammered out all the details, but the basic structure is there. It's a problem in efficiency—" The office door was suddenly pushed open and in peered a stout middle-aged lady in ranch mink. "Are there any more paintings in here? —Oops, Zelda, I think we made a mistake."

"You did," said Jerry, rising and closing the door.

"Lock it," said Leonard.

Jerry fumbled with the latch. "No lock," he reported.

"Oh, yes," said Leonard. "I forgot. We don't allow locks on writers' doors." He winked. "Eliminates funny stuff with the secretaries on the lower echelons, y'know?" He nodded at Jerry. "You sit in front of it, Jerry," he ordered.

"You bet," said Jerry, and hurried to move his chair. *What is this, Cousin?* I thought, watching him scurry to carry out orders.

Since when have you become a lackey at Screwy Lennie's beck and call?

"Where was I?" asked Leonard.

"You were with the basic structure," Jerry prompted.

"Oh, yes." Leonard nodded, turning back to favor me with his bulbous stare. "Walter . . . how would you like to be rich?"

"Excuse me, Leonard," I said. "I'll spare you running through this gavotte again. The answer is Yes, and now can we get down to cases? I'd like to get home to Connecticut before midnight. I've got a wife and kids waiting and a business to tend—"

"But not for much longer," said Leonard, pouring himself a tumbler of whiskey. "Soon we shall strike off those shackles, right?"

I blinked. "What does that mean?" I asked. "That I should get a divorce?"

He shook his head and smiled. "No, Walter. By shackles, I meant Science Associates, Inc."

The room was silent.

"I don't consider my business onerous, Leonard," I said at last. "I enjoy my work; things are going well; I get pleasure out of what I'm doing and—"

"—and now it's time to reap the just rewards of your labors, Walter," said Leonard.

The Scotch in my stomach had suddenly turned ice cold.

"I don't think I quite understand you," I said. "It sounds to me as if you're suggesting I retire."

"Not 'retire,' Walter," said Leonard cheerfully. "Sell out."

"Sell? What the hell for?"

"For a capital gain," said Leonard. "Actually, not sell. Merge is the technical means we'll have to use—"

"Now wait just a goddam minute!" I said, rising. "When did all *this* get decided?"

I looked stonily at Leonard and Jerry.

They looked stonily back.

What the pluperfect hell was going on around here?

Seconds ago, we had all been sitting quietly, the three of us, my cousin-partner and the man who had helped finance us, enjoying twenty-year-old Scotch. All working together toward the same end, to forge a strong small business . . .

But now, suddenly, I felt as if I were in an operetta, where, at a masked ball in old Venice, at the stroke of midnight everyone unmasks to reveal that the heroes are really villains and vice versa.

It was only 7:16 P.M. in Manhattan, not Venice, and there were no masks visible, and yet . . . why did I suddenly feel this wall of ice between us?

"Haven't you discussed this with Walter, Jerry?" Leonard was inquiring.

"Well, not specifically, no," said Jerry.

"Why not?" asked Leonard, too quietly.

"Yes, why not?" I demanded of my cousin. "Since when did you have the right to exclude me from top-level policy—"

"Now, Walter, take it easy, baby," said Jerry. "You've been up to your ass in work, and I didn't want to drag you away from it."

"Drag me away?" I cried. "I'm down in the hold stoking the boilers, and you—you're topside selling the ship! Merging away my interests! Partitioning Poland! Who the hell ever said you could take it on yourself to sell my business—"

"Part my business," said Jerry.

"And remember me," added Leonard.

"*You?*" I replied, and I was beginning to feel warm again, not from the lack of ventilation, either. "Why should I remember you?"

"Capital does have its privileges, old man," he said.

"How about *my* capital?" I snapped. "My investment may not be as large in dollars, but it represents a hell of a lot more manhours and sweat and—"

"Walter, baby, take it easy," repeated Jerry, putting a hand on my shoulder.

"And what kind of surprise party are you instigating here, Cousin?" I demanded, turning on him. "Is this what you call Furthering Our Best Interests, partner of mine? Why are you in such a rush to jump overboard?"

Jerry poured himself another Scotch. "Leonard's got a case, Walter," he said.

"Of course I do," said Leonard. "Walter, don't get emotional. You've worked hard, built up a business, made a success of it. Now you can merge, get out from under the load with an exchange of stock, and make yourself a hefty capital gain in the process. It's the American Dream. Why fight it?"

"Because I'd like to make this sort of decision for myself—" I began.

Somebody began pounding on the office door. "Get out!" called Leonard. "We're busy!"

"Who's in my office?" cried a voice offstage.

"I am and get the hell away from there!" yelled Leonard.

Silence. Then footsteps receding into the distance.

"Now here, in very broad strokes, is what I have in mind," resumed Leonard, no longer Screwy Lennie bawling through a locked door at a lackey, but once again Finch the Financier.

"When I'm ready to talk selling out, I'll let you know," I said.

"There's a very hot outfit on the Coast, small, yes, but growing like a weed," he continued.

"I'm not ready to discuss it," I said.

"Very shrewd financial connections, good management, bright guys up at the top."

"I'm not interested," I said.

"We'll meet with them, but of course that's only a formality. We'll have all the terms ironed out beforehand."

"I'm not going to be pressured like this!" I said.

"Then we'll sit down with Ed Harris—he's a friend of mine who's on their board, the power behind the whole operation—and finalize the basic move," Leonard went on implacably. "We're all going to come out of this smelling like roses."

I stood up again. "I don't like being told what to do!" I shouted. "That's why I went into business for myself!" I slammed down my glass in front of Leonard.

"You sound cross," he remarked.

"You got the message, old bunkmate of mine!" I said, and turned to my cousin who sat in front of the door. "Move, will you?"

"You want some fresh air?" inquired Jerry.

"No," I said, hauling him out of the chair and pushing him aside, "I want *out*." I threw open the door and stalked out into the crowd of tax-deducting art lovers outside.

Jerry came dashing after me. "Hey, Walter!" he said. "What're you so sore about? Come on, come on back—"

I shrugged off his grasp. "You Judas-goated me in here. I'll leave under my own power!" I said, and kept on elbowing my way through the drinkers, the munchers, and the gapers, headed for the lobby.

"Ah, come *on*, Walter," he persisted. "Don't be childish. Here's Leonard pulling strings—setting up a sweet deal for us—baby, aren't you being a little childish about this?" I kept walking. "Just because you and Leonard don't like each other is no reason for you not to be realistic about your future!"

We had reached the outer lobby. "Realistic!" I cried. "For Christ's sake, Jerry! We worked hard, we built something of our own—something we could be proud of. Didn't that *mean* anything to you?"

He stood in front of me, his glass of expensive Scotch still in hand. And shook his head.

"Oh, Walter," he sighed. "We're not at camp any more. These are the big leagues. And this is how they play up here."

"Sorry," I said, "I guess I'm not yet ready to join the Black Sox!" The elevator doors opened and I pushed past him.

A strange disease, corruption. Its symptoms are rarely obvious. It does not attack rapidly, but works its way through the conscience slowly. And, contrary to the drawings of Hogarth, corruption leaves no scars. The face of a corrupt friend is exactly the same face he possessed when you knew him as an Eagle Scout.

Or a counselor at Camp Ho-Ho-Ka.

The elevator doors shut.

I stood there, staring at the blank wall, slightly drunk, slightly tired, and rapidly losing faith in the Golden Rule.

"Was that an argument, or were you merely leaving the party in a huff?" asked a female voice.

I turned. It was Betty Lawrence, black tailored suit, chic hat, and inquiry on her face, standing next to me in the elevator.

"Don't worry," she went on. "Whatever you tell me is off the record, even though I *was* up there on business." She gazed intently at me. "Walter, you look as if you'd just lost your best friend."

"You might be right," I said.

12

In most of the gleaming windows of the new glass-fronted cubes along Park Avenue, the lights were on. Inside the functional high-rent towers, cleaning women were hard at work, dusting desk tops, emptying wastebaskets, stuffing sacks with crumpled-up notes, carbon copies, interoffice memos, bearing away the evidence of the day's corporate manueuverings.

By tomorrow morning at 4:00 A.M., all the visible signs of the past day's machinations would be gone, leaving time for the central air-conditioning units to blow the handsome office suites clear of the subtle odor of man's exploitation of his fellowman.

Then, at nine or so, the electric typewriters would emerge from beneath their covers, the power would pulse through the IBM machinery, errand boys would appear from Schrafft's with containers of life-giving coffee, and the whole process of business as usual would resume once more.

Betty and I walked slowly uptown. For almost eight blocks she remained silent.

"What would happen," I mused, glancing up at the endless blocks of tinted glass above us, "if this street ever felt a slight California-type tremor?"

"A highway paved with broken glass," she said. "But a boon to Libby-Owens-Ford."

"Not to mention mankind," I muttered.

"You're not in the warmest of moods tonight, are you?"

"No," I said.

"Well, I suppose those paintings would depress anybody," she commented. "Every time I reached for an hors d'œuvre, I caught a glimpse of one of those Torgens." She grimaced. "What a gantlet to run, merely to get a story on Big Business Moving into Fine Arts. By the way, Walter, what were you doing up there at Dooley-Finch? Are you a collector, too?"

"Of kidney punches and low blows," I said.

"Mmm . . . Would you like to tell Aunt Betty about it over dinner?" she asked. "Happily, my stomach is returning to normal. You may put me down as Entertaining Press. Everyone else does."

"I'm not hungry, but I'll feed you," I said. "And not out of the corporate pocket, either."

"I *am* flattered," she murmured.

The restaurant was small, French, with no prices on the menu, and the usual 40-watt amber bulbs in the lighting fixtures. I picked away at my Chateaubriand. Betty attacked hers with gusto, while I finished telling her of the outlines of Leonard's latest proposal.

"Excuse me for gorging like this," she said. "It's not that I don't sympathize with your point of view. It's merely that I know Leonard . . . and I know Jerry . . . and what they're trying to pull on you is such a drearily familiar story."

"Why the hell can't they leave well enough alone?" I complained. "Isn't it enough to build something? Everybody's doing well, making money, going forward. . . . Isn't that enough for now?"

"I was only your cousin's secretary, not his analyst," said Betty.

"Yes, but you warned me about him," I said, in an excess of masochism. "I wouldn't listen, but you had it all figured, didn't you?"

She sighed. "It's no fun being infallible. I guess that's why I'm still single. I haven't yet met a man who could stand the idea of marrying a self-employed Cassandra."

The waiter brought her a tray of rich pastries.

"They are *not* going to sell me out," I said grimly.

"But they are going to try very hard," she replied, her mouth full of Napoleon. "Finch is not the type who relishes No for an answer."

"Well, I have a safe-deposit box up in Connecticut full of engraved certificates that will keep on saying No to dear Leonard—" Suddenly I remembered; I had been out of touch with the stockholders for quite a while. Spurred by pangs of father-husband-provider-type guilt, I excused myself and left her to mop up while I called home.

The booth was small and painted in Chinese red. I was flushed from the Scotch and the lack of ventilation and depressed by the events of the past few hours. There were two phone numbers and descriptive graffiti scribbled on the wall. They conjured up visions of Bettina. And then I heard again Jerry's mocking voice: *"From where I sat . . . it seemed like merely a very bad case of scruples."*

He'd probably been thinking that about me for years.

Damn him.

"Hello?" said Marjorie, and I roused myself.

It was a bad time to call.

Buddy had been rude at the dinner table. She hadn't been able to find a new maid. Something was wrong with the station wagon; it clanked under the rear wheel. One of the girls on her committee was going to Europe for four weeks leaving her with all that extra work. And she hoped I was enjoying my trip to New York.

"Marjorie—" I began, and then stopped. It was too hot in the phone booth and too cold at home. "I'll tell you all about it to-morrow."

"What happened with Leonard?" she asked.

"Nothing," I said. "Nothing *yet*." I would have explained further, but one of the kids had started yelling and she had to go cope. "Where are you having dinner?" she asked when she came back on.

The Scotch had dulled my wits. I said, "I'm with Betty Lawrence." And instantly cursed myself for breaking the first rule of the businessman: *Always say: With two guys from Fort Wayne.*

But: "Oh. Betty," she said. "That's nice. How is she? Give her my best."

"You don't sound very jealous," I said.

"Jealous?" she answered. "Of you and *Betty?*"

Through the glass booth window I could make out Betty across the room, her face silhouetted in the soft light of the banquette. I had a sudden clear vision of the mountain trail behind the Riviera, of her rounded shape in those tight ski pants, of the warmth of her lips. . . .

"Yeah, I guess you're right," I said craftily. "She's the Good Scout type. See you tomorrow."

"Where are you spending the night?"

"Up at the apartment Jerry rented for us," I answered. "Take care of yourself, dear."

"I'm glad *one* of us is going to have a decent night's sleep," she said.

"She sent you her best," I said, as I sat down at the table.

"That's nice," said Betty.

"You think so?" I replied. "I found it kind of insulting."

She looked at me with surprised eyes. "Why?"

"Because if I were Marjorie, and my husband were out on the town with an extremely attractive single girl, I might just be a little more disturbed about it than she is," I explained. "How about a stinger?"

Betty didn't reply for a long moment.

"All right, Walter," she said. "I'd love one." She smiled. "And thank you very much."

When a man has been a monogamist for ten or eleven years, and (for whatever rationale he may choose) he turns predatory, he may discover something sad about himself as a potential seducer.

He is rusty.

He is out of practice.

Here I sat with a bright, eminently desirable girl in her early thirties. The next move was up to me. As we sipped our stingers, chatting of such matters as whether or not the next Congress might do something to help out Small Business, I rummaged through long unopened drawers of my mind for a proper gambit.

A hansom through Central Park?

No . . . we were hardly college students home for the holidays.

I let her tell me about depletion allowances in the oil and natural-gas industry, and contemplated another ploy: Let's Go Up to My Place for Some Soft Music on the Stereo and Some Honest Talk.

Tsk, tsk, Walter. So unoriginal. In her daily rounds, Betty must have encountered that one more often than the Dow-Jones average.

We moved on to the Excess-Profits Tax. I studied her attractive lines and wondered, How about the friendly hand on the knee opening?

No . . . too blunt.

142

She told me about the potential markets that would open up by 1970, when the Population Explosion went off, and I remembered another old stand-by, the Freudian Springboard. (Betty, I've been listening to you, and may I say something personal? You've got a *problem*. A warm female like you—you're *unfulfilled*. Why don't you let me help you break down that Block?)

But that one was now impaled on a Nichols and May record. . . .

So how *did* one go about it these days? Was seduction accomplished through Zen? Should we go see the latest Ingmar Bergman movie? Or did one take one's prey to a coffeehouse and discuss the Camusian alternatives to the futility of an existentialist society?

While I silently cursed myself for being so out of touch, suddenly I found myself yawning.

That did it. Betty broke off her analysis of the breakdown of the tariff laws. "Walter, darling," she said. "You're tired. Take me home."

I sighed and signaled to the waiter for the check.

And just as well, too, I thought, as I paid up. How stupid of me to believe that I could have risen to this occasion . . . at my age!

Not to mention what a fall from grace it would have been. Think of it. Me, a husband, a father of two, member of the Chamber of Commerce, upright citizen and pillar of the community, subscriber to *Business Week* . . . stooping so low as to contemplate adultery with this perfectly decent young woman!

I should be ashamed of myself.

But how could one feel guilty over mere wishful thinking?

She lived in one of the new apartment houses on the lower East Side. Sadly, resigned, I escorted her up in the elevator, then down the impersonal hallway to her door. She took out her doorkey, unlatched it, then turned to me.

"Thank you for helping me through a very dreary period," I said, holding out my hand.

"Where are you going?" she asked.

"Uptown," I said. "To brood on the duplicity of mankind."

"You could do that here," she said.

Then her arms were around me, and her lips were moving on mine. ". . . Schweik," she murmured, and kissed me hard. "Even *now*, a Schweik . . ."

Suddenly I wasn't tired any longer.

Somewhere in the middle distance I heard the sound of a door closing behind us.

All right, I thought, undoing the buttons of her jacket. Man can withstand just so much and then he gives up fighting.

Here is where I start being a bat boy for the Black Sox. . . .

13

It is nearly 10:00 P.M. In a small, comfortable two-and-a-half room apartment in a new building (cooperative, with tax benefits inherent in ownership) on New York's East Side, the bedroom door stands ajar. . . .

Ignore the array of intimate female apparel mingled with various items of men's wear, tossed hither and yon upon the carpet (new acrylic-fiber, wearing 22 per cent better than old-fashioned wool, and also costing 6.7 per cent less). Ponder not upon the unaesthetic attitude of the two shapes outlined beneath the rumpled sheet (purchased at the annual January White Sales a few months ago). Do not tiptoe compulsively into this quiet *chambre d'amour* to restore a semblance of order. (A hireling from Cleaning Power, Ltd., will arrive on the scene tomorrow at ten.)

Rather, let us leave this somewhat spent adulterer. Let him find rest, entwined in the competent arms and thighs of his new-found partner in dalliance. (He had always known she had a shrewd way with a dollar, but in the past hour or so she has revealed hitherto unsung talents.) Yes, let us leave him, relaxed warrior, to doze and to sleep off his classic postcoitus *tristesse* . . .

. . . while three thousand miles to the West of said nest, in an office in a large modern plant in California, where it is only 7:00 P.M., a certain Mr. Lenihan, Executive in charge of Production, his shirt-sleeves rolled up, a stubble of beard on his chin, and the butt of a seventy-five-cent cigar in his mouth, studies working drawings for a certain restricted project. Near him stands Mr. Beech, the Project

Boss of said project, and the subject under discussion is the completion of the pilot model of said project, a major component of which is Rocket Model XXX A, a major component of which is Engine XXXX 9-B, a major component of which is XXXXXX L-4 (modified).

Mr. Beech has just finished explaining to Mr. Lenihan that delivery dates on said project may have to be modified from the ones specified in the firm's contract with the Government. Mr. Lenihan has just replied that he would like to know just what in the hell has brought this about. Mr. Beech has replied that there is a little hang-up in Connecticut, at Science Associates, Inc., that outfit which is supposed to be shipping XXXXXX L-4 (modified).

Mr. Lenihan has replied that it is a hell of a note when a whole damn project has to hang fire on some miserable chicken-wire operation back East and why the hell did Mr. Beech let the firm get into this bind? Mr. Beech has replied that he is merely a human being, not an IBM machine, and that he has been on the phone for days trying to clear the log jam and that it will take time. And that is the reason that the cookie isn't crumbling properly.

Mr. Lenihan has lit his cigar and told Mr. Beech to calm down, that this isn't a personal reflection on his, Mr. Beech's, capabilities. He, Lenihan, knows what a hell of a job he, Beech, has been doing. In fact, he, Lenihan, has several times mentioned to the Boys Upstairs what a good job Beech has done holding various aspects of this screwed-up operation together with nothing but his bare hands.

Mr. Beech, somewhat mollified, has murmured an embarrassed thanks, and has added that he did not mean to lose his temper. What he was getting at before was how miserable it was to be at the mercy of some subcontractor in Dallas, who in turn is at the mercy of some subcontractor in Cambridge, Mass., who in turn is relying on some half-assed outfit in the backwoods of Connecticut.

Mr. Lenihan has agreed. Further, it seems that Mr. Lenihan has been giving the problem some little thought. Mr. Lenihan is not known in the industry as "Bulldozer" Lenihan for nothing; he has a reputation for being able to crack through such roadblocks, large or small. Mr. Lenihan has now informed Mr. Beech that he thinks he sees a way out of this mess.

Mr. Beech has sat down and listened patiently to the master.

Mr. Lenihan has added that it is a way out that might also have certain financial advantages to a loyal, tight-mouthed Project Boss.

Mr. Beech has continued to listen, his lips a firm, taut line.

Mr. Lenihan has outlined an amorphous plan. Supposing, he has said, one assumed that in that Connecticut outfit were thirty-odd pairs of hands, and one brain behind them. Supposing, further that that one brain were pulled out of that outfit, say, and brought to the Coast. Supposing, finally, it were set up in its own little shop, somewhere in the San Fernando Valley . . . backed with some financial capital, easily obtained from a local bank?

Now, said Brains could continue to function, to supply the firm for which Lenihan works, under assured contracts (assured by Mr. Lenihan), with daily production supervised much more closely by a crack boss a mere stone's throw away (Mr. Beech.) Thus, the Brains could supply all the XXXXXX L-4's (modified) that were needed, under a new set of designs that would eliminate patent suits, of course. The company would be happy, the Brains would be well rewarded, and National Defense could go forward.

Not to mention how this new little Brains, Inc., setup might spill over a little side income to Messrs. Lenihan and Beech's wives . . . in return for the know-how of Messrs. Lenihan and Beech.

Mr. Beech has mulled the idea over in his mind and decided that the old Bulldozer is making a lot of sense.

He has asked Mr. Lenihan if he knows the name of said Brains, back in Connecticut. Mr. Lenihan has said he will leave that sort of detail work to Mr. Beech.

Mr. Lenihan has risen and said he is glad they have had this little chat, that he hopes Mr. Beech will keep his lip buttoned about it, and that he also hopes that Beech will, in the near future, get the goddam ball rolling again.

Mr. Beech has fervently agreed to devote his best efforts to that end.

Mr. Lenihan and Mr. Beech have thus left the office, headed for the parking lot and their respective Thunderbirds, thence to their domiciles, and the meeting has been thus adjourned.

Now hurry eastward back to New York, to the upstairs floor of a well-known restaurant on Fifty-second Street. There, at a leather-lined banquette, moodily sipping Espresso and digesting their expensive dinners, sit two other conspirators.

"He'll come around, Leonard," says Jerry. "Give me a couple of days to work on him and I'm sure I can make him see our point of view."

"Your cousin," says Leonard. "Ha."

"He's upset, sure," says Jerry. "But that's only because he needs time to get accustomed to the idea. He's got to learn to live with it, don't you see?"

"He always was a stubborn bastard," broods Leonard. "Stuck-up, too. From the word go, a troublemaker."

"But he's made the business pay," says Jerry. "You can't deny that, Leonard."

"We have too much involved here to waste time playing Old Maid with him," says Leonard softly. "You realize we have committed ourselves to certain parties. Heavily."

Jerry eyes Leonard. "Now, come on," he says. "Are you suggesting I won't be able to swing my own cousin and his stock around to our point of view?"

Leonard shrugs his shoulders beneath his cashmere suit. "Not at all," he says. "You're a very fast fellow with the con, and the chances are that if anybody can, you can swing him around. But just supposing the slob stays stubborn . . . mmm?"

Jerry lights one of Leonard's cigarettes. "Leonard, don't worry," he says. "You'll get an ulcer."

"Okay," says Leonard dangerously, "I won't worry."

Jerry sits back against the leather. He is trying to decide which girl he should call for a little nightcap; he certainly doesn't want to spend all evening here with Leonard, who, powerful though he may be, is something of a wet smack. . . .

Leonard fingers the stem of his brandy glass and is thinking that maybe this idiot can swing his idiot cousin around after all, but that since he is smarter than both of them put together, prudence dictates that he protect himself from failure. In other words, insurance to protect *him* against loss.

Soon, Jerry yawns and excuses himself, ostensibly headed for the men's room, confident that he has put out the fire in Leonard's bailiwick. Moments later, he is downstairs in a phone booth, dialing Bettina's number.

While upstairs, Leonard is using a telephone that the waiter has brought, issuing orders to his broker in Pound Ridge. . . .

148

Some sixty-odd miles to the north of Fifty-second Street, in a drafty bedroom in Connecticut, Mrs. Leatrice Yerkes lies recumbent, but not asleep, three feet away from her husband Basil, who has just arrived home from an eleven-hour day at his workbench, where he has been putting the finishing touches on a project the nature of which he has never revealed to his wife.

Leatrice has just completed an eleven-hour day on a project known as Raising This Family Without a Father To Help Me, and she is more than willing to discuss *that* with *Basil*.

"Basil Junior is going to have to have his tonsils out," she is saying. Basil Senior sighs and murmurs something indistinguishable in reply. "The doctor says he should get out of this damp climate," she continues. "The doctor says this house is too drafty for children like ours who are croup-prone. The doctor says this house isn't doing *me* any good, either."

". . . hsmhharff . . ." murmurs Basil, dropping off to sleep.

Leatrice reaches a tentative hand across the gap between the two beds. She finds her husband's bony forearm. "Basil," she says softly.

Basil groans.

Leatrice puts a foot onto the floor and winces at the cold. "Basil," she says again, "I'm coming over to talk to you."

"Whaddabout?"

"About moving," says Leatrice with a burst of sudden determination as she lifts the blanket from her husband's bed and insinuates herself under it. "To a dry climate."

Now journey exactly thirty-one miles to the south of the Yerkes split level.

Here is the antique-paneled study of an opulent Georgian mansion on Heathcote Road, in Scarsdale, New York. There, on a Robsjohn-Gibbings sofa, a plumpish psychoanalyst named Dr. Lothar Schreck puffs placidly on an expensive Romeo y Julieta which he has helped himself to from the humidor in the corner. The lady of the house, a somewhat agitated young matron named Mrs. Leonard Finch, née Caroline Handelman, sits next to him, clutching at Dr. Schreck's tweed lapels, her ample figure tightly encased in an elaborate lace-figured peignoir. A flow of angry protest gushes from her as if from an uncapped oil well of wrath:

". . . and he pays no attention to our children, he barely says hello in the morning, he never comes home to dinner, God forbid he should call and have *me* come into town! No— You know what I am? His housekeeper, his laundress, the chauffeur for his kids, hostess, doorkeeper—and what do I get in return?" She covers her eyes with fluttering fingertips. "As far as the physical side of our marriage is concerned—"

Dr. Schreck reaches over to pat Mrs. Finch's hand. "Sh-sh, *Liebchen*," he soothes. "About that, we've already done a little something, mm?"

"Yes . . . and *thank* you, Lothar." Mrs. Finch sighs fervently.

"*Nein*," the doctor murmurs gallantly. "Thank *you*." He kisses her hand.

"Oh, Lothar," she groans. "Without you I'd be completely miserable. . . . A doll. A puppet. A wind-up toy he thinks he can keep happy with a charge account at Saks. Or some jewelry. Or a new fur."

Dr. Schreck assumes a pained expression. "Materialistic answers . . ."

"Not so materialist!" says Caroline. "*One* charge. *One* piece of jewelry. *One* mink—a lousy stole!" She rises and begins to pace. "This farce is over. This marriage is ridiculous! I'm a grown woman. He can't keep me on a leash any more!"

"He can in New York State, *mein Schatz*," says Dr. Schreck. "Haven't we been all through this? He is a dominant personality who insists on having things strictly his own way. An infantile personality."

"Lothar," says Caroline. "Stop with the analysis. Have you ever figured why Leonard won't give me a divorce? I mean, on a basic level?"

"Dominant personality," repeats the doctor. "I once lectured to a group in Minneapolis on the subject."

"It's not that complicated!" says Caroline. "Leonard won't divorce me because if he does he'll have to make a settlement. And why won't he do that? Because Leonard is just plain *tight!*"

"Mmm . . . an anal erotic?" suggests Dr. Schreck.

"I don't know *what* he does for kicks," says Caroline. "But I do know that's why he won't cut me loose. In simple fiduciary terms, it would cost him too damn much."

"Mmm," says Dr. Schreck, puffing on the two-dollar cigar. "An ugly situation. Classic in its Grecian simplicity."

Caroline sits down. She drops her head on Dr. Schreck's shoulder. "Lothar," she says, "what do you think are the chances of Leonard ever going to a good psychoanalyst?"

"Rotten," says Dr. Schreck. "And speaking as a busy professional man who has his hands full of people who need help, *Liebchen*, I must ask, why bother?"

"Because," says Caroline, her forefingers playing with a lock of Dr. Schreck's sparse gray hair, "he has all that bottled-up tension, and you've had such success with other cases of it . . . and I was just thinking, after a couple of months in the hands of the right analyst Leonard might just decide that his silly wife Caroline was holding him back from going on to bigger things. Mmm?"

Dr. Schreck rises, shaking his head. "Caroline!" he says righteously. "What a venal idea! Even though I am only an analyst, I have taken the Hippocratic oath, and when I did, I—"

"Yes, darling?" whispers Caroline, rising and kissing the doctor's earlobe. "You what?"

Dr. Schreck stares at the paneled walls. His eyes take in the expensive furnishings of the room, the Matisse above the mantel, the formal gardens outside, the second family Mercedes parked in the driveway, barely visible through the window. He glances down at the affluent matron fastened firmly to his side. Dr. Schreck is suddenly tired of listening to an endless parade of disturbed patients. He is suddenly willing to spend the rest of his life listening to one wealthy one.

"However," he says thoughtfully, "the man does have problems. You see, that anal erotic pattern *could* be a manifestation of much deeper drives beneath."

"A divorce," Caroline murmurs into his ear, "with a handsome property settlement for me and the children . . ."

The good gray Dr. Schreck absently runs a hand across Caroline's ample posterior. "Mmm. Come to think of it," he says, "I just may have some time open for the unfortunate man. Wednesday mornings at nine?"

While a few hundred miles to the south, in the living room of Brigadier General H. R. Mowbray's apartment in Washington, D.C., a quiet little bridge game is just breaking up. Brigadier General Mowbray and his wife have been entertaining Major C. C. Willoughby, of his staff, and Mrs. W. The Willoughbys have just managed, through careful misplaying, to lose the sum of $6.55 to their hosts, and in a burst of jovial camaraderie the game has come to an end. The ladies have adjourned to the Mowbray kitchen to bring out the customary refreshments, while in the living room the two officers are putting away the bridge table and policing the area.

"By the way, General," says Willoughby, lowering his voice, "have you had a look at the progress report on that you-know-what project in Connecticut?"

"I've been so damn busy," complains the general. "Bring me up to date, boy."

"Right, sir," says Willoughby smartly. "Everything is under control. Our flanks are fully covered in case of failure—"

"Failure? We can't afford a failure," scowls Mowbray.

"Of course we can't," says Willoughby. "But if there *is* one, I've gone ahead with the Complete Alternate Schedule of Recommendation, strictly according to the lines you outlined last week."

"The schedule I outlined last week?" says General Mowbray. "Hmm."

"At our meeting on Tuesday," prompts the major. "You suggested that if we should run into any snags up in Connecticut when we test the you-know-what, we should already have alerted you-know-who to the problem so that it could be shifted you-know-where, remember? And if I may say so, it was damned clever of you to think of it."

"You may say so," says General Mowbray absently, putting the bridge cart away. Silently, he is congratulating himself on having such a thorough man on his staff.

"But typical, sir. Well, they're all alerted," says Major Willoughby. "They'll have to get up pretty early in the morning to catch *our* section napping, eh, sir?"

"Damn right," says the general.

His wife emerges from the kitchen, bearing a plate of pastry, followed by Mrs. Willoughby with the coffee. She offers the plate to Major Willoughby. "Here," she says. "Have a lovely whipped-cream tart."

Major Willoughby glances at the tart, and in his mind's eye it suddenly resembles a silver oak leaf. "Yes," he says, jovially. "I think I will!"

"Take two!" urges General Mowbray. "You've earned them."

"If you say so," says Major Willoughby modestly.

Back in the small bedroom in the apartment in New York (co-operative for the tax advantages), the prone male figure beneath the sheet opens one eye as he emerges from the depths of a refreshing, dreamless sleep.

What am I doing here in this strange bedroom? the man asks himself. How did I get here? And who the hell is this fragrant creature whose soft form lies inches away from me?

Slowly he becomes oriented. He is in bed with Another Woman. He is a philanderer. It has been a most pleasant departure from the norm. He should feel dreadfully guilty about what he has done. But he does not.

The bedside clock says 12:10. It is late. Habit takes charge. He should get up and dress, go home and get into his own bed. Get a good night's sleep so that he can arise tomorrow and go forth to cope with the world and the evils of the next day. He must return to the helm of his little ship. Who knows what has happened since he left the plant this morning? What calls? What crises? Supposing—

He stirs, softly, so as not to awaken the sleeping beauty beside him. The dalliance is over, and now he must needs away, into the night.

He is clumsy. His movement rouses his hostess. She stirs. "Walter?" she murmurs.

"Sh-sh . . ." he says tenderly. "*Sleep.*"

He feels her arm go around his waist, an arm with a surprising strength that tugs gently, pulling him back into the tumbled bed. "You're always *going* somewhere," she says.

"I've really got to," he apologizes, but the arm is joined by a second arm that reaches around his back to pull him downward.

"You can't go yet," she whispers in the darkness. "Why, it's just the shank of the evening."

The man from Connecticut, a few moments ago driven by habit and obligations, makes a remarkable discovery about himself: he has just developed his second wind.

The hell with it, he thinks, pulling the lady closer. . . . Nothing out there can be as important as what's about to happen *here.* . . .

153

$$14$$

___

AND, in the following A.M., behold the licentious breadwinner, dragging himself home to Connecticut after an evening of forbidden fruit.

What is he doing?

Instead of hastening home to cope with the snags, the foul-ups, all the assorted industrial goofs that are certain to have mushroomed in his factory . . . instead of wrestling with the ethical and/or philosophic problems involved in either joining with or fighting off Leonard and Jerry in their proposed scuttling of Science Associates, Inc., . . . instead of hurling himself full-tilt into the completion of XXXXXX L-4 (modified) . . . where is he?

He is wasting valuable time shopping.

And what is he out to purchase?

Just a little something for his dear wife.

Consider how this man is driven.

He has just spent what his ever-loving will undoubtedly consider (and with a certain amount of justice) was a wonderful night on the—on the town.

Can he walk in the front door of his happy home empty-handed? No, he cannot, for in her eyes he will then be an Unthinking Bastard, inconsiderate of his wife's feelings at having been Left Out. And what is more important, in his *own* eyes he will be an Unthinking Bastard.

So, in order to quiet his noisy conscience, he staggers somewhat blearily downtown in search of a gift for his Marjorie.

Which really presents a problem. What the hell to bring?

Something warm and whimsical, an amusing trifle, a *bibelot,* a box of assorted nylons, perhaps? Look there in the window, sheer black panties with two hands embroidered in silhouette . . . Over in that window, a set of scented satin closet hangers . . . How about that mink-covered change purse, guaranteed to raise eyebrows when Madame presents it at the Grand Union check-out stand?

(O Thorstein Veblen, thou should'st be with us at this hour!)

I spent an hour or so browsing past windows full of such expensive trivia, and then I heard the voice of my conscience: Walter, you should be ashamed of yourself. After what you have done, how can you repair the damage with a silly five-dollar whimsy?

No, dammit, the girl was entitled to something better!

You bet.

I'd been a dissolute louse, and she's entitled to the very best, dammit!

I turned and headed for Fifth. I would splurge some of my newly gotten wealth on my dear, sweet, loyal, long-suffering wife and helpmeet. Yes, it should be something ostentatious—like a Bonwit Teller *robe de nuit.* No, clothes she'd rather buy for herself at Loehmann's. All right, then, it should be perfume. Chanel, Balenciaga —Christmas Night—yes, a whole damned cask of it!

But perfume wasn't the answer. One couldn't expiate one's sins in a cloud of imported musk. No, jewelry was the ticket. I turned toward Cartier's, determined to find something expensive for her wrist or her neck or her ears . . . and then I changed my mind again. Dammit, whether or not she was aware of it, that dear girl had been Betrayed. Yes, Wronged! She deserved the very best. In an excess of self-torture, I hied myself off to Revillon Frères, to pick her out the ultimate—a small cape, no; a jacket, no; halfmeasures were an evasion. A mink coat, full length, with attached hood! Nothing was too good for that dear child. I'd walk in the door, hand her the expensively wrapped box with a low bow, kiss her hand, and say, Here, my sweet, a little something for you that's long overdue.

But then I thought of the inevitable reaction:

Oh, darling, how absolutely beautiful! Then the lovely eyes begin to narrow. . . . And tell me, Walter, what have you been up to these past twenty-four hours?

No, if I went overboard and brought her what she deserved, then I was signing my own death warrant.

Somewhere between the Doubleday Book Store and Revillon Frères, there had to be an apt Guilt Present.

Marjorie opened the package and took out the album of Frank Sinatra and Ella Fitzgerald duets. Then she smiled. "Thank you, dear," she said. "What's in the other package?"

"A working model of an Atomic Pile, complete with 417 detailed plastic parts, a small bag of imitation fissionable material, and a certificate attesting to membership in the Atomic Engineers Club, suitable for framing."

"Just what I've always wanted," she said.

"Sorry," I told her, kissing her cheek, "but that's for Buddy."

"Mmm . . . you're feeling guilty," she remarked.

"Guilty? At what?"

"At not having spent much time with him lately," she said. "Oh, well, I suppose you *have* been busy."

We were upstairs in the bedroom the following noon. She was seated at her dressing table, which was piled high with documents and notes pertaining to the Community Chest drive, and I was changing out of my city clothes into a working outfit, preparatory to my return to the factory.

"Oh, I've been busy, all right," I said.

"Are you going to accept Leonard's offer to merge the business?" she asked.

My fingers froze at the buttons of my shirt.

"Who told you about that?" I asked.

"Jerry," she said. "He says you walked out of Leonard Finch's office in a real huff."

"Wh—*When* did he tell you that?"

"Oh, he dropped by this morning," she said. "He wanted to see you and talk with you before you went to the plant." She scribbled on a pad. "Didn't the two of you stay at the apartment last night, dear?" she asked casually.

"No, we didn't," I said, hoping to skirt the issue of my previous evening's bed and/or board. "And I wish he'd mind his own damn business. He's got one hell of a nerve coming here to open all this up with you."

"Well after all, dear," she said, "I *am* a stockholder. I suppose Jerry was just trying to keep me informed on the latest developments."

"I'll keep you informed!" I said. "And this is no development; it's just a simple conspiracy whereby Leonard opens the valves and the company sinks slowly to the bottom!"

"With a nice capital gain for all concerned," observed Marjorie.

"Mmm-hmm," I said. "I see he's *really* filled you in."

"Well," she said, lighting a cigarette, "he said he didn't see any harm in giving me a few details. Inasmuch as you didn't give Leonard much of a chance to go into them last night at his office."

Oh, very shrewd of Jerry. Under the guise of Dear Kindly Cousin and Old Family Friend, he was making an end run around me to propagandize my wife. "By the way," she was adding, "where *did* you spend the night?"

"At a hotel!" I said, crumpling up my dirty shirt and tossing it hastily into the laundry closet. Luckily, there did not seem to be any incriminating carmine smears in evidence. . . . "Listen, honey," I hurried on, "I don't know exactly how Jerry presented all this, but I know what a fast talker he is. I'm sure, when he got through, you had a technicolor picture of Leonard Finch as Dag Hammarskjöld, Jerry as Adlai Stevenson, and what they're up to as being of benefit to the little people everywhere. With me in the part of Just Plain Molotov, a stubborn, malicious bastard. But that ain't the case. Not at all."

"Then what is the case, dear?" asked my wife.

"Do you want to listen to it with an open mind?"

She nodded.

"Okay then," I said. "Here it is, very quickly. These two saviors of humanity are really out to make a quick buck, pure and simple. Mostly for themselves—"

"And for us, too," she added.

"Sure—at the expense of dumping the entire business!" I said. "Booting out the window our whole Science Associates, Inc., lay-out, just like that!"

Marjorie looked up from her table full of charitable works. "But you could always start up another business, couldn't you?" she asked. "I mean, aren't you getting a little emotionally involved with a rundown factory and a bunch of hired hands who'll take the slightest opportunity to quit you and go across town if another plant raises its hourly rates?"

"Yes, I am," I said.

"Why?" she asked.

I was thinking out my answer as I spoke. "I guess because it's a business that *I* set up, that by the sweat of my own brow and some capital I dug up *I* got rolling, a business that functions efficiently because of *my* efforts."

Marjorie nodded slowly. "I think I can understand that," she said. "You feel as if it's your child."

"Yep," I said. "So you can understand why I got so sore when they suggested disowning the kid."

"But what I *don't* understand," Marjorie continued, "is how, in this year of 1960, you've suddenly become such a romantic. The object of the capitalistic system is to make money. That's what they taught us in college, right?" I nodded. "Well, here's a chance to make lots of it. Enough to heal all your wounds."

"Marjorie," I said, "despite what Jerry may have tried to tell you, I have absolutely no prejudice against taking a large profit. But I've also found out something about myself. I like being my own boss. And I want to hang on to this business as long as I can."

Marjorie sighed. "But isn't it a fiercely competitive field?" she asked. "With the big fish eating up the little fish every day? How long can you hang on before you're *forced* to merge, or sell out?"

Oh, he had done a thorough selling job, hadn't he?

"Listen, honey," I said. "As long as you're so interested, let me give you a few quick facts. Every day I go over to that factory, I walk into the lion's den. We've got suppliers that ship 98 items when the order reads 104. . . . I'm surrounded by local politicians who have their hand out for fire ordinances and zoning deals and God only knows what else . . . shop stewardesses whose only ambition in life is to squeeze the most pay out of me for the least amount of work . . . corporations waiting to get their hands on our patents and steal them as soon as they can break them down and adapt Basil's latest ideas. I know exactly how tough it is to be a Small Businessman in this day and age. It's murder. And it gets more ruthless every day!"

"So if you can pull out with a big fat chunk of security in reward for your efforts," she argued, "all the more reason why you should, right?"

"Wrong," I said.

"Why?"

"Because I am not yet ready to throw in the towel!" I said. "And when I am, *I* want to be the one who decides that we should run up the white flag, not Screwy Lennie sitting on his overstuffed can in that overdecorated layout on Park Avenue!"

Marjorie sighed. "I don't know. . . ." she said. "Maybe it's just because I grew up with a father who never built anything substantial of his own. But dearest, even though I respect your desire to make your own decisions, don't you think you're being a little too quixotic . . . in a very tough neighborhood?"

I stared at her. "Then you want me to go along with their deal?" I asked.

"I didn't say exactly that," she said.

"You didn't have to!" I told her.

"Now, Walter, just a moment," she objected. "You're jumping to conclusions—"

"Just because your father was in and out of the red all his life doesn't mean that *I* have to operate like Gus the Hurrying Salesman!" I snapped.

"You can leave my father out of this!" she replied, her lips tightening. "I merely mentioned him because I wanted to show you how *I* felt—"

The phone on her table rang and she picked it up. It seemed that someone on the other end was calling about plans for a fund-raising Flower Show. Angrily I knotted my tie, snatched up a tweed jacket, and started for the bedroom door.

"Just a second, Marie— Walter, when will you be back?"

"I don't know!" I yelled, starting out the door. "I've got to go to the plant and find out if I still have a business left!"

What an irony. I had brought her home a Guilt Present . . . and now *I* was the one who felt wronged.

15

Small Business Topics, pages 17–19, February 1961.

HORATIO ALGER RIDES AGAIN

A Saturday morning coffee break that spawned a million-dollar business.

Sounds like an economics student's dream?

Yes, but this one panned out. A going concern that came to life and grew with such speed that the business world is still rubbing its collective eyes in amazement.

Two years ago, it didn't even exist. This year, the baby wonder should (if present projections and estimates prove out) ship electronic devices worth over a million dollars.

That's the amazing history of Science Associates, Inc., not yet out of its swaddling clothes, but a profitable beehive humming happily in an abandoned firehouse in southeastern Connecticut.

How did it all happen?

"There are times when we ask ourselves the same question," grins youngish (42 years old) Jerome Teel, Executive Sales Manager and Vice President of this sizzling-hot stripling outfit. "That is, when we get a few spare minutes. Actually, we've grown so fast we really don't get much chance to sit back and figure out *how* it all happened."

He leans back in his battered chair—the inner executive chambers of Science Associates, Inc., are currently located in the corner of an abandoned furnace room—scratches his sandy crew-cut hair, and thinks while groping for an answer. "I guess maybe we were just too naïve to worry over how tough it would be to start up a small business in this era of giant corporate structures. See, my cousin Walter Fleming, who's the real workhorse of this outfit, had run into Basil Yerkes, a brilliant electronics engineer who had a couple of interesting notions kicking around in his fertile brain. One Saturday, the three of us sat down over a cup of coffee—and an hour later we'd decided to toss all our ideas into the same hat. . . ."

This month, the hat into which Messrs. Teel, Fleming, and Yerkes dropped their ideas had blossomed into a firm which employs 42 employees and whose roster of steady customers reads like the Dun & Bradstreet report on American manufacturers.

Press Sales Manager Teel further for an insight into what was the industrial hormone responsible for such amazing growth, and he will light up an expensive pipe (his only new vice) and modestly tell you that he believes it was old-fashioned teamwork.

"We haven't time to be bothered with rigid organization," he says. "We exist on steady give and take. I remember back when I was a counselor at a summer camp. First few days, we were just a bunch of scrawny city kids who'd never played anything together. But I'll never forget our coach, a grizzled old gent named Uncle Ted, a retired baseball player. They just don't grow Uncle Teds any more. He took nine or ten of us and molded us into a winning baseball team by the end of only two weeks. How? With the application of one secret that Uncle Ted taught us kids . . . one that I've never forgotten. *Teamwork*."

I rang the doorbell of the Yerkes home, a somewhat weather-beaten Cape Cod colonial. Silence. I rang again. The front door was opened no more than an inch or so and the baleful eye of Mrs. Yerkes peered out at me. "Go away," she said. "I have the dog tied up, but at a moment's notice—"

"Why, hello there, Mrs. Y," I said jovially. "I've been trying to reach your house—"

"The phone is off the hook."

The door began to close, but I wedged a toe into the opening. "I understand Basil is home today. Do you think I could speak to him for a moment or two? It's very important."

"No, you could *not*," she replied, and there was stainless steel in her voice. "I wouldn't dream of disturbing him."

"I know Basil's been working awfully hard," I pleaded, "but the pressure should be off soon—"

"*Hard!*" she exclaimed. "The man is half dead from overwork!"

"But Mrs. Yerkes, we have a test date to meet—"

"He doesn't eat properly, he never gets any sleep, he's wasting away to a shadow!" she cried. "Why, he's become a complete stranger to the children, not to mention what this has done to our home life. Oh, I wish he'd never gotten involved with two slave-drivers like you and your cousin—"

"Mrs. Yerkes," I interrupted, "this is hardly the time or place for an emotional brouhaha. I *must* see Basil."

"Emotional, you call it! A brilliant man is ruining his health, and all you're interested in is profit, profit, profit—"

Behind her, I heard Basil's voice rasp, "Let me talk to him, Leatrice."

"No!" cried that lady. "Go back to bed, Basil; look at the hollows under your eyes!"

Basil pushed her gently aside and opened the door. His bony frame was draped in a sacklike robe; he needed a shave, and his eyes were indeed red from lack of sleep. "What is it, Walter?"

"I didn't mean to interrupt your rest," I said. "God knows I want you to take care of yourself, old friend, but I have a message in the office that Willoughby called from Washington for a definite date. Obviously, the boys are getting very itchy for their modification. What can I tell them?"

"Oh, God," sighed Basil. "Tell them we'll be ready to test Monday."

"*Are* we ready?" I asked.

"Who the hell knows?" he replied.

"Jesus, Basil," I said, softly, "if *you* don't, who does?"

He groaned. "Listen, Walter, get off my back, will you? You know what these deals are like. You skull it through, slide-rule it out, make the drawings, build it from scratch; you flip on the switch and then you pray. . . ."

"In the old days, yes," I said. "But we're not playing the wheel at Las Vegas this time. We're under the gun. Do you have doubts? If so tell me *now*."

Basil peered at me. "If I had," he asked, "what could you do about it?"

"I don't really know," I said. "Maybe call Willoughby and stall—postpone the test—then you and I could lock ourselves away and prove it out for ourselves first." I tugged hopefully at his frayed bathrobe sleeve. "How about that? We could go down to the shop together—"

"Maybe," said Basil, and then his arm was pulled away. He himself vanished from sight, to be replaced by Mrs. Yerkes.

"Basil, you go back to bed!" she commanded, and then turned the full force of her wrath upon me. "Mr. Fleming, you leave this poor shell of a man alone! His health may mean nothing to you, but he's all we have, and he's not going to *cripple* himself."

"Just for a couple of hours," I pleaded.

"Not for one minute!"

"Basil!" I cried. "Call me at the office—"

The front door was closed in my face.

"This is urgent!" I yelled. "It's a matter of National Defense!"

Click went the latch, and a locked door was between me and my prime, not to say sole, source of engineering technology.

". . . None of us could knock a four-bagger, or make a put-out on the diamond without knowing that the other fellow was there to back him up," Teel reminisces. "That's how it is here at Science Associates, Inc., today: just one smooth, well-functioning team. Take labor. Most of the people here in our shop never worked before in electronics. They came to us some months ago with no previous training. They were ordinary housewives, seamstresses, domestic workers, most of them with only a high school education. Now they've become skilled assemblers of highly complicated mechanisms." Teel smiles. "They take great pride in the quality of their work, of the uses to which we've put their native New England ingenuity. And I'd like to add that we on the management end are just as proud as they are of their daily accomplishments. . . ."

"If it's about the coffee machines, Mrs. Polacheck," I said, "the repair man promised faithfully he'd be here this week. Now, if you'll please let me get back to my office—"

The stocky shop stewardess blocked my path. "Mr. Fleming," she said, "the issue of the coffee machines and the short-changing is getting to be a hot potato, sure, but we can table that for the time being because there's also the matter of the bowling-team uniforms—"

"Talk to Mr. Teel," I said, trying to work my way around her. "I'm in a bind on a delivery, and I can't discuss it—"

"You're not refusing to negotiate, are you?" she asked wickedly.

"Mrs. Polacheck," I said, "come see me next week and we'll thrash it out."

"Because there's also the matter of air conditioning," she said. "and the towel machine in the rest rooms. And also we've got problems at the Inspection Department."

"Inspection? Why, that's where we're paying the highest scale!" I protested. "What could possibly be the beef in there?"

Mrs. Polacheck shrugged. "I won't deny that you pay a more *adequate* rate there than anywhere else in the shop," she said, "but you're not giving money away. Let's not forget how tough it is."

How could I ever forget how tough? And how crucial. There, in a small soundproof, dustproof cubicle, six of my most adept girls tested out all of the tiniest components of XXXXXX L-4 before it was put together—in particular, the wax-covered tiny box known as Subassembly 3389. Inside that box, which is roughly the size of a domino, were eighteen miniaturized circuits, all jammed together. Should a Subassembly not test out properly, it became the tedious problem of the lady tester to peel away the wax covering and then, with the aid of a jewelers' glass and tiny tweezers, to take apart, piece by piece, the entire assembly, in order to discover the offending infinitesimal flaw.

Tests had proved that no man could stand the demanding inner strain of this work; as a matter of fact the very best girl we had trained to do it could last for only a two-hour stretch before putting down her tweezers and releasing the tension with a loud scream.

"Okay . . . it's hairy in there," I conceded. "But we've always made generous concessions to the girls. What's the trouble now?"

"They've been running their own unofficial check," said Mrs. P. "It seems that the Flaw Rate has gone up 17 per cent in the past two weeks. And as their representative, I'm taking it on myself to sound you out on the possibility of a raise. Say between 8 and 10 per cent."

I stared at her. "Mrs. Polacheck," I said, trying to keep my voice from cracking, "*if* the Flaw Rate on Subassembly has risen 17 per cent, it would seem to me, dammit, that the ones responsible for that lousy record are the girls in Production who are putting Subassembly 3389 together. And if *they*'re the ones responsible, then by what sort of twisted logic can you come to me with a straight face and suggest that *Management* should increase Inspection 8 to 10 per cent an hour to compensate for the sloppy work in Subassembly?"

Mrs. Polacheck shook her head sadly. "That is a pretty lousy attitude, Mr. Fleming," she said, "and if I didn't know you better, I'd say you was turning anti-labor."

"I'll show you how anti-labor I am," I said. "I'll make you a fair deal. Let's put a penalty clause in effect on the mistakes made in Production"—her face began to darken, but I was too angry to pay attention to the storm warnings—"and the proceeds from that penalty clause don't go to us, but are applied to the pay envelopes, pro rata, of those girls, Marie, Phyllis, Arlene, Agnes, and the others in Inspection!"

"Mr. Fleming!" she bellowed. "That's positively the most reactionary suggestion I ever heard! *Cutting* pay!"

"It's not cutting at all!" I yelled. "It's an equitable redistribution! We're the ones who're paying—"

"Equitable!" replied Mrs. Polacheck. "I'll tell *you* something. That's just the kind of equitable that causes slowdowns!"

"Are you threatening to pull your people," I demanded, "in defiance of a written contract?"

"I never said nothing about pulling nobody," she said, her eyes narrowing behind the steel-rimmed glasses. "But I'm telling you now, if this sort of dangerous talk gets around, and the girls hear it and get all emotional and nervous and decide to pull a wildcat walkout on you, don't come crying to *me* for help, Mr. Fleming, because *I* already warned you about your attitude!"

She began to waddle back to the entrance of the shop. "Wait!" I yelled. "What's this nonsense about a wildcat walkout? You know that's specifically forbidden!"

She did not answer, but disappeared through the double doors. Click went the latch, and now there was a closed door between me and the prime, not to say sole, source of my labor. . . .

". . . and not only teamwork, but respect for the other fellow's capabilities," continues Teel. "We were all drawn together in the first place because we knew and appreciated what the other fellow could do. So, on an hour-to-hour basis, we get a valuable kind of give-and-take here in the shop that's missing from some of the bigger corporate operations with which we're constantly in competition. We're faster, more adaptable, and thus we get, if you'll excuse my giving you another old baseball expression, more room in which to swing."

"But dammit, Dominick, I want the pockets on the jacket to *slant!*" Jerry was saying into my telephone. He was sprawled in my chair, his feet up on my desk. "I mean, who ever heard of side vents with straight pocket flaps?"

"Jerry, I've got to talk to you!" I said.

He smiled and waved a hand at me. "Be with you in just a minute, Walter boy—"

I pulled the phone from his hand and hung it up. "Now!"

"Just a *second*," he protested. "That was long distance!"

"Yeah, and it's vital, I'm sure," I said. "Who the hell asked you to go see Marjorie and pitch Leonard's proposition to her? Since when have you become my family counselor?"

He stood up. "Walter, baby," he said. "You sound cross again."

"Cross!" I said. "Oh, no—I'm over that. Now I'm furious! Mrs. Polacheck is out there tearing up the labor pea patch; the Army's coming next week for tests that probably won't be ready; Basil is locked up in his house with his wife standing guard over him; the whole joint is coming down around our ears, and you're on long distance arguing about your damn pocket flaps!"

He lit a pipe. "You know, you behaved very badly in Leonard's office," he said. "It took me almost the whole evening to smooth his feathers down. And by the way, dear cousin, where did you disappear to after you left us last night, mmm?" He winked.

"Forget that," I said. "We've got more important things to discuss. When Willoughby gets here, we've got to be sure the modification's ready—"

He frowned at me. "You know," he interrupted, "lately I don't understand you at all. Here you are, up to your ass in all this trivia, people climbing on your back, crap piling up on your desk, and all it means is that you're on your way to an early ulcer—but I honestly believe you *enjoy* it."

I looked at him. "What the hell do you want me to do," I asked, slowly. "Just throw up my hands and walk away?"

"No . . . don't throw up your hands," he said, a slow sly smile spreading over his face. "Hold them *out*. Like so." He made a cup of his two well-manicured hands. "And then, just stand there and let Leonard drop a load of well-deserved capital gain into them, sonny."

My cousin, Jerry-One-Note . . .

"I don't want to discuss that deal!" I snapped. "I've got enough trouble around here to keep me busy for the next month—" I snorted angrily. "Of course, if you wanted to pitch in, it just might take a little of the load off my back. . . ."

He was yawning. Then he sighed, shook his head slowly, and knocked out ash from his expensive pipe. "Walter," he said, "most men go their whole lives waiting for a brass ring that never comes. Now here it is, dangling right in front of you—and here you are, so happy playing big executive that the ring is going to zip right on past you."

"I'm not *playing* big executive!" I yelled. "This is a business—one that we dreamed up together, remember?—a business of our own—"

He waved a deprecating hand around the cluttered room. "Sure we did," he said. "And look at us now. General Motors, right?"

"We're growing," I said defensively. "Look at our stock."

He laughed cynically. "The public will buy anything with the word Science tacked onto it these days, Walter. So please don't give me the stock market as a barometer of anything except public stupidity. And as for our future, we're strictly fat little fish waiting to be swallowed by a bigger fish."

My stomach was churning and the taste of my luncheon cheeseburger was sour in my mouth. "What in the hell has gotten into *you?*" I demanded. "You're talking like some cheap barroom cynic."

"Correction," he said coldly. "Realist. I'm being realistic, but you're still playing as if the world were the Rover Boys in Big Business. Listen to me. There are two kinds of people in this miserable society: Cringers and Grabbers. If you want to turn down loot and security and a nice fat nest egg for your future and stay a simple-minded Cringer—in this drafty rathole of a factory—*okay*. God knows I've tried to pull you out of it, but"—he shrugged and emptied his pipe in the old china plate we used for an ash tray— "but just because *you* won't budge, don't expect *me* to stand pat. I'm getting too old to be virtuous. If there's loot lying around loose, waiting to be stuffed into my bank account, then stand back, Buster, here comes a Grabber!"

"Jesus," I said finally, "I don't know what Leonard's disease is, but it certainly is catching."

Jerry picked up a new Borsalino hat from the top of the filing cabinet. "I'll tell you one thing more, because we're still cousins and I feel sorry for you: When the Grabbers leave you standing in the cold breeze without your pants on, remember, I tried to warn you. . . ."

I swallowed to fight back the nausea. "Jerry," I said, unbelieving, "it sounds as if you were trying to threaten me with something. What?"

He shook his head. "Threaten you, baby? Like I said, we're still cousins—"

"—and partners?" I demanded.

"I'm merely trying to warn you, schmuck!" he yelled, and, eyes averted, he stamped out of the room.

Outside, there was the steady hum of machinery from the factory proper, punctuated only by sporadic footsteps in the hallway and the rattle of office typewriters. Everything operating at normal tempo.

Or was it?

I got up and ran out into the hall. "Warn me about what?" I shouted.

No answer.

I heard the outside door slam shut.

There was more than simply a door between me and a cousin in whom I'd reposed friendship and trust since my childhood.

Suddenly, between us, there had arisen a wall.

". . . What else is happening at Science Associates, Inc.?

"Not much else that can be printed here in this brief summary of success. Too much of S.A.'s product is veiled in official Pentagon secrecy.

"But one thing becomes readily apparent to anyone fortunate enough to spend a couple of rewarding hours in this bustling little Connecticut dynamo-outfit.

"In this converted firehouse there might just be one of those infant outfits that have the pleasant habit of exploding into a major corporation—one of the Texas Instruments, one of the Litton Industries, one of the Thompson Ramo-Wooldridges of the next five years.

"Launching pad, a coffee break.

"Horizon? Unlimited."

16

I STOOD in front of the mirror, running the electric razor across my weary face and rehearsing my opening remarks for today's test.

"C. C., old man, sit yourself down over here by this bench while Basil uncorks his latest little beauty." No, perhaps a little too chummy for that stone-faced man from the Pentagon.

"Major Willoughby, may I have the pleasure of presenting to you the latest development of Science Associates, Inc.?" My God, that sounded like a butler calling off the arrivals at a formal ball.

No, I had better try and play it down the middle of the road. "Major Willoughby, you're here, you're a busy man, and we're ready" (pray God) "so let's get started."

Buddy poked his head into the bathroom and stared up at me. "Hi, stranger," he said.

I reached over and patted his shoulder. "I have been a little seldom around here lately, haven't I?"

He nodded. "I haven't seen you since my model Ford Thunderbird, my P-38 Lightning, *and* my classic 1931 Duesenberg roadster. How are things at the plant?"

"Don't ask," I said.

"Gee, we had a good time there that day," he said. "I kind of wish I could go back with you again. Today?"

"What about school?"

"Vacation," he said.

"Again?" I asked. "It seems as if you just got through with one."

"This is spring vacation," he said. "Then two weeks from now

170

there's a teachers' convention, three days off. Then another week and we're through."

"Lately it seems like school is just an interruption between vacations," I commented.

"Sure. So can I come over today?" he asked.

"Of all the days in the whole year," I told him, "this might be the absolute worst." I snapped off the razor and began to dash after-shave on myself.

"A crisis?" he asked, picking up my razor and eying it.

"Not yet," I said. "Just keep your fingers crossed."

He ran the cutting head of the razor across his smooth cheek. "Don't rush it," I told him fondly. "After you get to the point where you have to shave, it can become a terrible bore."

"Oh, I wasn't thinking about shaving," he said. "I was thinking about an electric razor with a built-in tank. Then, while you're shaving, it's just a squeeze, and powee, cool refreshing mint pours across your cheek."

"You're either going to be an inventor or a great advertising man," I told him, and went into the bedroom to hunt for a tie in the closet.

He followed me. "Put on that gray with the red stripes," he suggested.

"I don't like that one," I told him.

"I love it!" he said.

Impulsively, I handed it to him. "Here," I said.

His eyes lighted up. "For me?"

Feeling like one of the Rockefeller brothers, I nodded.

He draped the tie around his neck, and he could have been a young matron caressing her first set of fox.

"Pop," he asked, his hands beginning to knot the silk, "are we really rich?"

I found myself another tie. "I guess so," I told him. "At least, the last time I looked, we were."

"That means lots and lots of money, huh?" he asked, knotting the tie.

"On paper, at least," I said.

He stared proudly at himself in the mirror. "Funny," he said. "I've thought and thought about it, and being rich doesn't make me feel any different."

I looked at Buddy, in his faded chinos and gay sports shirt, the gray tie and the red stripes hanging, a violent color clash, from his thin neck.

Sweet naïve boy, I thought. You are of the age when the word "rich" means some more coins in the pocket and the passport to the movies on Saturday, larger purchases of Tootsie Rolls and comic books and more shelves full of motorized models. Of course being rich doesn't make you feel different. Yet.

But give it a little time, and *rich* will begin to mean something.

Wait, wait until it means college, with your own checkbook and the security of a three-figure bank account while others sweat it out on scholarships. That MG you will drive, and the corsages and stingers and theater tickets you will buy for your various lady friends. . . . Wait for their fond mamas, who (having read a credit report secured from Dun & Bradstreet through Papa's downtown office) will make you welcome as a potential candidate for marriage (affiliation?) with their dear negotiable daughter. . . .

Then there will be the tailors who murmur your measurements to an assistant as you fondle cashmeres and expensive mohair, fawning clerks who bend over your foot and slip on it the very best grade of calf and kid. Wait for the rubbery smile of the headwaiter and the brisk salute of the parking-lot attendant. See how the doors swing open for you and remain shut for the rest of the herd. . . .

And you will keep on learning what *rich* means, Buddy. Later it will be the membership at the best country club, the right to buy a house in the best part of town, the seat in the private club car, the two in help, the two cars in the garage, the two months off each year for a good solid vacation. . . .

And perhaps, later, when your son is growing up and learning to ask questions, *he* will ask *you* what it means, exactly, to be rich. And you, by that time, comfortable, ingrained quiet Old Money, will gently chide him for his question: "Son, it really isn't polite to discuss money. What I mean is—one just *has* it, that's all." And he'll smile cheerfully and run off to his club, leaving you with your monthly report from the bank's Trust Department.

"Pop," Buddy said, bursting my bubble image of his happy future, "it's such a nice day. Do you really have to go to the plant?"

"If you want to stay rich, I do!" I said. And immediately regretted my remark when I saw his expression. "But hold it—" I said, trying to repair the damage. "We can have breakfast together. Maybe we can even cook it ourselves."

He nodded eagerly. "Sure we can. Mommy fired the new cook again. Or maybe she left. I can never keep track any more."

We went down the stairs together.

"I know what rich is like," Buddy said, half to himself. "It's ever since it happened, we never see you very much. . . ."

Ah, yes, I thought, brought up short. That's the footnote you forgot to add to your projection.

Rich also means children who learn to grow up and do without parents who are generally somewhere else, making more money . . . money that their children will use in later years for analysts . . . who will try to help them unravel the roots of why they grew up to hate their parents.

"Come on, we'll scramble some eggs," I told my son, "and as soon as this test rat race is over and done with, you and I have a fat date with the New York Yankees!"

We were finishing our omelet—a special recipe invented on the spot by Fleming *père et fils*, consisting of eggs, cream, chives, and a liberal sprinkling of Chef Boyardee's best grated cheese, when Marjorie came through the kitchen from the garage. She put down an armload of bags from the supermarket. "Good morning, Buddy," she said, and continued on her way inside. "Oh, by the way, Walter," she said at the door, and her voice made ice form on my wings, "did Betty get in touch with you?"

And, leaving that cryptic depth charge to detonate behind her, she continued inside.

"Betty?" I called brightly, "Betty who?"

No answer.

I sipped my coffee. Hold it, boy, I told myself. Let's not panic. Play it very carefully now. This is the classic situation from the Molnar comedy . . . except that this is Connecticut, not Vienna, and your wife is not Lynn Fontanne, and you, unfortunately, are not Alfred Lunt.

Marjorie returned and grimly began to stow away the load of groceries.

"Betty Lawrence," she said. "How many Bettys do you know? Or perhaps I'd better not ask."

"Oh. Betty *Lawrence*," I said.

173

"She seemed very anxious to talk to you," said Marjorie.

"Our friend from Riviera-in-the-Mountains," I said.

"*Your* friend," said Marjorie, stowing meat into the freezer compartment.

"Betty, eh?" I said. "Bright girl. Not very pretty, but a sharp mind. Mmm . . . I wonder how she's been since we saw her at the Riviera."

"She said she *had* seen you," said Marjorie, stuffing fresh supplies of cold cereal into the cupboard. "In New York." She slammed the cupboard shut. "Last week."

"Oh, *yes!*" I said. "Don't you remember? We had a bite together. She was in that crowd—up at Leonard's office. You know, at the art show."

"Oh?" replied Marjorie, stacking Jell-O into another cabinet with precision. "What was she doing there in the first place? I thought Betty was a *financial* writer."

"Well, this was one of those tax deals," I said, pouring more coffee and hoping that the slight quiver in my hand was not evident.

"She's called twice," said Marjorie. Another cabinet door slammed. "Are you and she going to be involved in some—tax deal?"

"Me in a tax deal? *Ha,*" I chuckled. "That's funny." I got up, ever so casually. "Hm . . . I can't imagine what Betty would want. Can I help you with anything, dear?"

"No," said Marjorie. "I certainly don't know what she wants, either." She moved away to stuff soap flakes into the cabinet beneath the sink. "I told her you were at the plant working late. At least, that's where you *said* you'd be last night—"

"Of course I was at the plant! Where else would I be?"

Marjorie glanced at the dinette table where our son was bent over his collection of blue stamps, a juvenile Silas Marner.

"I don't really think we ought to discuss that here, do you?" she asked. She thrust a loaf of bread into the breadbox, slammed it shut, and vanished into the dining room.

The best defense is a strong offense . . . even in Molnar.

"What does *that* mean?" I said, following her inside.

My wife had proceeded into the study and was now seated at the desk. On it was the latest collection of charity card files. She began to riffle briskly through one of them.

"Honey," I said, forcing amiability into my voice, "aren't you making a mountain of this molehill? I mean, supposing Betty Lawrence did call me—"

"Oh, yes," said Marjorie. "She also said she'd like to talk to you right away because she had something very important to discuss, and that she'd be in meetings all day today, but there was a private number where she could be reached. She didn't want to talk to you at the plant; she wanted to speak to you *privately*."

"Sounds very ominous," I said, trying to remember how Alfred Lunt would have read the line.

"Yes, doesn't it?" replied Marjorie. "I wrote the number down somewhere." She continued to riffle through her card file.

"May I have it?" I inquired.

"Certainly," said Marjorie. She pawed at the papers on the desk. "Oh, I do hope I haven't mislaid it. Since it's so important that you and she talk, I certainly wouldn't want to—"

"Sweetheart," I said, adopting a devil-may-care attitude as I unclenched my teeth, "you're behaving as if I'd been seen at the Harwyn Club with Zsa Zsa Gabor. . . ."

"Yes, angel," she said, tossing papers from one side of the desk to another. "Aren't I?"

I watched her for a moment. She began to pile match folders into a corner. "Is it written on one of those?" I inquired.

"You seem terribly anxious to get in touch with her," she remarked.

"The woman called me twice," I observed mildly. "She said it was important."

"Too important to give *me* the message," she murmured, tearing up envelopes and tossing them away.

"Marjorie darling," I said, "I'm late. Let me help you. Did you write it down on something specific?"

"Walter, dearest," she sighed, "it's the strangest thing. I must have some sort of a block because I can't seem to remember. Oh, well, I'll work on my card file and perhaps it will come back to me—"

I repressed a definite homicidal impulse.

"All right, pet," I said. "You're jealous. You resent Betty's call. Did it ever occur to you that Betty is one of the shrewdest financial minds in the country and that she has access to a hell of a lot of sources of valuable inside information and that she might just be calling me with a piece of news or a tip or pertinent gossip? That her call has nothing to do with my fair white body, or hers, or the secret midnight rendezvous we're contemplating, but involves Science Associates, Inc., a somewhat profitable business that I am trying to operate?"

Good Lord—now I *was* Alfred Lunt! And with no previous experience, either.

"Yes," said Marjorie, holding out a match folder. "It has. Here is the number."

I glanced at the folder. On it was scrawled a set of indecipherable numbers.

"Would you mind translating for me?"

"Certainly," she said. "That's DR—no, it's TR—8—no, that's a 3—3-1988. TR 8—no, it's 3-1933."

"You said *88!*"

She nodded. "I was wrong. It's 33. See, my 3's look like 8's some days, and this was one of them." She moved the telephone over toward me. "Here, dear, go ahead and call. TR-3-1933."

Frantically, I dialed. 1-1-2. 2-1-2. T-R-3-1-9-3-3. (Small wonder AT&T stock has soared. The company makes the money and the customers do all the work.)

Ring . . . ring . . . ring.

Then a gravel voice said, "Hy and Billy's Busy Bee Delicatessen; this is Sol speaking; hurry up, we're taking inventory—"

I hung up.

"She wasn't there?"

"That was a wrong number, dear," I said.

"Oh, what a shame," she murmured, intent on her card file. "Well, if Betty should call again I'll tell her you're at the plant. . . .That *is* where you'll be, isn't it?"

I suppose I should have been feeling guilty. After all, beneath the oxford of my white button-down shirt, my chest bore a large subliminal "A"—but my guilt wasn't strong enough to keep me from wallowing in a rage of righteous indignation.

"Yes, dear. That is where I'll be," I said unpleasantly. "Over at my industrial pleasure dome, where I can now pick up where I left off at 2:00 A.M. this morning arguing with Basil—or grappling with Mrs. Polacheck—or waiting to see what dear Leonard has up his sleeve— while at the same time I will cross my fingers and pray that Basil's new device meets the contract specifications. And when I get over to the daily festival of fun and games, I want you to know how much I appreciate the feeling that back here on the home front I have everyone's firm support. I tell you, it gives a man strength to go on."

I started out.

"Walter!" Marjorie called, and ran around the desk to block what I thought was a very effective exit.

"I'm late," I said. "The orgy is half over."

"I didn't mean to be so bitchy." She sighed. "And I know how rotten it was of me to take it out on you. And I know what the books all say about tension in successful executives. But look at it from my point of view. Hell hath no fury, et cetera . . ."

"If I've et cetera'd you, dear," I said, "it's been in a good cause. Remember, Russian technology . . ."

She put her arms around me. "I'm as patriotic as the next girl," she said into my chest. "But there have been a lot of nights lately when I wouldn't mind if you and I did a little lagging behind the Russians."

My hostility ebbed away, leaving me holding my wife and a double portion of guilt. "I'm sorry, honey," I said. "Pretty soon this will all be over and we can relax together."

"Why did I have to marry an indispensable man?" she asked, and kissed me. "Have lunch *home*," she whispered into my ear.

"I can't keep Major Willoughby and our whole space program waiting," I muttered.

She ran her hands under my jacket and raked her nails across my back. "But in such a good cause," she breathed.

"You're making things very difficult."

"Funny, I thought I was making them easy."

Well, I thought, holding her close, if the Russians beat us, at least we'll go down happy. . . .

I was on my way to lock the door when Buddy poked his head in.

"Excuse me, please," he said. "I knocked twice but you didn't answer. Sorry to interrupt, but I've audited all the books, and we now have enough blue stamps to get me a decent microscope."

"Fine, fine," I said, patting his shoulder. Little did the kid know how much his country owed him. "I've got to go."

"How about you, Mom?" he asked. "Can you take me to the Redemption Center?"

His mother patted her hair back into place. "All right, dear," she said, forcing a cheery note, and lighting a therapeutic cigarette. "But for the sake of your future wife, think about giving up science and taking up sports as a career instead, will you?"

"Wish me luck, folks," I said.

"Luck," said Marjorie, reluctantly settling down once more to her card file. "And *hurry* back, dear."

"Knock it out of the ball park," said Buddy.

"Out of your mouth into God's ears," I said, and went marching as to war.

17

Classification: SECRET
From: Major C. C. Willoughby
To: Brig. Gen. H. R. Mowbray, Chief of Section
Subject: XXXXXX L-4 (Mod.) 6/14/60
             (Held at Science Associates, Inc., Contractor A, Bay-
             port, Conn.)
             Ref: Contract 871–98 A9, dated 8/13/58
Copies: Five
Distribution: None
Appended: Five (5) typed copies, transcript, tape recording of
             test session, held at factory, Science Associates, Inc.,
             Bayport, Conn., 6/14/60

1. Undersigned has returned from Bayport, Conn., and hereby submits his official report.

2. Before proceeding to undersigned's recommendations as to further action on above-named project, it is suggested that appended transcript of tape recording, made at the scene of the test, be read.

Tape Recording of Test Session, 6/14/60. Present (security clearance granted): Walter Fleming, executive of firm; Basil Yerkes, executive project designer and engineer; Mrs. Hilda Bostwick, clerical assistant; Jerome Teel, executive of firm; certain unidentified voices.

Time of test: 11:26 A.M.
Transcript follows:

FLEMING

Good morning, Major Willoughby. Sorry I'm a little late, but a few things came up at home; you know how it is. How about some coffee?

WILLOUGHBY

No, thanks. We're late as it is and I'm on a tight schedule. Where's Mr. Yerkes?

FLEMING

Oh, isn't Basil here yet? That's strange; I thought I saw him outside when I came in, didn't I, Mrs. Bostwick?

MRS. BOSTWICK

I'm sure he's somewhere out in the shop, Mr. Fleming. I'll just go look.

FLEMING

Good. Oh, and on your way out, Mrs. Bostwick, would you check to see if I've had any calls from New York this morning? I'm expecting a very important one.

MRS. BOSTWICK

I haven't seen any on your pad but I'll check.
(*Door closes.*)

FLEMING

Now let's see. Here's the little baby, and she's all rigged up waiting for you people. We can go any time, but I sort of think it's best if Basil himself runs the test for you, don't you, Major?

WILLOUGHBY

As you like, but I'd prefer to get on with it as soon as possible.

FLEMING

I'll just move these packing cases to one side. We're a little cramped for space these days, you know, getting set to supply you people. There. Now we've got a little more room to swing. By the way, Major, what's that gadget here in your attaché case?

WILLOUGHBY

A tape recorder.

FLEMING

Oh. You're recording the proceedings for posterity, eh?

WILLOUGHBY

No, I use it for my files. And my report. To eliminate the possibility of misquotation. Any objection?

FLEMING

Oh, no. Very efficient idea. What sort of rig are you using here?

WILLOUGHBY

A simple transistorized job.

FLEMING

Damn clever little gadget. One of the Japanese models. They certainly do good work. Undercut us on price, too.

WILLOUGHBY

It was a gift. From one of my classmates who's stationed overseas.

FLEMING

Mm. Bought it at the PX, too, I'll bet, at a nice discount. Say, do you think your friend might—

WILLOUGHBY

Mr. Fleming, do you think we can get on with the test? I have to be
in New Jersey by four.

FLEMING

You're sure you couldn't use a fresh cup of coffee? We've just installed new machines out there, and they serve up a nice hot cup.
Amazing what they're doing with vending machines, don't you
think?

WILLOUGHBY

Amazing. But I'll skip the coffee and we can get started.

FLEMING

Sure. Let's see—
(*Door opens.*)

MRS. BOSTWICK

Mr. Yerkes is just pulling in, Mr. Fleming.

FLEMING

Oh, that's fine.

MRS. BOSTWICK

No calls from New York at all.

FLEMING

By the way, where is Mr. Teel?

MRS. BOSTWICK

I have no idea, sir. He never checks with me. Would you and the
Major care for some coffee?

FLEMING

That would be a fine idea.

MRS. BOSTWICK

And how does the Major take his?

WILLOUGHBY

Only with his meals, thank you.

FLEMING

Bring him some anyway, Mrs. Bostwick.
(*Door shuts.*)
Damned efficient woman. Ex-WAC, you know. You people do a great job on them.

WILLOUGHBY

Thank you.

FLEMING

I tell you, Major, there are times when I wish I had a whole staff trained the Army way.

WILLOUGHBY

You have trouble with your other people?

FLEMING

Oh, no. What I meant was, well, that girl does the work of three.
(*Door opens.*)
Ah, here's Mr. Yerkes, now. Basil, you're a little late.

YERKES

Sorry. One of the kids is down with the flu or some damn thing, and I was up all night changing sheets. Oh, hi, Major.

WILLOUGHBY

Good morning.

YERKES

Come to see if our little gismo here tests out, mm? Well, we're waiting to find out the same thing.

WILLOUGHBY

You haven't run preliminary tests on it?

FLEMING

Naturally we have! What Mr. Yerkes means is that we're all set to turn over the modification to you for approval and get right into production. Correct, Basil?

YERKES

Yeah.

WILLOUGHBY

Because I hardly think any of us is in a position that allows for levity, gentlemen.

FLEMING

Major, this is a damned serious thing, and I want you to know we've been breaking our asses—I mean, working night and day to get it right. I mean, to keep things up to standard.
(*Door opens.*)

MRS. BOSTWICK

Here you are, gentlemen. Coffee.

FLEMING

Oh, good.

184

WILLOUGHBY

No, thank you!

YERKES

Don't fight; I'll take it.

FLEMING

These coffee machines are certainly an improvement over the old
eyewash, eh, Basil?

WILLOUGHBY

Gentlemen, if you *please*—

YERKES

Don't pop a circuit, Major; we're all set. I'll just check the power
output here. Okay. And the test board over here. Walter, where the
hell is that power jack?

FLEMING

Isn't it there?

YERKES

Some moron dumped a whole carton of crap here in the corner and
I can't find a thing.

FLEMING

Mrs. Bostwick, who put that carton there?

MRS. BOSTWICK

I really don't know, sir. I'll go out and check with Plant Management.

YERKES

Don't bother. Nobody in this pigsty knows anything about anything. Ah, here's the jack. I'll plug in.

FLEMING

Major, do you want to sit over here and takes notes on the performance data?

WILLOUGHBY

I'm perfectly comfortable on this crate, thank you.

YERKES

All right, here we go. You know the setup. What we did was to jam everything into this miniaturized XXXXXX here, and even though she's half the size of the previous XXXXXX, she should be able to handle up to the 5th, or let's see. I made notes here somewhere. Oh hell, it's in my desk at home. Anyway, she'll take whatever load you give it. I think.

WILLOUGHBY

Without failure?

YERKES

Well, that's what we're here to find out, isn't it?

WILLOUGHBY

I beg your pardon?

FLEMING

Major, you and I will check the Tote Board together, right? Basil, let's go.

YERKES

Shall we pause for a moment of prayer?

FLEMING

Basil, the Major is on a very tight schedule.

YERKES

Oh, for God's sake, I was only— All right. Power switch on. Here we go.
(*Door opens.*)

VOICE

Mrs. Bostwick, there's a long-distance call for Mr. Fleming.

FLEMING

I can't take any calls.

MRS. BOSTWICK

Close the door, Miss Duffy.
(*Door shuts.*)

WILLOUGHBY

What sort of plant security do you people have around here?

FLEMING

It's okay, Major, the girl is cleared. Mrs. Bostwick, have Leo Banks stand outside the door and keep everyone out.

MRS. BOSTWICK

Right, Mr. Fleming.
(*Door opens and shuts.*)

YERKES

Okay, she's warmed up fine. Now, I'll proceed to test. Circuit A. Circuit B. What's your reading on the Tote Board, Walter?

FLEMING

32-34-36. Load Factor B.

WILLOUGHBY

32-34-36. Load Factor B.

YERKES

So far, so good. Now I'm going to increase the load. Circuit C. Circuit D. Now what does she show?

FLEMING

42-44-46. Load Factor B2.

WILLOUGHBY

42-44-46. Load Factor B2.

YERKES

Well, well. I guess our little darling functions after all, eh? Take her away, Major.

WILLOUGHBY

The contract specifies an optimum Load Factor of B4, gentlemen.

FLEMING

Ah, but under normal operating procedure, that would never be necessary, Major.

WILLOUGHBY

Mr. Fleming, I do not draw contract specifications. I am merely here as representative of the Defense Department to make sure that they've been met.

YERKES

You want optimum load, you'll get optimum load. Walter, stand by the Tote Board. Here we go.

FLEMING

52-54-56. Load Factor B4! There you are, Major!

WILLOUGHBY

52-54-56. Load Factor B4. Hmmm. What's that smell?

YERKES

What smell?

WILLOUGHBY

I smell something overheating. Or is it burning?

FLEMING

Probably somebody outside burning trash or—Basil, cut the power!
She's overheating. The danger light—

YERKES

For God's sake, why the hell— Must be faulty wiring somewhere in
the XXXXXX. Or maybe here in the—

WILLOUGHBY

I knew I smelled something burning.
(*Door opens.*)

FLEMING

Mrs. Bostwick, get me Marie and Phyllis from Flaw Inspection on
the double! Tell them I want them in here right away!

MRS. BOSTWICK

On the double, Mr. F.
(*Door shuts.*)

FLEMING

Now, let's not get excited. Whatever it is that's overheating, I'll get the girls to check it out and we'll rewire and set it right back upon the test rig, right, Basil? Basil?

BASIL

Who the hell knows.

FLEMING

We have a very efficient Flaw-Testing setup, Major. I'm delighted you'll be able to see it in action today.

WILLOUGHBY

You have a high rate of flaw in production, Mr. Fleming?

FLEMING

No more than anyone else in the same field, Major. Human error, you know.
(*Door opens.*)

FLEMING

Ah, here they—

VOICE

Mr. Fleming, can you take that New York call?

FLEMING

No, I can't. Miss Duffy, where's Leo Banks? Where are the girls from Flaw Testing?

VOICE

I don't know. I'm all alone out there in the office trying to run the switchboard and everyone's gone for lunch and it's like a crazy house.

FLEMING

All right, Miss Duffy, I'm sure somebody will be back.

MRS. BOSTWICK

Mrs. Polacheck, you can't go in there!

VOICE

Mr. Fleming, Mrs. Bostwick here says you want Marie and Phyllis from Flaw Inspection.

FLEMING

That's right, Mrs. Polacheck, and what business is that of yours?

VOICE

They're eating lunch. It's twelve-oh-seven. P.M.

FLEMING

Well, they can have lunch later. This is an emergency.

VOICE

When the girls are on their lunch hour, I can't allow them—

FLEMING

Go get them!

VOICE

—to show up in here until twelve forty-five. P.M. Unless you're prepared to pay Lunchtime Replacement.

FLEMING

We'll discuss that later! Now go get them. Oh, hell, I'll go.

VOICE

And another thing, Mr. Fleming, this isn't their assigned duty by contract. This here is a *special* test setup.

YERKES

Oh, for God's sake, I'll rip the damn thing apart myself. Where are my glasses?

VOICE

Mr. Yerkes, you can't do that. That comes under the heading of Flaw Testing and—

FLEMING

Listen, dammit, he's the man who put it together and he can damn well take it apart if he wants to.

WILLOUGHBY

Mr. Fleming, what has happened to your Plant Security?

VOICE

Oh, you're slamming the door on negotiation, is that it?

FLEMING

I am not slamming the door on anything, Mrs. Polacheck. I've got a test rig to check out!

VOICE

Mr. Fleming, that New York call says they have to talk to you.

FLEMING

Mrs. Bostwick, you take it. Tell them I'm hung up.

MRS. BOSTWICK

Right.

VOICE

And I'm warning you, if Mr. Yerkes there goes to work on that rig, I'm going to have trouble making the girls listen to reason!

192

WILLOUGHBY

Madame, are you cleared for Plant Security?

VOICE

Why, I never heard such a terrible accusation! Me, Ida Polacheck, 100 per cent American and worked in the scrap-metal drive during the war. I'm as patriotic as—

YERKES

This damn circuit is soldered wrong.

VOICE

You never gave the girls in Production proper time to do their jobs. You rushed them.

FLEMING

I will talk to you later, Mrs. Polacheck!
(*Door shuts.*)
Listen, Basil, can *we* rewire—
(*Door opens.*)

VOICE

And I'm going to report this as a violation of our basic agreement!
(*Door shuts.*)

YERKES

Sure, we can rewire, but not now.

FLEMING

Why *not* now?

YERKES

I've got to get home to help out the wife when the doctor comes to see the kid.

FLEMING

Your kid can wait!

YERKES

The hell he can.

FLEMING

Listen, you never paid any attention to your kids before; what's the big crisis at home all of a sudden? You're a partner in this outfit, aren't you?

YERKES

Yeah, and I've been thinking that over, too. I'm getting a little tired of you guys working my ass off.

FLEMING

Us working your ass off? For Christ's sake, you've got stock, haven't you?

YERKES

I've got to go.

FLEMING

Wait a minute, Basil, give me an answer.

WILLOUGHBY

Gentlemen, I think we'd perhaps better call this test off for now.

FLEMING

No, we won't, Major! We'll have this straightened out—

WILLOUGHBY

I am due in New Jersey at four. It's obvious we can't move ahead here.
(*Door opens.*)

MRS. BOSTWICK

It's a Mr. Handmacher from New York, Mr. Fleming.

FLEMING

I can't talk to him. Listen here, Major—

MRS. BOSTWICK

I'll tell him. He said to tell you that the bid had dropped to 3½ and the asked was 4.

FLEMING

I don't know what the hell that means. Listen, Major, what about an extra forty-eight hours? We can be rewired by then, Basil's kid will be out of the woods, and we'll retest. Basil?

YERKES

I'll call you later.
(*Door shuts.*)

WILLOUGHBY

I couldn't possibly take it on myself to promise you that, Mr. Fleming. I'd have to get in touch with General Mowbray.

FLEMING

Fine, let's go put in a call.

WILLOUGHBY

But he won't be back from Dallas until tomorrow noon.

FLEMING

Well, meanwhile, what's the status here? Where do we stand?

WILLOUGHBY

Well, ah, that is one of the things we'll have to take up at the next staff meeting.

FLEMING

All right. Red tape is red tape. But you're the Project Officer; you'll have to make a recommendation. What's it going to be?

WILLOUGHBY

Well, I could hardly commit myself *here*, Mr. Fleming. I'd, ah, have to draw up a report and weigh all the considerations, pro and con, and then—

FLEMING

Dammit, we tested out to 52-54-56, Load Factor B2. Look, Major, *are we in or not?*

WILLOUGHBY

You're insisting on a direct answer?

FLEMING

You bet I am.

WILLOUGHBY

Please let go of my coat.

FLEMING

Excuse me. Look, I'll turn off the tape recorder and you can tell me off the record—

WILLOUGHBY

There's nothing said here that can't be recorded.
(*Door opens.*)

VOICE (TEEL)

Well, say, look who's here! Having a little brawl and didn't invite me?

FLEMING

The absentee partner. Where have you been?

TEEL

Overslept. Hi, Major, are we all straightened out and squared away with Uncle Sugar?

WILLOUGHBY

In a sense, yes.

TEEL

What does that mean in plain English, pal?

FLEMING

He won't explain it to you, but I will. It means we're nowhere, that's what it means! Up the creek without a paddle and no contract extension and a virtuoso engineer who's taken a powder, and—

TEEL

How the hell did all this happen?

FLEMING

What would you care? You and Leonard don't give a goddam what happens here anyway!

TEEL

Now Walter, take it easy; don't go off half cocked.

WILLOUGHBY

Well, gentleman, if we're finished—

FLEMING

No, I'm not finished! I've got something else to say into your efficient little Jap tape recorder. Can all you boys down there in Washington hear me? This is a small businessman talking. Remember me? The backbone of the economy? I'm trying to deliver the XXXXXX L-4 to you. Maybe I am a good soldier Schweik like Betty says, but I figured that's all I know how to do—take on a job and do it—

WILLOUGHBY

What soldier are you referring to, Mr. Fleming?

FLEMING

—deliver the goods and worry about the profit *later*. What did I do wrong, gents? Don't you want me for the backbone of the economy? What the hell is it?

TEEL

Don't mind Walter, Major; he's a little tired and he's been under a lot of tension.

FLEMING

How would you know what I've been under? You and your glib double-talk.

TEEL

Walter, baby, calm down.

FLEMING

I'm tired of calming down! If I calm down long enough I'll end up bankrupt!
(*Door opens.*)

VOICE

Mr. Fleming, I don't want to disturb you, but there's a policeman out on Water Street putting tickets on everybody's car for overtime parking.

FLEMING

Ask him if he's cleared for Plant Security. Right, Major?

WILLOUGHBY

Gentleman, I'm sure there's nothing to be gained by—

TEEL

Don't worry, Miss Duffy, I'll fix it. I've got connections downtown.

FLEMING

Good, good! Connections. That's all that matters. Right, Jerry? Go ask the connections what to do about the plant here that's all geared up for production—forty people sitting on their cans waiting for the major and his staff meeting. And while you're at it, ask your connections about the overhead and the rent.

TEEL

Walter, baby, it didn't *have* to be this way.

WILLOUGHBY

Gentlemen, you'll be hearing from our section, oh, I would say, within a week at the outside.

FLEMING

Don't call us, we'll call you.

TEEL

Well, Major, that's how the circuit breaks, eh?

WILLOUGHBY

You hit Mr. Teel!

FLEMING

Hard.
(*Door opens.*)

VOICE

I just want to inform you, Mr. Fleming— Say, what's Mr. Teel doing on the floor?

FLEMING

Get out of here, Mrs. Polacheck.

VOICE

You better not threaten me, Mr. Fleming. The girls have just held a short meeting and decided in view of the abuses they have suffered they have no choice but to walk out in protest.

FLEMING

Tell them to start walking. The Unemployment Insurance office is six blocks that way.

MRS. BOSTWICK

Here's fresh coffee, gentlemen.
(*End of Tape Transcript*)

3. In view of the current unsatisfactory status of the XXXXXX L-4 (Mod.) project (Ref. Contract 871-98 A9, dated 8/13/58), as revealed fully in the above transcript of Test Session, 6/14/60, and due to various factors of delay, insufficient standards of quality control, and substandard labor procedures, it is the considered recommendation of the undersigned that, pending final staff action on any contract renewal, this Section continue and finalize Section III of Complete Alternate Schedule of Recommendation (Ref. 5/10/61, Document 367, Classified SECRET).

4. In compliance with procedures as approved in said Complete Alternate Schedule of Recommendation, this Section has already transmitted all pertinent information and/or drawings and working documents pertaining to the successful completion of XXXXXX L-4 (Mod.) to the Alternate Contractor as specified on Page 6, Paragraph A, namely, Tech Instruments, Inc., 4581 Orange Avenue, Redwood Grove, California.

5. Preliminary contract negotiations, pending Staff approval, have already been held with Tech Instruments, Inc.

6. Staff approval of the foregoing is requested at earliest convenience so that the XXXXXX L-4 (Mod.) project may be successfully completed.

Signed: C. C. WILLOUGHBY, MAJ., U.S.A.
Ass't Chief of Section

18

Leo Banks poked his head into my office.

"Everything's locked up tight inside, Mr. Fleming," he announced. "Isn't it about time you were going home?"

"I had a few things to clear up here at my desk," I told him. (*General Fleming's Farewell Address to the Troops,* or *Down The Rabbit Hole: The Story of an American Failure. Notes To Be Read at the Sheriff's Sale.*)

He nodded. "Say, Mr. F.," he inquired, twirling his passkeys, "I've been meaning to ask you. The wife and I have a few bucks salted away in the savings bank and we were wondering, do you think this is a good time to buy a little bundle of Science Associates, Inc., stock? I mean, from what I hear, since you people put it out on the market, it's gone up pretty good."

"And it's come down pretty good, too," I said.

I had reached Mr. Handmacher some time after the disaster in the Test Room.

"Hello, Mr. Handmacher, this is Walter Fleming. You've been trying to reach me?"

"Fleming? Fleming?"

"Science Associates, Mr. Handmacher. Bayport. Remember?"

"Oh, that one," groaned Handmacher.

"I got some sort of message about bid and asked. . . . Was it 3½ bid and—"

"That was before lunch. Down to 3 now. We're offering what

202

we've got at 4. What'd you say, Fred? Some more just came in at 3⅞ths? Tell 'em we'll try and sell it but the market is soft—"

"Mr. Handmacher, what the hell is happening?" I cried.

"That's what I was calling to ask *you*, Fleming. I haven't had such a day since Goldman Sachs broke in '29—God forbid I should remember! You got trouble up there or something?"

"No trouble," I lied. "Business strictly as usual," I added, which was no lie.

"Then who's dumping all this stock?" he demanded. "It's been showing up by the truckload from all over the place!"

"Can't you tell who owns it from the names on the certificates?" I asked.

"These are in brokers' accounts," he said. "What, Freddy? Los Angeles? Tell 'em to wait a minute—"

"Listen, Mr. Handmacher," I said, doing mental arithmetic, "three bucks a share is better than a poke in the eye with a sharp stick. Maybe I'll give you an order to sell a few thousand for my account. What do you think?"

"Sell a few thousand?" Mr. Handmacher laughed a hollow laugh. "To who?"

". . . I could sell you a lot of stock right now, Leo," I said. "If you weren't my friend, that is. I could sell you enough to paper your whole living room at two bucks a share. But if you're looking for a more solid investment, why don't you buy a book of tickets on the Irish Sweepstakes? I hear that pays off every so often."

Leo stared at me in the half-light, perplexity writ large on his honest face.

"What happened?" he asked. "Last week it was up around eighteen or nineteen, wasn't it?"

"That was before the pin was applied to the balloon," I said.

. . . A pin in the hands of Leonard Finch? Trading behind dummy accounts spotted in various cities? Selling in concert with Jerome B. Teel, youngish (42 years old) crew-cut Sales Executive? And perhaps even including some shares held in the none too steady hands of Basil and Leatrice Yerkes, Joint Tenants?

Later in the afternoon, I'd called the Yerkes residence.

"Ah, there, Mrs. Yerkes, how's the little fellow? Fighting his way back to health, I sincerely hope?"

"He's better," said Mrs. Y. "Not that *you'd* care."

"Oh, but I do care," I protested. "And I care about Basil. Do you think I could speak to him for a moment?"

"He has nothing to say to you," she replied.

"But I have something to say to him," I said. "I merely called to apologize. Surely you won't stand in the way of my doing the decent thing, Mrs. Yerkes?"

In the background I heard a murmured debate. It continued for almost thirty seconds, and then I heard Basil's rasp. "What do you want?"

"Basil, baby," I said, "in the heat of crisis I may have said some things to you today that were absolutely uncalled for—"

"Yeah," said the engineering partner. "You sure did."

"—and I want to apologize to you," I said. "You're a sensitive, hard-working, intelligent fellow, and I had no right impugning your honest instincts as a father and a provider."

Silence.

"And Basil, baby," I added, "there's nothing much wrong with our modification that a couple hours' hard work in the shop won't fix, right?"

"Ordinarily, no," said Basil.

"Fine, fine," I said. "Take your time, get a good rest, make sure Basil Junior is completely well, and then let's get back with it. Okay?"

"I'll tell you after I've seen my lawyer," said Basil.

"What are you seeing your lawyer about, Basil?" I cooed. But the coo came out a croak. My throat was suddenly quite dry.

"Leatrice says when you pull out of a partnership deal, there's all sorts of legal junk," said Basil. "Before we leave for the Coast, I want to get everything straightened out properly."

"Pull out of *what* partnership?" I choked. "What are you doing to me? Just because we had a squabble in the Test Room—a little misunderstanding—"

Silence.

"Listen, you softheaded genius, we built a business around your brain; you've got everything locked up in it; you can't go running off with all that know-how and peddle it to our competitors!" I yelled.

But Leatrice Yerkes had replaced Basil on the other end. "Please stop harassing my husband!" she said. "He's well past the stage where he has to accept any more abuse from the likes of you. If *you* don't appreciate his special talents, I'm sure there are others who will."

"I'm coming over there. I've got to talk to Basil!"

"The door will not be open," she said. And hung up.

"I dunno," said Leo Banks. "I guess I don't understand High Finance. I better stick to earning a living the hard way." He trudged out.

"Move over," I muttered.

Betty Lawrence had finally reached me an hour or so ago. "I'm sorry," she'd apologized. "I've been locked up all morning in an industrial conference and couldn't get to a phone. Walter, why didn't you call me back last night?"

"It's a long and tedious story, dear," I said. "Something out of Molnar."

"This is no time to be witty," she said. "I've been trying to reach you to warn you. Something fishy is going on. The word is out that you're having some sort of internal difficulties, and all week long they tell me there's been heavy selling. *Is* there something wrong?"

I told her.

"Oh, brother," said Betty.

"You mean, oh, cousin," I said bitterly. "Do a little digging and I'll bet you find dear Jerry is out of Science Associates stock and home free. And dear uncomplicated Basil—somebody got to *him*, too. Or Leatrice. Now she can move them all to a warmer climate . . . and I have a good suggestion for her, too. . . ."

"I'm supposed to be so smart," Betty wailed. "I should have figured this out last *week!*"

"They were smarter," I said. "Don't you see? They knew the Good Soldier would be so busy with his nose to the grindstone that he wouldn't have time to notice their shenanigans. . . ."

"The bastards," she murmured. "I'm going to call a man I know at the SEC."

"To lock the barn door?" I said. "Forget it. They're not bastards. They're simply intelligent investors with inside information who took a legitimate profit. Leonard's clean, isn't he? Didn't he offer me a way out? Is it his fault that I'm such an idealistic nitwit that I wouldn't sell out on his terms?"

"He's still a bastard," she said.

"You don't get to be Leonard Finch without being one," I sighed. "He just sat down and figured out that if I wasn't going to budge, then what the hell, he'd unload and go around the roadblock. It's the American Way, dear. You can write an article on it for the Sunday section, but your editor will probably object because it's a little too downbeat."

"Oh, Walter," she said, "it isn't completely a disaster. You've still got a factory, and machines . . . and a solid small business."

". . . . getting smaller by the hour," I added.

"Walter, I've got to get back inside for the closing speech," she said. "Why don't you come to town in the morning and we can talk? I have a few friends that *aren't* bastards, I can have them up for cocktails and maybe we can pull a few strings, get you a contract for something else—"

"Not until I get a new engineer," I said. "Right now I'm still in a state of shock. Maybe next week. Meanwhile, I've got to figure out if we can meet the current pay roll. You know, these girls get very high rates for sitting around and waiting for the boss to come up with a government contract. . . ."

So there I sat, alone in my office, a man in a bathtub with the plug removed and the last of the water running down the drain. . . .

I picked up the phone and dialed my house.

Buddy answered. "Hi, Pop," he said. "Did you knock it out of the park?"

"Yep, and lost the ball in the bushes," I told him. "Tell your mother I'll be home in half an hour and she should get into something interesting from Loehmann's. I'm taking her out to dinner, Valkyrie style."

"Valkyrie what?" he asked.

"It's in the encyclopedia," I said. "You can look it up."

I hung up and thought to myself: You're all wrong, Fleming. Stop telling your kid to look things up. The world he's going to

206

graduate into doesn't run things by the book—not unless some lexicographer from the Ford Foundation is compiling the definitive dictionary of greed. Teach him to look in the back for the answers.

I snapped off the lights and went out.

Outside, all the office equipment was properly covered, the desks were clear, and the staff had evacuated the premises for the night. Leo got up from the waiting-room bench where he had been browsing through a month-old copy of *Time*, and unlocked the front door for me.

"Mr. Fleming," he said, as I went out, "I've been thinking. If it dropped down to two, like you say, isn't there a good chance the stock would go *up* again to three or four, maybe? Isn't *that* a good gamble?"

I climbed into my Marci-10, having first pulled the parking ticket from the windshield wiper and tossed it into the gutter. "Maybe," I admitted. "But right now, I like the Irish Sweepstakes better."

I headed for home.

19

The same Hungarian waiter at the Inn poured the final three inches of our second bottle of Piper Heidsieck '52 into our glasses, dividing it most equitably, upended the bottle in the nearby bucket and padded softly away, leaving us alone.

"Well, now," said my wife, raising her glass, "to what shall we drink this time?"

I stared at her through a haze of fine grape. Up to a few seconds ago, I had been letting the alcohol waft me gently away, soothing and blunting my synapses. We had eaten well and I had even been able to dredge up a few chuckles based on a description of Mrs. Polacheck's facial expression when I'd told her off at noon. . . .

But now, quite suddenly, I felt hopelessly depressed.

"Come, come," said my attractive companion. "No use letting this good wine go to waste. I mean, how much longer can we indulge ourselves in expense-account binges, eh, old friend?"

"Back to Good Old Guckenheimer for us," I muttered.

"It does the job just as well," said Marjorie. She eyed me. "I know what's wrong with you, dear. You are beginning to feel some pain, correct?"

I nodded. "Then what better time to toast?" she asked. "I'll order us another bottle. Here. To Gertrude Ederle, Conquerer of the English Channel—"

"You're doing your level best to behave like a true Gray Lady," I said. "And I appreciate every bit of it. But it's no use, honey. I'm past therapy; I'm in shock." And I wanted to add: *I am an unfaithful cad who does not deserve your tender ministrations.* . . .

"I know what else is wrong with you, Walter Fleming," said my wife, articulating carefully. "You are feeling inadequate, right? The beautiful edifice you constructed in that abandoned firehouse in Bayport—that lovely going concern has come slightly unglued, and you are thinking the roof is about to cave in, and the whole debacle is all your fault, correct?"

"Oh . . . I've had a little help from others," I muttered.

"Now listen, Walter," said Marjorie, setting down her glass. "I want to tell you something. *Listen* to me."

"I *am* listening to you," I said.

"You are looking at me but you are not listening to me," she accused.

"How could you possibly tell that I wasn't listening to you?" I asked.

"Because I have been married to you long enough to know that vacant look you get in your eyes when you are looking straight at me but thinking about something that needs checking in the shop or some other damn thing, and that was exactly the look you were just giving me, and when I am trying to tell you something, something very important, I expect the common courtesy of a little attention. Do you understand me, my sweet?"

"You're raising your voice, dearest," I said.

"So I am," she said. "And now you are listening, aren't you? You *are* listening to me, aren't you?"

"Yes, angel, I am listening to you and I am not thinking about anything else and if my eyes are vacant it is merely because they are not focusing too well," I said.

"You can go to an optometrist tomorrow," she said, and drained her glass. "Now. What was I about to tell you?" She blinked. "All these interruptions. Oh, yes. It was about us. Now. I have observed that there are lots of women who stand behind successful men, and they are known to one and all as The Woman Behind the Man. I, unfortunately, am not such a woman."

"You're not?"

"No, I am not," she said, "and if you thought I was when you married me, you have been cheated. I am simply a simple person who found a guy and fell in love with him and got him to marry her knowing that she would never be his pusher or his manager or his driver or whatever else it is that these women do in order to be dominant forces behind their husbands, see?"

I thought briefly of a dumpy little girl with braces, in a black pleated skirt, seated beneath the branches of a large spruce tree, long, long ago. . . .

"Now. Having established that fact about *me*," said Marjorie, "—whew, it's getting warm in here—let us now proceed to an examination of *you*, sir."

"Must we?"

"Yes, we must. You, Fleming, are a throwback to an earlier era. Another time. You are a gentleman. You are courteous. You are kind. You are—"

"—trustworthy, loyal, brave, clean, and reverent."

"Shut up. Hard-working, and you believe in the Golden Rule and you take people at their face value, and you are, to use a dirty word, honest. Honest as the day is long. Honest to a fault. Honest—" She stopped to search for another expression.

"Injun?" I offered.

She glared at me. "No!" Then she smiled. "Yes! *Injun*. Very apt."

"Why?"

"Because you are one of a dying race."

The waiter had come hovering back. With a queenly wave of the hand, Marjorie dismissed him. "We are *talking*," she said. "You may have the table shortly." He withdrew, his tails between his legs. "Now," she demanded, "have we established the fact of your honesty?"

"For the sake of argument, yes," I said.

"Forget argument. Just agree with me. It saves time. You are an honest man, right? Right. Just now you have been put upon. You have allowed yourself to be had, flim-flammed, gulled, diddled, cozened, hornswoggled, bamboozled, and painted into a corner by a pack of unworthy footpads. So?"

"And then some," I muttered. "Must we rehash—"

"Now. Listen to me, Fleming, old husband. I have a very strong feeling that this experience may well leave its mark upon you. You are middle-aged and impressionable. It is quite possible that you will wake up tomorrow morning with a slight hangover *and* something else."

"I don't need anything else," I said.

"Shut up," she advised. "And that something else will be what they are fond of calling Disillusionment."

"Who?"

"They," she said. She pointed a finger at me. "You will have come to the conclusion that since the world is full of crooks, there is nothing left to do but join them. Starting after breakfast tomorrow morning, you will embark on a career of cheating, infighting, dirty pool, and stepping all over anybody in your way. Am I correct in that assumption?"

"I don't really know," I protested. "Can't I wait until tomorrow to find out?"

"Let us please not equivocate," said Marjorie. "I know you rather well, and I sense the emergence of a new Walter Fleming, a man *au courant* with the wave of the future. Walter the Quick. Walter the Shifty. Walter Weasel, blood relative to Jerry Teel, the Artful Dodger, who—" Suddenly, she was blinking, and I saw tears in her eyes.

"Honey . . . what are you crying about?"

"Because I don't want you that way!" said Marjorie. "I don't want you changing your spots into that other crowd of Walters!"

"Well now," I said, "let's be a little realistic here."

"Let's not!" she replied, hiccuping slightly.

"Because it does seem as how there is no room for much honesty in the major leagues."

"Then I say, back to the bush leagues!" she said. "I for one could not care less about the capital gains and the minks and the charity drives and the trips to Europe and the big houses with the two in help you can never hire anyway, and the flower arrangements *and* the buying clothes at those damned Fifth Avenue prices! I don't need it and I don't want it, and neither do you. And if you're sitting there needling yourself on to a career of nastiness because you're carving out an industrial empire with your bare hands for the wife and kiddies at home, then *forget it*, Walter!" She glared at me. "We are not in the empire market. Not if when we get there I look around and see what a creep you turned into. See?"

I focused clearly on Marjorie's intent face for a long moment. She stared back at me. I could remember all the faces I'd seen of my wife: the face with the braces . . . that face the first morning we'd awakened together in her brownstone apartment . . . her face at the Lying-In hospital . . . the face she'd averted because of her jealousy toward Betty Lawrence . . . and now this face, a new one.

"Still buying my copy of the *Saturday Evening Post*, eh?" was all I managed to say.

"You haven't answered me," said Mrs. Fleming.

"I shall take the matter under advisement," I said, "but I want you to know that you have made one hell of an impression on the Board of Directors, Madame."

"I . . . was not being funny," she said.

"Neither was I," I replied.

"I will not trade you in for a new model, merely to be rich," she reiterated. "It is not that good a deal. Do we understand each other, Buster?"

"I think so," I told her.

I could learn to love this new face too.

"Good." She rubbed her knee against mine beneath the table. "Now," she said happily, "let us have brandy and coffee and toddle along home to bed. On second thought, let us skip the brandy and the coffee and toddle along to bed that much sooner."

"All rightee," I said, and signaled the waiter for our check. "It is, after all, still our house until we miss a mortgage payment whilst old Dad is out peddling shoelaces door to door." I sighed.

"Pooh," said Marjorie, trying to repair her lipstick in the candle-light. "Who ever heard of a citizen of your stature being foreclosed upon? I mean, who else has *two* septic tanks, mm?"

I squeezed her thigh with mingled feelings of love and guilt. "I don't deserve you," I murmured.

"Of course you don't," she agreed. "Come along. Mother is quite ready."

I signed my name to the check and added a hefty tip. What the hell, if Pompeii was about to have it, let its last moments be gaudy ones.

I helped her up. "May I add one footnote to your valedictory address, baby? Just who—I mean whom—are you kidding about not being The Woman Behind the Man . . . mmm?"

"Don't talk dirty," said Marjorie, allowing me to lead her out.

We were standing on the porch of the elaborately unostentatious, expensive dining establishment, waiting for the parking attendant to bring my Marci-10 around when the shiny new Bentley drove up to the door.

Not so much of a coincidence, really. Remember, it was a soft June night, and he'd come home from the city for once. She'd probably had a pitcher of cocktails ready, and after he'd had a few she had been able to persuade him to take her out for dinner, if not to the city; then she'd settled for a pleasant drive north to that elegant place she'd read about in *Cue*. Then they'd undoubtedly got lost on the unfamiliar roads below here and wandered back and forth. Now they were tired, the drinks had worn off, and here they were, silent, hungry, glaring at each other as they stepped out. First, a plumpish, overdressed lady, then, from behind the wheel, a very familiar old friend.

I felt the adrenalin course through me—or could it be the champagne that made me step forward, my heart pounding?

"Are you the owner of this trap?" he demanded. "I'm Mr. Finch from Scarsdale. I called and made a reservation—"

"Screwy Lennie," I said.

He stopped and peered at me in the darkness. I have to give him credit for it; he didn't twitch a muscle. "Walter Fleming," he said. "Oh, yes, you do live up here in the woods, don't you?"

"Live and used to work," I said. "Take off your glasses, Screwy Lennie; I'm going to beat hell out of you."

His wife gasped.

Leonard backed away. "Now just a minute," he said, his voice quivering ever so slightly.

"Take them *off*," I said, following him. "I wouldn't want your lawyers claiming I took unfair advantage of you—"

"You're behaving like a jerk!" protested Leonard.

"You bet I am," I said. "A stupid country bumpkin who'd just been double-crossed by a gang of double-breasted city thieves. *Take off the bifocals, Lennie.*"

"Caroline, call a cop!" cried he.

His wife stood still, watching attentively

"Caroline!" he yelped. "This bum is going to attack me!"

"I heard," she said. "I don't know why he's going to hit you, but whatever it is, I'll bet you've got it coming to you!"

"Honey," Marjorie trilled from the porch, "here's the man with our car. . . ."

"Just one second, dear," I said, reaching out a hand and seizing Leonard's hand-sewn lapels. "Now, here it comes, you conniver," I told him, as he tried to pull free. "You've wrecked my business. Now it's my turn to do *you* a little mayhem."

"Big talk!" he sneered. "Go ahead, you stupid son of a bitch, with your ideals and your mealy-mouthed crap. You haven't got the guts—you and all the rest of those nitwits down at the campfire who thought you were better than *I* was—"

Talk about vendettas! Weren't the two of us setting some sort of new record?

"You were a thief then and you're *still* a thief!" I rasped.

"Yes, but a successful thief!" he yelled. "You've got the lily-white hands, sure, but *I've* got the loot. And I can buy and sell you by the pound because you're *stupid*—don't you know that?"

We stared at each other, nose to nose, breathing hard.

He was right, of course. This was undoubtedly the way of my world. No matter how much of a little island of accomplishment I might be able to dredge up out of hard work and effort, above me, taking his 40 per cent off the top, there would always be a Leonard Finch.

Sure, I could belt him, break his glasses, humiliate him, knock him flat on the pavement, but what about tomorrow? Would the architecture of society change and our positions be reversed?

Of course not.

So what would be the point of hitting him? I'm a nonviolent type anyway.

So I let him go.

Straightening up, he brushed his lapels.

"Don't you ever do that to me again, Putz," he said. "If you do, I'll see to it that you never earn another dollar. Just remember your place around Leonard Finch. I knew you didn't have the guts to hit me, you cheap nickel and dimer." And he turned scornfully away.

So I didn't hit him. I kicked him in the behind instead.

An easier target to find in the dark.

Some time later, Marjorie giggled in the darkness of our bedroom. "Really," she said. "The two of you . . . like *schoolboys*."

"Or tentmates." I sighed.

". . . attacking a man from the rear when he wasn't even look-ing." She chuckled. "Aren't you ashamed?"

"Not really," I said. "He'd just done the same thing to me day before yesterday, remember? That day when we were still rich?"

"Hm-mm . . ." said Marjorie. "Is it tomorrow *already?*"

"Yes, dear," I said. "Let's get some sleep. . . ."

She moved closer to me. "In a moment . . ." she said.

I awoke around five, just as the light was beginning to seep through the clouds on the eastern horizon.

The house was still asleep. I tiptoed downstairs and made myself a cup of instant coffee. The revels now were ended, and I had a day to face at the factory in Bayport . . . a day I wouldn't wish on anybody.

Oh, well, I thought, settling down in the living room, I could probably devise some sort of consumer-goods item to manufacture . . . something salvaged from the components of the XXXXXX L-4 (modified). A pocket electronic cooking thermometer? A tran-sistorized fire alarm, maybe? Perhaps some sort of toy. Toys were big sellers if one could dig up just the right gimmick. . . .

Next to the television set on the coffee table, I spied a large, in-tricate drawing. "Design for an Interstellar Space Receiver," was the description, in Buddy's bold block printing. Smiling fondly, I eyed my son's work.

Then fell to studying it.

Who knew?

I mean, every small new electronics business has to start *some-where*, doesn't it?

(Continued from front flap)

Mr. Wilk's second novel is a fitting successor to his successful first, DON'T RAISE THE BRIDGE (LOWER THE RIVER). Once again wild financial stratagems, innocuous sex, and an outrageously funny plot are blended in an all-purpose mixer with special attachments marked Satire, Farce, and Burlesque. But this time a dash of bitters in the form of disenchanted social comment makes RICH IS BETTER a more substantial book.

MAX WILK, who describes himself as an angry middle-aged man, was born in New York City in 1920 and received his B.A. degree at Yale in 1941.

He has been in the TV field, as writer and producer, for more than eleven years. He has also been a theatrical press agent, and has written motion picture and TV scripts, short stories, revue skits, and a Broadway play.

$3.50

"I have been poor and I have been rich," Joe E. Lewis once remarked, "and believe me, rich is better."

But Walter Fleming, small businessman and normal neurotic, had cause to wonder. Partner in an electronics business in a small New England community, Walter is suddenly—thanks to the development of an electrical gadget that turns out to be a vital component of a supersecret Defense Department project—rich beyond the dreams of avarice. Strictly speaking, he should be riding high, wide, and handsome; and for a time he does, in a brand-new European sports car de luxe.

But the route is not altogether scenic. Some of the blots on the landscape: one partner, a cousin, with a taste for high living; another partner whose engineering genius is impaired by an overly protective wife; a lovely wife who deeply mistrusts their abrupt affluence; a disturbingly attractive Other Woman; a vindictive Amazon who speaks (loudly) for Labor at the shop; an impatient Army major whose approval of the improved model of the aforementioned gadget is all-important— these and other exacerbations make Walter wonder if the game is worth the candle . . . even a solid-gold candle.

(Continued on back flap)

4179